Advance Praise for
Art Geeks and Prom Queens

"I love Alyson's use of dialogue. It's acerbic and vicious and bitchy. Totally realistic, in other words, without a false note."

—Catherine Forde, author of *Fat Boy Swim*

"A book about life in the fast lane . . . The reader cheers for New York transplant Rio as she wanders through a minefield of peer pressure in a quest for popularity and a place to belong. Slick and hip!"

—Lurlene McDaniel, author of *My Secret Boyfriend* and the *Angels in Pink* series

Praise for
Faking 19

"Gloriously, outrageously funny . . . *Faking 19* is *Feeling Sorry for Celia* with an L.A. edge."

—Jackie Fischer, author of *An Egg on Three Sticks*

"Deliciously funny and irreverent. I couldn't put this down!"

—Niki Burnham, author of *Royally Jacked*

"I loved *Faking 19*. . . . A totally convincing look at one teenager's broken world, and how she reaches inside herself to fix it."

—Joe Weisberg, author of *10th Grade*

Also by Alyson Noël

Faking 19

art geeks

and

Prom Queens

art geeks

and

Prom Queens

Alyson Noël

 St. Martin's Griffin ⚑ New York

www.stmartins.com

Book design by Irene Vallye

Illustrations by Sarah Hughes

ISBN 0-312-33636-5
EAN 978-0-312-33636-3

10   9   8

In memory of Beryl Rothstein,

1928–2004

Acknowledgments

Thank you to my family and friends for their endless supply of enthusiasm and support; to my editor, Elizabeth Bewley, for her sharp eye and impeccable taste; to the long-ago classmates who stood by me when I was the bullied "new girl," and as always, thanks to my husband, Sandy Sherman, who fills each day with magic and makes everything possible.

art geeks

and

Prom Queens

One

"Oh, no. You are not wearing that," my mom says, barging into my room and invading my privacy as usual.

I'm sitting on the floor, rolling my eyes and tying my shoes. I mean, the fact that she despises my faded, old Levi's and "Cape Cod Crew" sweatshirt (that is now so faded and peeled it reads " ape   Crew") is reason enough for me to love it. "Mom, it's fine. Trust me," I say, making a mental note to get a lock on my door ASAP.

"No, Rio, it's not fine. You've got to make a good impression on your first day!"

"I know what I'm doing," I say, glaring at her as she plows through one of the open boxes like it's a sale bin at Barneys.

"Here, why don't you wear this?" She holds up the denim mini-skirt and sparkly tank top she gave me right after she broke the news about moving, as if it were no more than a simple costume change, and that they weren't really wrecking my life.

"Forget it." I shake my head and push it away. "There's no way I'm showing up on my first day at a new school looking like a Hilton sister."

"This outfit is adorable, and you've got the figure for it," she says, holding it against herself and looking in the mirror.

"That outfit will get me *killed!* All the girls will *hate* me if I show up in that."

"This outfit will get you *noticed!*" She raises her eyebrows at me.

"Then why don't you wear it?" I roll my eyes at her white terry-cloth short shorts, matching hoodie, and sky-blue Ugg boots, which have apparently become her new "O.C." uniform. "Besides, it's only *January*," I remind her.

"Yes, and it's already seventy degrees out. People here dress for the weather, *not* the seasons."

" 'Cause there are no seasons in this freaky place," I say, suddenly hating her all over again for dragging me across the country, far away from everything I know and love. I mean, we've only been here a week, but it may as well be a year. I'm completely miserable and it's totally my parents' fault.

If my dad hadn't decided to move to the Newport Beach office, and my mom hadn't insisted on throwing out all of our "heavy, New York furniture" before replacing it with "California-lite," I wouldn't be sleeping on the floor and getting dressed out of a box. And from what I've already witnessed of her own extreme beach-bunny makeover, I've got a sick feeling she's going to decorate the entire house with nothing but yoga mats and water bottles. I swear I miss my old bed almost as much as I miss my old friends.

"Well, if you insist on wearing sweats, at least let them be designer." She reaches for the new hot-pink Juicy Couture sweat suit she bought me two days ago.

"Mom, no! I'm totally gonna be late!"

"Good, you'll make an entrance!"

"Yeah, only in high school they call it 'being tardy,' and it's frowned upon," I say, surrendering to her sales pitch against my better judgment.

When I'm dressed for the second time, in the outfit of *her* choice, I notice she's staring at my shoes, eyes filled with disapproval.

"Forget it," I tell her. "I've compromised all I can. Now would you please just drive me to school?"

"Not until I put on my lips."

I roll my eyes, grab my backpack, and run down the stairs and out the front door to the new white convertible Jaguar that's sitting in the driveway. I throw my bag on the floor, fasten my seat belt, and just sit there and wait while she locates the perfect shade of lip gloss that will offset the blue in her eyes (made even bluer courtesy of Bausch & Lomb), the blond in her hair, and transform her back into the fabulous Jahne Jones, former almost-supermodel, that she was twenty years ago.

In my mom's world, lip gloss is definitely more important than getting me to school on time. I swear, her priorities are a total mess.

Okay, so this is the movie-trailer version of my life. I'm sixteen but almost seventeen, named after a Duran Duran song (which was some big-deal group in the eighties that you might have heard of, depending on whether you watch VH1 or MTV). My mom dated one of the members for three weeks back when she was a model, but she's very vague about which one. Still, sometimes I fantasize that it was the really cute one and that he's actually my real dad, and that any day now he'll come claim me and take me away from this crazy house. But the reality is it probably wouldn't be any better, since rock stars aren't exactly known for their stability.

My real dad is "very busy making money for my mom and me and the people that work for him and their families," as well as "upholding the law by defending the innocent," which is the line he's been giving me for every missed school function, birthday, and holiday since I can remember. I mean, he's a defense attorney, but he probably travels more than a rock star, and sometimes I think Larry King and the camera crew at CNN get to talk to him more than I do.

I feel guilty for saying that (even though it's true), because the fact is we're pretty close, and he's my only ally against my mom. But the problem is he's gone so much that I'm usually left to fight my own battles, and believe me, it's exhausting.

I'm an only child and we have no pets because "animals may look cute from a distance, but they're destructive, shed, shit, and throw up" (that was a direct quote from my mom), and except for the shedding part, it's probably the same reason why I have no siblings.

And today is the first day in my new school, but it's not the first day *of school*. It's actually the first day back from winter break. And it totally sucks because I was pretty much hoping just to blend in and go unnoticed, but now I'm gonna be the late new girl in the hot-pink Juicy sweat suit, and you just can't blend when you're late and pink.

My mom slams the brakes in front of the administrative office, and I look at my watch and shake my head. Twenty minutes late.

I grab my backpack and then nervously run my hands through my long, honey-blond tangled hair, redo my ponytail, and open the door.

"Rio?"

"Yeah?" I look at her without even trying to hide my annoyance.

"Do you want me to help you find your class?"

"Mom, please. I'm not in kindergarten. Jeez." I shake my head and glance nervously at the empty campus.

"Okay," she says, in a hurt voice designed to make me feel bad. And it does. "What time do you want me to pick you up?"

I look at her sitting there in the Jag, and I know she means well, but I go, "Don't pick me up, Mom. Please don't pick me up. I'll find my own way home."

"Okay," she says, shrugging and looking away like she doesn't care, but I know she does.

"Are you gonna be okay today?" I ask, climbing out and closing the door between us. It's weird how I worry about her sometimes. It makes me feel like I'm the parent.

"I'll be great! But you better get to class. You're twenty minutes late you know!"

Then she puts the car in gear and speeds away.

Two

I sling my backpack over my shoulder and head to the office so I can inform whoever's inside that I'm new, late, and have no idea where I'm supposed to go next.

I pull on the heavy glass door, walk inside, lean against the counter, and wait for someone to notice me. This woman with severely bleached hair and a starched white blouse with tiny pink flowers squints at me and says, "And how can we help you?"

"Um, I'm new here. It's my first day, and I'm not sure where I'm supposed to go," I tell her.

She turns to her computer and taps a few keys. "Name, please?"

"Rio."

She stops. "Like in Brazil?"

"Like in the song," I say, tired of always having to answer this question.

She knits her brows together like she's trying to remember how that one goes, then she shakes her head and says, "And your last name, Rio?"

"Jones."

"Very good. Well, I see that you're scheduled to be in AP English. You do know you're twenty minutes late?" She gives me a stern look.

I look at my watch and shrug. "Um, actually I think it's more like twenty-five."

"We'll let it go today. But tomorrow be on time." She looks like she means business.

"I promise."

"C'mon. I'll walk you." She reluctantly sets down her coffee cup, and sighs as she rises from her desk.

"Oh, you don't have to do that. I can find it," I tell her.

"Are you sure?" she asks, pausing in her ascent, which makes it pretty obvious she'd rather stay.

"Definitely."

She hands me some papers, and by the time I'm standing in front of the classroom door I'm in a total panic and I wish I'd let her come with me. But I have to do this, so I take a deep breath, grab the handle, and when I go inside I can feel like twenty pairs of eyes checking me out, including the teacher.

"Hi. Um, I'm supposed to give you this. I'm new." I hand her the pink slip the office lady gave me. Then I just stand there and wait and hope I don't look like a total reject as I stare at the walls that are covered in orange-and-brown construction-paper leaves that say "Fall into Literature."

"You go by Rio?"

I nod.

"You know you're late? Class is half over." She runs her fingers through her short, brown, practical hair and peers at me through metal-framed glasses perched on the end of her nose. Her skin is so pale and translucent it looks like it was carved from a bar of glycerin.

"I know. I'm sorry," I say, rubbing my arm like I always do when I'm nervous.

"Okay, well I'm Mrs. Abbott, and there's an empty seat right over there."

I walk over to where she was pointing, slide into the empty second-row seat, unzip my backpack, and pull out my favorite pen and the notebook I used at my old school. On my last day, all of my friends signed the cover and seeing it now makes my throat go all tight, and my eyes start to sting, and I wish I'd bought a new one. So to distract myself, I flip my pen upside down and watch the miniature New York skyline float by in a cloud of glitter, and then I flip it the other way, sending it back where it came from. But it doesn't cheer me up.

Mrs. Abbott goes back to the chalkboard and starts writing stuff on it and I know I should concentrate and copy it all down, but I can feel the girl at the next desk totally staring at me. And it makes me nervous and self-conscious.

I pull my zipper all the way up, making sure my chest is completely covered, since in the last year it's gone from nonexistent to Jessica Simpson proportions, and I'm not entirely happy about it. Not to mention the five-inch growth spurt that has me clocking in at just under five feet ten, and my new, shiny, straight teeth no longer covered in thick metal braces. I mean, this is what it must feel like for those *Extreme Makeover* contestants. Only I didn't ask for any of this. And it might sound crazy, but I was actually way happier as a short, chubby, acne-splattered, flat-chested dork.

Even when people would look at my mom and then me and then back at my mom, and whisper, "Is she adopted?" it didn't bother me. Really. It was just a lot easier when I was the type of girl no one wanted to be like and everyone ignored. Because that kept their expectations low, so I could just be myself.

But now that I look different people are starting to treat me different. And it always makes me feel like I'm disappointing them by being a big geek, instead of glamorous and exciting like my mom. Also, I can't stand the way they always stare at me.

Like right now.

I take a deep breath, look over and smile and try to seem friendly. But she doesn't smile back.

She just taps her fingers against the chunky knit sleeve of her cheerleading sweater and looks me up and down.

And all I can think is: *I'm dead.*

When the bell finally rings I grab my backpack and hurry into the hall in search of my new locker. Okay, it's not like I have anything to put in it yet, but I figure I should at least know where it is. So when I finally find it, I'm spinning the lock trying to make sure the numbers are lining up in just the right spot, and I hear someone behind me go, "So."

I turn and face the cheerleader from my English class. Her sweater is turquoise, white, and green, which I guess are the school colors, and in the middle is a fuzzy white megaphone that says "Kristi!" in black cursive letters.

"Hey," I say, not sure if she's being friendly or menacing.

"Your locker's, like, right next to mine." She stares at me with these piercing blue eyes, holding some books against her hip with one hand, while twisting her long dark-brown hair around and around the index finger of the other. And she's so petite, pretty, and perfect, I feel like Shrek in comparison.

"Really?" I say, trying to appear excited about this new piece of information.

"Yeah, that one's mine." She points to a locker two rows over and one row up.

"Oh, okay," I say, smiling and nodding even though I have no idea where this is headed.

"So what's your next class?" she asks, checking out my clothes, shoes, watch, backpack, and earrings.

"Um, AP Art," I say, squinting at my class schedule.

She looks at me for a long moment and I'm starting to feel really uncomfortable when she finally goes, "Well, ciao!" and gives me this little wave with her hair-wrapped index finger.

As I watch her walk away I realize I have no idea what just happened, but I know it can't be good. Because let's face it, girls like Kristi just don't talk to girls like me.

Three

When I walk into AP Art, I'm the last to arrive even though I tried to be early. So I go across the room and introduce myself to my teacher, Ms. Tate, and it's kind of weird, because she looks really similar to my art teacher from my old school, with her mass of dark wavy hair falling almost to her waist, hardly any makeup, and at least three piercings in her right ear (there may be more but I can't tell because of her hair).

I hand her my paperwork and after looking it over she taps a pencil against the faux-wood grain of her desk like she's deciding something important, then she stops tapping, and tells me to take a seat at the long table in the corner.

I consciously avoid the curious stares of the other students as I sit on the vacant chair next to a skinny girl with chin-length, choppy, red hair and a cool vintage outfit that has so much going on it's hard to take it all in with just one glance. When she looks at me with these heavily black-rimmed eyes I sort of press my lips together in a pathetic, nervous, no-teeth smile. I guess after my strange encounter with the cheerleader I'm feeling a little shy. But unlike Kristi, she smiles and says, "Hey, I'm Mason, and that's Jas."

I look across the table to where she's pointing, and sitting there is like the cutest guy *ever*. Okay, maybe not gorgeous in that perfect

Hollywood "spray-on tan personal trainer Brad Pitt in Troy" kind of way. But definitely cute in that "real person who goes to your school and he's sitting right in front of you right now" kind of way.

He's really tan, with sun-streaked brown hair that falls just short of his incredible, long-lashed, topaz eyes. And when he smiles my heart stops.

Temporarily, but literally.

And so determined to be cool I say, "Hey, Jas." Only it comes out sounding like "Hey, Jath!" Like I have a speech impediment or something. *Which I don't!* But now he probably thinks that I do. Great.

After Ms. Tate takes roll call she tells everyone just to continue with their projects. Then she comes over and sits next to me on the edge of the long wood desk, and even though she's thin and petite, the desk creaks really loudly when she does that, like it's gonna break or something.

"So, Rio," she says, picking off pieces of white lint from her black cotton smock. "We're all working on a series of projects, some of which will be chosen for the upcoming art show held every year in Laguna Beach. You're getting a late start, but I'd still like you to try to contribute something. This year I've had each of the students pick a theme, value, or idea and then express it in a medium of their choice."

"Can I use photography?" I ask.

"Sure. Whatever you like. The darkroom is over there." She points to a door across the room that has a sign on it that says DARKROOM. "I'm sure Mason or Jas will be kind enough to show you around."

So, of course, I immediately picture Jas (Jath!) "showing me around," then I feel myself turn bright red when I realize he's looking right at me.

Ms. Tate smiles and says, "I'm looking forward to seeing your work." Then she rises from the table slowly and carefully so that it doesn't creak again. But it still does.

When she's gone, Mason leans across the desk and says, "You're into photography?"

"Yeah." I nod. Then I look over and see Jas looking at me, so I quickly look away.

"Who do you like?" he asks.

YOU!!!

But luckily I just say, "Um, well, I love how Irving Penn shows the beauty in the most simple things, and how Annie Leibovitz gets right inside the soul of her subject, oh, and Helmut Newton's work is so amazing." Okay, I could go on and on but I make myself stop before I go too far and out myself as a total geek. I mean, most people my age have no idea who I'm talking about.

"Helmut Newton rocks." Jas nods.

"And I love Irving Penn," Mason says.

"You do?" I ask.

"Yeah, and Herb Ritts and Bruce Weber and Richard Avedon and Mario Testino. Wouldn't that be the greatest job? To be a photographer?" Mason says.

"Totally," I say, wondering if I should tell her how I met Herb Ritts once when he photographed my mom. But I don't want her to think I'm bragging, so I don't say anything.

"So where'd you move from?" she asks.

"New York."

"Wow, I've always wanted to go there. What's it like? Is it better than here?"

"I don't know yet." I shrug, even though I know it is.

"Anywhere's better than here," she says, rolling her eyes. "You'll see."

"Don't listen to her." Jas shakes his head. "It's not so bad. We've got great weather and awesome beaches. Have you been to the beach yet?"

"I've driven past," I tell him.

"You've *got* to go to the beach. Do you surf?"

"I've gone boogie boarding in the Hamptons." I shrug.

"You should come with us at lunch," Mason says.

"Where?" I ask. "Surfing?"

"No, we're going to Jas's house. He lives right at the beach and he's a great cook, he'll make you whatever you want."

"But is there enough time? I mean, I thought we couldn't go off campus," I say, sounding like a law-abiding good citizen. *Gag, why did I say that?*

"Technically that's true," Mason says. "But we're skipping the assembly, so there's plenty of time."

"No worries," Jas says.

And when he smiles and pulls his fingers through his bangs, exposing all of his gorgeous face, there's no way I can say no.

$\mathscr{F}$our

Jas lives in a gated community with a private beach, in a house like you see on the cover of *Elle Decor*. It's like this big, sprawling space on a cliff overlooking the ocean, and it's filled with all these really cool masks and paintings and sculptures and all this foreign-looking ethnic stuff that Jas says he and his dad have collected on their travels around the world.

So I go, "Around the world?"

And he goes, "Yeah. Last summer we went to Morocco."

Wow. The only traveling I've done is the usual summer exodus to the Hamptons, two Christmas trips to the Caribbean, and countless train rides from my old house in Scarsdale to Manhattan. Not that I'm complaining, but it hardly seems as glamorous as Marrakech.

As he's busy grabbing food from the fridge, Mason wanders off to the bathroom, leaving me alone with him and it makes me kind of nervous. So I pick up this silver-framed picture of a dark-haired woman. Her mouth is spread wide with laughter, and her eyes are all crinkled up so I can't really tell what color they are. The blue green of the ocean is right behind her, and it's a really good picture, so I go, "Who's this?"

Jas turns from the fridge and squints briefly at the photograph. "Oh, that's my mom. I took that the summer we went to Greece. I think that was in Mykonos."

"You took this?" I say, impressed. "It's really good, really natural."

"Thanks," he says, turning from the fridge and juggling an armful of Tupperware containers.

I reach out and catch the one from the top just before it falls to the ground and ask, "So where is your mom?"

"She died of breast cancer four years ago," he says, opening the containers and spooning the contents onto these square black plates.

"Oh, I'm sorry," I say, feeling like an idiot. "I didn't know."

"It's okay." He shrugs. "How could you know?"

"Do you have any brothers or sisters?" I ask, trying to change the subject.

"No, it's just me."

"Me too," I say. "I mean, I'm an only child too. But I always wondered what it would be like to have a little brother or sister, you know?"

"Yeah." He nods. "Me too."

We look at each other for a moment and it seems like he's about to say something more, but then Mason comes into the kitchen and goes, "Let's eat in the backyard. It's so nice out."

I'm holding my plate in one hand, a glass of iced tea in the other, and I'm just about to sit on this lounge chair when this yellow Lab comes charging toward me and sticks his cold, wet nose straight in the crotch of my hot-pink sweatpants.

Oh, god.

I can't push him away since both of my hands are full, so I lift my knee up high, trying to shield myself, as I shove him (gently but firmly!) with my foot.

But he's very determined, and refuses to give up, so I end up hopping around in this totally uncoordinated, one-legged dance, trying to dodge the dog without spilling my drink or the food on my plate.

Mason starts cracking up so hard she's doubled-over, but Jas is really embarrassed, and he comes running over and goes, "Holden, stop it! You know we've talked about that."

He drops his plate on a chair, grabs Holden by the collar, and drags

him away. And I swear, you can actually hear the dog whining and scraping his nails in protest the whole way.

Holden reluctantly settles in the shade next to Jas's chair, but he
continues to look at me with these big, sad, brown eyes. "Sorry about
that," Jas says. "He means well, but he has really bad manners."

"Did you name him after Holden Caulfield?" I ask, casually wiping
a bubble of canine juice from my crotch and trying to act like I'm not
totally mortified.

"I did." He nods. "Kind of embarrassing now, but it seemed like a
good idea four years ago when I got him."

I smile nervously and look down at my plate. "Um, what is this?"
I ask.

"Endive and watercress salad with mustard-seed vinaigrette, baked
rigatoni with sausage and Portobello mushrooms, followed by a piece
of pear and dried cherry cobbler for dessert," Jas says, smiling.

"Do you guys eat like this every day?" I ask between spoonfuls,
thinking how I could definitely get used to this.

"Only when Jas supplies the leftovers," Mason says, eating her
dessert first.

I'm chewing my pasta and looking at my two new friends, and the
Jacuzzi right next to us, and the ocean right below us, and it seems like
such a postcard-perfect image of O.C. living, that I start to feel better
about being forced to live here. I mean, maybe it won't be as bad as I
thought. It's only my first day and I'm already having an awesome
lunch with the cutest guy I've ever seen in real life. I can't wait to tell
Paige.

After lunch Jas stacks the plates and takes them inside, and when
he comes back out he has a box in one hand and a thick stack of papers in the other. He hands Mason the papers and sets the box on the
end of his lounge chair, then he lifts the hinged lid and pulls out a bag
of weed and some rolling papers.

I just sit there and watch him casually lick the edges and twist the
ends, then light it up and take a deep drag. When he passes it to me
he's still holding his breath and like a ventriloquist with his lips barely
moving he goes, "Do you smoke?"

Well, the real answer to that question is probably no, even though

I did it a few times before with Paige and Hud. But that was back in junior high when we found Paige's sister's not-so-secret stash hidden in a Nirvana album jacket.

Because her sister was really pretty, four years older, and would barely ever speak to us, we were in total awe of her. So we used to sneak into her room when she wasn't home and look at all of her cool, "grown-up" stuff. She had this stack of vintage eighties albums, even though everyone else was into CDs, and we liked to look at all the covers and vote on who was the most kissable. I always voted for Bono because I thought that he was not only cute but also *a good person*. But Paige voted for Adam Ant because she said it was just about kissing, not marriage, so it was okay to just go for looks.

So this one day we're looking at the picture on the *Nevermind* jacket of the naked baby swimming after a dollar bill, and we're thinking about poor, misunderstood Kurt Cobain, when Paige tipped the album on its side and three joints fell out. She quickly scooped them up and held them to her nose, and after one sniff she looked at me, and her eyes went wide, and without saying another word, we stuck the joints in my backpack and raced over to Hud's.

We found him in his backyard in the tree fort his mom kept threatening to tear down, and the three of us lay on the rough wood floor and smoked one of them 'til there was nothing left. Then on a dare, I climbed down and snuck into his house, and when the maid wasn't looking I grabbed a brand-new box of double-stuffed Oreos and ran it back to the fort. We lay there eating and laughing until it was dark, and then we hid the other two joints for future use.

But all that happened like way long ago, and I haven't really done it since. But not wanting to look like a total geek, I go, "Yeah, I light up every now and then."

And then I pinch it from his fingers, take a long, deep drag, and go into a major hacking coughing fit that's so bad it wakes up Holden, and Mason has to lean over and slap me on the back a few times until I stop. When I calm down my eyes are all watery, and my face feels like it's all red, and there is absolutely nothing cool about me now.

After passing it around a few more times, Jas stubs it out, and Mason shows me the papers she's been holding. Apparently they used to work on the school newspaper, *The Sea Crest Chronicle*, but last year when Jas wrote an article protesting the war in Iraq it sparked a whole lot of trouble. All of a sudden parents started calling the school to complain and threatening to pull their kids out unless something was done.

"They said I was anti-American and didn't support the troops. Can you believe that shit?" Jas says, shaking his head.

Mason goes, "Yeah, and since I was the editor, we both got called into the office. So we go in and we're sitting right across from the principal and he looks at us and says, 'The parents are upset.' So I just shrug you know, 'cause like, what do I care, right? It's not like my mom was upset. And then he goes, 'I want you to write an apology.'"

"And I go, 'forget it. I quit,'" says Jas.

"I told him, 'me, too,'" says Mason. "And we walked out. Then after a while we realized we missed working on it but we didn't want to go back so we started a 'zine. We call it *The Sea Crest Chronic*, and we write whatever we want. Because we don't have to answer to anyone."

She hands me a copy and I'm looking through it when Jas says, "At first it started really small with maybe like twenty copies, but then it started to get out there, and people seemed to like it, so we started printing off a couple hundred. It's mostly just us, but sometimes we invite other students to contribute music reviews, artwork, opinion pieces, just whatever, as long as it's interesting."

"Yeah, it's like the only ones still reading *The Chronicle* are the jocks and cheerleaders since they've pretty much taken it over and filled it with stuff about themselves."

"Can I keep this?" I ask.

"Of course," Jas says, standing up. "But we should bail now."

So Jas parks his Toyota Prius (the same kind of hybrid car that Leo and Cameron drive!) in the student lot, and we nonchalantly head for the gate surrounding the campus. The secret to coming and going, they told me, is just to walk with authority, like you have every right to be doing this.

But just as we're approaching the gate, Mason and Jas are in front and I admit, I'm totally checking out his back view, when Mason casually drapes her arm around his shoulder, leans in, and says something so softly I can't hear it.

And then they laugh.

And it makes me wonder: *Are they boyfriend and girlfriend?*

Ohmygod. I can't believe I just now thought of it. I've been so into how I felt about Jas that I wasn't even thinking that they could be a couple. Uh, *duh?* They're together all the time, with school, and lunch, and the zine, and now watching their little inside joke, I can't believe what a total idiot I am. I mean Hel-*lo?* It's *so* obvious.

And when Jas puts his arm around Mason and pats her on the shoulder, well that just happens to be the exact same moment I'm supposed to step onto the curb.

Only I don't.

Because I'm completely obsessed with watching Mason and Jas engage in what I now recognize as *foreplay!*

And when my knee hits the ground, immediately followed by my right hand, and then my chin, I start cracking up. Maybe it's the pot. I don't know. But I can't seem to stop laughing.

Then Mason goes, "Oh, shit."

And Jas goes, "Are you okay?"

And school security says, "What's going on here?"

Five

Detention. On my first day of school. Detention for an entire week, when I've never been in any real trouble in my life! I mean, I've always been the kind of girl that teachers can depend on, and kids nominate for hall monitor. So being sent to the principal's office is all new to me.

I tried telling Principal Chaney that I was totally unaware of the off-campus rule. That Jas and Mason were just doing me a *big* favor by getting me something out of his car. But no way was he buying it.

"You're not going to call my mom, are you?" I asked, right before he dismissed us.

But he just looked at me and said, "This is a very bad way to begin your school year. I hope I don't see you in here again."

Then he picked up the phone and called my mom.

When I get home an hour and a half after school let out, my mom is pretty fired up.

I'm halfway up the stairs when she goes, "Rio?"

Shit. I pause in midflight.

"I think we need to talk." She's standing at the bottom of the stairs holding a water bottle in one hand and a damp towel in the other.

"Um, what about?" I ask, clutching the banister.

"I think you know."

I surrender. I let go of the banister and begin the long walk down the stairs toward ultimate doom.

I'm standing in front of her, bracing for trouble, when she shrieks, "What happened to your face?"

"What?" I panic, my hands racing to my cheeks. And then I remember how my chin hit the pavement a few hours earlier. "Oh, this? It's nothing," I say, patting it gently. "It's just a scrape. I fell."

She looks at me for a moment, eyes full of judgment, then she shakes her head and says, "The school called."

"I know."

"And what do you have to say for yourself?" she asks, using her damp towel to tap at a ring of yogalates sweat that's formed around her neck.

"Um, not much." I shrug.

"Rio, this just isn't like you." She shakes her head in frustration. "Do you have any idea how much we are spending on your education? Tuition to your little private school is costing us twenty-two thousand dollars a year, and that's just tuition! It doesn't include the extras like books and clothes and activities."

"Dad can afford it." I glare at her.

"That's not the point. The point is that it's a *privilege* to receive an education like that and I will not have you throw it all away. When I was your age—"

"Yeah, I know," I interrupt her. "When you were my age, you were working as a model to put food on the table for you and Nana. You walked sixty blocks in the New York snow, just to save on cab fare." I roll my eyes.

"Well, it's true, Rio. I didn't have the advantages that you do."

Well you seem to be doing all right now, Mrs. Louis Vuitton–Yogalates!

But I only think that, I don't say it.

"How'd you get home?" she asks, peering at my chin like it may hold the answer.

"Some friends drove me," I say, studying the toe of my tennis shoe as though it's fascinating.

"And who are these friends of yours?"

"Jas and Mason. They're just some kids from school."

"Are these your detention friends?" she asks.

Okay. Now I know what this is really about. It's not about breaking school policy, or exorbitant tuition, or even the possible negative effect of detention on my academic standing.

Oh, no.

It's about hanging with *the wrong crowd.*

In my mom's world, being popular with the princess posse takes precedence. And the fact that I've never belonged to a group like that *really* bugs her. But I just say, "Whatever," and roll my eyes again. Mostly because I know how much she hates it when I do that.

She's gripping her bottle of Evian so hard it makes a crackling sound, then she dabs at some sweat on her forehead and says, "I don't like your tone, young lady. And let me tell you something else, your father is not going to be at all happy when he hears about this. He is working on a very big case right now and the last thing he needs is to hear this."

"So let's not tell him," I say, looking right at her.

She stares at me for a moment, and I'm waiting for her to really lay into me. But when she doesn't, I go, "Can I be excused?"

When she nods, I bolt upstairs to my room and close the door firmly. But I don't slam it 'cause that's just asking for it.

I throw my books on the floor and rush over to my laptop, which is perched on a sturdy box in the corner. And when I check my e-mail I'm totally disappointed that my in box is empty.

So I tool around the Internet for a while, looking stuff up, and when my computer finally beeps I check my mail again. And I'm feeling all excited, until I see that it's just a note from my dad. Not that that isn't nice, because he's back in New York, and I haven't seen him for over a week. But still, it's not the same as getting something from a friend.

I hit reply and tell him how I started school today, and about my new art project, but somehow I totally avoid mentioning detention. Then I tell him how much I miss him, and to hurry home.

And then Paige instant messages me.

PAIGE: How'd it go 2day??????
ME: Awesome!!! I got detention! ☺

And the pathetic thing is, I do think it was awesome, because up until today nothing ever really happened to me. I mean, I've always just gone along and blended in. But now I'm in a new school, making a new start.

I can be whoever I want to be.

$\mathcal{S}$ix

The next morning when I'm getting ready for school my mom "suggests" that I wear this new Michael Stars T-shirt she bought me, and I don't even fight it. I just put it on, with the 7 for All Mankind (whatever the hell that means) jeans she also "suggested," then I sit quietly on the edge of my bed while she attempts to cover my chin scab with her tiny, little makeup brush and a pot of Chanel concealer. And even when the final result is just a big, nasty, *beige* chin scab, I don't protest. I just smile, grab my backpack, and let her drive me to school.

Then the minute she drops me off, I head straight for the bathroom where I cover the T-shirt with the " ape   Crew" sweatshirt I had stashed in my backpack and go over to the sink, where I wash all the beige off my chin so that it's back to being purplish red, but at least it looks natural.

When I sit at my desk in English I'm hoping that Kristi won't stare at me all through class again. I mean, I'm so dressed down there's really nothing to see. But she does it anyway. And every time I get the courage to look over and confront her she looks away.

After class when I'm switching out books at my locker, I glance over toward her locker where she's talking to these two other cheerleaders. They're laughing hysterically at something she said, and it's kind of obvious that Kristi's like the CEO and they're competing to be her apprentice. I mean, just because I've never been popular, doesn't mean I don't get how they operate.

But while I'm standing there watching them and thinking all this, Kristi looks over and sees *me* staring at *her!*

Oh, god. Now that I've been caught I know I have to do something fast, but I just continue to stand there like the biggest geek on the planet. And then Kristi says something to her friends and they all turn and stare. Then the redhead waves and they all start laughing again. So I quickly slam my locker shut and make a run for my art class. Real smooth, I know.

When I get to our table Jas isn't there yet, but Mason is. So I lean toward her and whisper, "Did you get in trouble?"

"Yeah," she says. "You?"

"Totally." I roll my eyes. "My mom gave me this big lecture about disadvantaged youth, how lucky I am, and how much they spend on this school. Please." I roll my eyes and shake my head.

"I'm here on full scholarship," she says. "I live with my mom in a tiny apartment in Costa Mesa."

Silence.

She's looking right at me, but I don't know how she can even see me because I'm like half an inch tall now and I'm choking on my own foot. "Sorry," I whisper. *God, I really am a spoiled brat.*

"Whatever." She shrugs.

Jas arrives then, and completely unaware of our girl-on-girl tension, he says something funny.

But it's one of those moments when you're busy inside your own head, listening to a continuous play of the stupid, hurtful, snotty thing you just said. So you can't really hear the words that were just spoken to you, but you can tell by the delivery that you're supposed to laugh.

So I do.

But apparently a little too loudly, 'cause Jas looks at me strangely and a bunch of students turn and stare, and I'm thinking maybe I should just hang out in the darkroom until graduation.

I guess this upcoming art show is like a pretty big deal. Mason really wants to go to an art school like Parsons or something, so she's pretty serious about working on her portfolio and not wrecking her chance at a scholarship by getting into any more trouble. At least that's what she said right before getting up from our table and heading for her easel.

Then Jas got up and went over to the potter's wheel, and with his hands immersed in clay, he looked completely gorgeous and intense. So before I could do or say anything stupid I asked Ms. Tate if I could walk around campus and see if I could find something inspiring for my own project.

She hands me a hall pass that's dangling on a long string, so I slip it around my neck, grab my camera, and head out.

In New York, my old school was like this big, imposing brick building that you entered at eight and left at three, and you rarely saw any daylight in between. But here, it's the exact opposite. Instead of one big building, it's like several smaller ones made of smooth beige stone with green-tinted glass windows, and they're all connected by these sun-dappled, rambling walkways lined with flowers on one side and color-coordinated lockers on the other. There's even a view of the ocean from the lunch area! I mean, it looks more like a resort than a high school, but then everything in Newport Beach is so polished and glossy and new (even the people!) that sometimes I wonder if we've accidentally moved to Stepford.

I head out to the big athletic field behind the gym where there are some guys running around the track. And as I stand there watching them take the corner, I contemplate doing a whole "motion, speed, and glory" kind of theme. But since I'm not really into sports, I doubt it will hold my interest.

I'm resting my camera against my shoulder, and trying to come up with something creative, when I notice Kristi and company sitting on the grass just a few feet away, and they just stop what they're doing (inspecting their cuticles and gossiping) and stare.

It's the first time I've seen Kristi out of her cheerleading ensemble but there's no doubt it's her. She's wearing the same kind of terry-cloth drawstring shorts like my mom wears, a pair of silver Nikes, and a T-shirt with a picture of a seagull on it that says "Sea Crest High School" (which is what they make us wear when we do PE), and her long dark hair is in two braids. Her two friends are like total clones of her except that apprentice wanna-be number one has brown eyes and long red hair in two braids, and number two has long brown hair with major blond highlights, but I can't see her eyes because they're hidden behind a pair of big, black Versace sunglasses.

So then all of a sudden they lean in really close to one another and give me this big fake smile and wave. And it seems really strange. And I'm not sure what to do. So I just sort of stand there and give a little wave back.

And then Kristi goes, "Hey, Brazil. Take the picture already!"

Brazil? Oh, very cute. And then I realize they're posing for me. But I don't really want to photograph them. But I also know that actually telling them that would make me a social casualty for the next two years (if I'm not one already).

So I fake-take it.

And then I go, "Thanks."

But when I turn to walk away, Kristi says, "I didn't hear it click. You better take another."

So I go, "Oh. Really?" And then I peer at the camera, angling it in all these different ways, like I'm looking for a defect.

Then Kristi says through clenched teeth with her lips barely moving, "Just take another one before my face cracks from smiling."

So I do.

And this time when I push down on the shutter it makes that click-ing sound, and the second it's over she goes, "I need to approve that before you use it for anything."

Like I'm with *The Enquirer* and she's Jennifer Aniston. But I don't say anything. I just nod and walk away.

Lunch is definitely the scariest part of the day. It's like thirty-five min-utes of unstructured hell for the new girl. And even though I started the day thinking I had two new friends, the fact is now I'm not so sure.

By the time I got back to class Mason and Jas were already gone and I had no idea where to find them. So I turned in the hall pass, expecting Ms. Tate to be mad that I was gone that whole time, but she just smiled.

And since I snuck off campus yesterday, I'm not really sure what the lunch rules are, but I know they exist because every school has them. It's like, you can't just walk up to some random table and take a seat, since everyone is so segregated into such carefully designated groups, that you can't just assume you'll be welcomed.

Not to mention that my mom made lunch for me today, and I'm not sure if that's cool or not. I mean, how embarrassing would it be to sit at the wrong table and pull out a sandwich made by Mom's carefully manicured, self-tanned hands when everybody else is hitting the vending machines. It may sound paranoid, but it's those little moments that label you forever.

And I'm not used to worrying about stuff like this, 'cause at my old school it was just me, Paige, and Hud (I know, you already know that, but please play along), and we didn't really care what everyone else thought. I guess you could say we were geeks, but it didn't matter. But now that it's just me, I admit, it kind of matters.

But I'm also hungry.

And how stupid would it be to not eat my lunch when I'm hungry? So I grab the bag out of my locker and figure I'll just go sit in some shady spot near the lunch tables so I can check out the action without actually putting myself on the front line. And as I'm walking over there I hear someone go, "Hey, Rio!"

And I turn to see Jas waving at me. So of course I immediately change direction. As I'm walking toward him he's looking right at me and it makes me all nervous, so I look up for a moment at this banner that's hanging overhead that says in turquoise-and-green letters:

Winter Formal!
This Saturday!
Don't miss it!

And when I'm right in front of him he asks, "Do you like movies?"

Ohmygod! He's asking me out! I knew it! Deep down inside, I *knew* he wasn't dating Mason!

So I go, "Um yeah, I *really love* movies!" As I mentally prepare for the best (okay, first), date of my life.

"Great," he says, smiling and wrapping his arm loosely around my shoulder as we walk down the hall, with me acting all casual, like I'm totally used to having gorgeous guys who smell amazing ask me out on dates.

And when we get to the end, he opens the classroom door and goes, "We're having a film club meeting and we need more members. Are you interested?" He looks at me, waiting for an answer.

"Uh, sure," I squeak, clutching my lunch bag and following him into a room filled with five other people who *really love* movies.

I don't know how I did it, but I managed to get through the rest of the day (including detention), without doing anything majorly stupid. But mostly because I stayed very quiet, and I didn't look at Jas.

So as I was walking to the parking lot, where my mom was supposed to be waiting, I turned on my cell phone just in time to listen to a message from her telling me how she was running late, and that I could either: a) wait *or* b) call a cab.

A cab? Is she kidding? There are no cabs in Newport Beach. 'Cause from what I've seen you can't even live here unless you own a Mercedes, a Jag, or a Hummer. So I sit on the curb, deciding to wait, and just as I'm calling to tell her that, Kristi walks up.

"Hey, Brazil," she says, standing in front of me, holding a Louis Vuitton bag with one hand and shielding her eyes from the sun with the other, so as not to disturb the Chanel sunglasses that are carefully placed in her hair.

"Um, it's not Brazil, it's Rio," I say, pausing between numbers.

"Why are you still here?" she asks, looking at her watch, then back at me.

"I had detention," I tell her, even though it's really none of her business.

She raises an eyebrow and looks me over. "So what are you doing now?"

"Waiting for my mom. She's late."

"Don't you have a car?" she says, eyes going all wide like she just found out something really juicy.

"No." I shrug. "I don't have my license yet."

"You're joking." She says it like a statement not a question.

And I press my lips together and raise my shoulders in a slightly more animated shrug than the previous one.

"Oh, my god. We totally have to fix that."

We? I think. But again, I don't say anything.

"Come on, I'll give you a ride."

"No, that's okay," I say. "She'll be here." But deep down inside I wonder if it's true.

"Come," she demands, dangling her keys.

And I hesitate for a moment. Then I get up and follow her. But not because she's that powerful, but because my mom is that unreliable.

"So where do you live?" she asks, starting up the engine of a silver convertible Mercedes.

"Over on Playa del Sol. Is this your car?" I mean, I'm amazed that someone in high school would drive this.

"I wish. It's my mom's. Mine's a TT Convertible, but it's getting customized," she says, pulling out of the student lot. "So I live nearby. I'm on Vista del Mar." She looks at me and smiles in a way that's not exactly warm, but not entirely evil either.

"Oh, I think Jas lives on that street," I say, just trying to make conversation and *not* because I wanted to say his name out loud.

"Jasper Klein? You know him?" Kristi asks, narrowing her eyes.

"Uh, yeah," I say, looking out the window, because she's making me uncomfortable.

"How do you know him?"

"We have AP Art together," I say, turning to watch the road for her since she's still looking at me.

"So how do you know where he lives? Have you been to his house?"

"Just once." *God, why is she interrogating me?*

"Oh, well then you must have seen my house, because I live right across the street." She smiles brightly, but there's something behind it.

I just shrug.

"So are you guys going to Winter Formal together?" she asks.

"What? Jas and me? I don't think so. I mean, no, definitely not." *Oh, that was cool.* "Why, are you going?"

"Duh? Of course I'm going." She rolls her eyes and shakes her head.

I just look out the window then because I really don't know what else to do, and I'm beginning to wonder if she's only driving me home so she can gather information to use against me later. I mean, not to sound paranoid, but really, why would a perfect, popular girl like her want to hang with me? It's like one minute she's being nice, and the next she's making fun of me 'cause I asked her about the dance. I'm beginning to feel like I'm caught in a game I don't know the rules to.

When we finally turn onto my street I've never been so happy to call this place home. "Um, it's the one at the end, right there." I point at my house, then hurriedly remove my sweatshirt and shove it inside my backpack.

"You live there? Wow, that house is like, major. What does your dad do?"

"He's a lawyer," I say, gathering my books, anxious to get out of here.

"Really?" She looks at my house again like she's trying to add it all up.

"Okay, well thanks," I say, climbing out of the Mercedes just as my mom pulls into the driveway. Great.

"Rio, you could have called. I went all the way to your school." She's lecturing me, but peering at Kristi.

"Sorry," I say, trapped between two luxury cars.

"Is that your mom?" Kristi whispers, watching her get out of the Jag.

"Uh, yeah. Mom, this is Kristi. Kristi, my mom." I watch them exchange nearly identical perfect teeth smiles, then I go, "Okay, see ya."

"She looks really familiar," Kristi says.

But I don't acknowledge it. I just wave good-bye and go inside.

So, of course, like the minute I walk in the door my mom goes (in her animated voice), "She seems really nice!" Then she looks at me waiting for confirmation.

"She does? How can you tell? From the Mercedes?"

"Is she a friend of yours?" she continues, ignoring my comment.

"Not really."

"Well, she must like you or else why would she drive you home?" she asks hopefully.

"Got me." I head upstairs.

"What's her last name?" She's following right behind me.

Jeez, I can't believe her. We've been here like what? A week? And she's already familiar with the local who's who. "I think it's Wood," I say, going into my room and throwing my books on the floor in the corner since I *still* don't have any furniture, which is getting really old by the way.

"Wood. Wood," she says, squinting at the wall. "I think there's a Wood in my yogalates class."

"I don't doubt it." I boot up my laptop and make myself comfortable on the floor.

"Rio, you're not e-mailing Paige and Hud are you?" she asks, standing over me, all disapproving.

"No," I lie. "I'm doing homework."

"Good. Because, we live *here* now, and it's really time you made some friends at your new school. Kristi seems really nice and I think you should give her a chance."

"Mom, can I please just do my homework?" I point at my computer.

"Of course," she says, smiling. "I'll let you know when dinner's ready."

And the second she leaves I instant message Paige.

Seven

The next day in AP English I'm sitting at my desk when Kristi looks over and says, "Hey, Brazil."

But I don't correct her this time because I know she knows my real name. She's just trying to be all cute or something.

"Is your mom Jahne Jones?" She stares at me, waiting for an answer.

And while I'm hesitating, Mrs. Abbot says, "Open your books to page one twenty-five. Hunter, would you read for us starting with the second paragraph?"

And luckily I'm off the hook for now. Because I don't know if she meant Jahne Jones from her mom's yogalates class, or Jahne Jones former almost-supermodel. And the truth is, I don't really feel like talking about either one.

My mom is complicated. Well actually, my mom is pretty simple, it's our relationship that's complicated. I mean, it's not that she's a bad person or anything because she's not. It's just that she's extremely interested in things that don't really do it for me. Like she's really into shopping, and I don't know why, but even though I like nice things, I think wearing a ton of labels is kind of embarrassing. She's also really into her looks, and I never feel comfortable with mine.

But now that I'm taller and my braces are gone, people are starting to say we look alike. Which I guess is a compliment, but to be honest, I'm not really comfortable with that kind of attention like she is. It's like, my mom lives to be in front of the camera, but I'd rather be behind it.

And for the record, Jahne is *not* her real name. She was born Jane Jones. But when she became a model they thought that was too plain so they added an *h* and changed the pronunciation to *Jah*-ne. She started traveling the world on fashion shoots when she was only fourteen, so she didn't really finish high school, but she took her GED and she reads a lot so she's not stupid.

Because of her job she met all these famous people, like rock stars, movie stars, and other models you might have heard of, and even though she was once on location with Christy, Linda, Cindy, Naomi, and Claudia, she never quite made it to their level. She's more like someone people vaguely recognize but they're not sure why.

Then, when she was around twenty-four, she was on a flight from L.A. to New York, and sitting in first class right next to her was Griffin Jones (her future husband/my dad). They started dating, blah blah blah, and within three months they got married and she didn't even have to change her last name. (I just hope somebody had the good sense to make sure they're not related or something because how gross would that be?) When she had me at twenty-five and a half, they moved to the 'burbs and that was pretty much the end of her modeling career.

Anyway, I know my mom would love it if I came home and told her about the question Kristi just asked me, and that's exactly why I won't tell her. Because then she'll start asking me about her every day and she'll end up all disappointed when Kristi and I don't become best friends. Since that will never happen. Girls like Kristi don't hang with girls like me. And my mom always makes me feel like my choice of friends is one big disappointment. It's like, I'm never popular enough, stylish enough, or cool enough to please her.

But I don't care. I mean, I may look like my mom now, but I still think more like my dad.

When the bell rings Kristi slams her book shut, grabs her things, and leaves the room without once looking at me.

See? What did I tell you?

———

At lunch I follow Mason, Jas, and some other guys from the film club to this grassy area behind the art building. And despite it being only January, the day has grown hot and bright. So I take off my sweatshirt, throw it on the ground, then sit on top of it and peer inside my lunch bag.

Mason takes a bite of her Snickers bar, then lies back on the grass and closes her eyes, and Jas looks at me and goes, "So what's going on after school?"

"Um, I don't know." I shrug, biting into my turkey and avocado sandwich and refusing to read anything more into that since I've been down this path before. "Don't we have detention?"

"After that," he says.

"I have to work," Mason says with her eyes still closed.

"Where do you work?" I ask. I had no idea she had a job.

"Urban Outfitters. It's in Costa Mesa."

"That's cool. Do you get a discount?"

She nods, still not opening her eyes.

"What about you?" Jas asks. "Do you want to come by and hang out? I can teach you to surf."

"Isn't the water freezing?" I ask.

"I'll lend you a wet suit." He smiles.

"Okay." I shrug, and take another bite of my sandwich, trying to act like I'm not really excited about that, even though I am.

So we're sitting in the sun and Mason's dozing, and Jas is sketching, and the three guys from the film club are talking about that movie *Garden State,* which I make a mental note to rent, when Kristi and Company and a couple guys easily recognizable as jocks walk right by us and go, "Fucking stoners."

Then one of the jocks throws an orange at us that just misses Jas's head. And then they all start laughing.

And as they're walking away Kristi's looking back at me, but I turn to Jas and go, "What was that about?"

"Class wars." He shrugs, ignoring the orange sitting on the ground right next to him, and continuing with his drawing.

"What do you mean?"

"They hate us," he says, shrugging.

"But why? We weren't bothering them."

"They hate us because we're not like them, and we don't want to be like them."

He continues sketching, but I just sit there staring at the orange, wondering if it's really that simple.

$\mathcal{E}$ight

So after detention I go to Jas's house. I called my mom earlier when I was sure she wouldn't be home, left a message telling her not to pick me up 'cause I was hanging with friends, then turned off my cell so she couldn't call me back. I know that sounds sneaky, but it's the only way to deal with her. I mean, she really has no boundaries.

When we get to his house I'm all nervous to see that his dad is there, but Jas introduces us and his dad is really nice, and pretty much the exact opposite of my dad. Not that my dad isn't really nice, because he is, but Jas's dad is like a "cool dad." He has brown hair with touches of gray that he wears kind of wavy and longish, and his face looks a lot like Jas's except for the eye color. His are really dark brown, where Jas's are more golden-bronze. And I'm not trying to be all poetic and creepy and love-struck, it's just a fact that Jas's eyes look like topaz.

Anyway, his hair was all wet because he said he just came in from surfing! I can't imagine my dad surfing. I mean, the few times we got him to lay on the beach at our old house in the Hamptons he always had a stack of legal papers at his side and would end up on his cell phone talking strategy, barely noticing that there was an ocean in front of him. But it's not like he's boring or anything, he just takes his job very seriously. Because it is.

But Jas's dad, Seth, is standing there talking about how the ocean is all really high curl or swell or whatever, and watching them talk they seem more like friends than father and son. Then Jas tells him that I just moved here from New York.

So his dad goes, "Some of the best restaurants in the world are in New York."

I just smile, because people say that, but really, how would I know?

"My dad owns a few restaurants in Newport and Laguna," Jas tells me.

And I go, "Oh."

Then his dad says it was nice meeting me and to have fun, and he disappears into another part of the house.

Jas looks at me and goes, "So, you ready for your lesson?"

"I don't have anything to wear."

He shrugs. "I can lend you some shorts, a T-shirt, and one of my old wet suits. How tall are you?" He squints at me.

"Almost five ten," I admit, feeling kind of embarrassed.

"I should have something." He nods. "Follow me."

My first surf lesson was so not *Blue Crush*. I totally sucked. And even though Jas was really patient and nice about it (not to mention it being a good excuse to get him to put his arms around me and hold me steady), after wiping out on my third baby wave, and choking on salt water, it was pretty clear that I'm no surf Betty. So I called it quits, and swam to shore.

I'm sitting on the sand watching Jas and I guess I never really noticed before (being from a place that worships Derek Jeter and not Kelly Slater), but surfing is like this incredibly beautiful sport. I mean, it's almost poetic, like man and nature melding together in one perfect, seamless moment.

I reach into my bag, pull out my camera, and take what I hope will be some really great photos of Jas in the middle of the curl (or whatever they call it). And then I get up and head over to the tide pools and take some close-ups of sea urchins, hermit crabs, and things like that.

As I'm heading back, Jas is walking toward me with his board under his arm, and he looks so amazingly cute that I make sure I use my very last shot on that.

"Hope you weren't too bored," he says, sticking his board in the sand, unzipping his wet suit, pulling it down to his trunks, and rubbing his hair with a towel.

"No, it was great," I tell him, trying not to drool over his tight, tan abs. "I think I got some good shots."

"So how'd you like your first lesson?" he asks, grabbing his board and leading me up the steps to his house.

"I think I have a long way to go."

"It takes practice." He nods. "I've been surfing since I was a little kid. My dad used to put me on his board with him."

The stairs lead right up to his backyard and when we get to the top, Jas stops, pulls off his wet suit, and drapes it over one of the lounge chairs we ate lunch on the other day. So I unzip and wriggle out of mine too, and I do it quickly since I'm on high alert for Holden the crotch-sniffer. But I don't see him anywhere, so I relax and follow Jas through the sliding-glass doors, and into the kitchen.

I'm standing next to the sink, and I feel really bad because the tank top and shorts I'm wearing are so wet that I'm dripping water all over the Spanish tile floor. So while Jas looks for something to drink, I drop my towel on the ground, and use my foot to kind of slide it around and dry it off. "Um, I'm dripping everywhere. I'm really sorry," I tell him.

"No worries," he says, closing the fridge, and turning to hand me a bottle of beer.

But when I go to take it from him I notice he's looking at my chest, and his face is all red. And when I look down, I see why.

Talk about a wet T-shirt contest!

Ohmygod! Everything is on display! I quickly fold my arms across my chest and say, "Um, I think I better go change now."

And he just stands there looking at me with his mouth kind of open like he's about to say something, but I leave before he can.

As he's driving me home we're mostly quiet, but I'm not sure if it's because he's tired from the surfing or if he's embarrassed because just ten minutes ago I was pretty much topless in his kitchen. And when we finally get to my house, he looks at me and says, "See you tomorrow."

And I go, "Okay." And it's like I can feel him watching me as I walk to the door, but when I look back, he drives away.

As I walk in the house I'm braced for my mom's inevitable inquisition. So I quickly pop a breath mint and run through my made-up story. But when I go into the kitchen I see I won't have to use it.

"Oh, good, I want you to meet my daughter, Rio." My mom is sitting at the white, plastic, temporary kitchen table across from some lady who I've never met but looks strangely familiar.

"Rio, this is Kristi's mother, Katrina. We're in yogalates together."

Oh, god, that's why she looks so familiar. She's like Kristi with fake boobs and Botox. "Hey," I say, noticing that she's staring at me almost as hard as her daughter does.

"Were you working on the Winter Formal decorations, too?" And then without even waiting for a response she looks at my mom and says, "The girls are so excited about the dance! You should see the adorable dress Kristi's wearing." She shakes her head and smiles at me, and I smile back, kind of. "Did you get your dress yet?" she asks.

And before I can even answer, my mom says, "Well, Rio's still getting settled in. This is only her third day of school." Jeez, she sounds so defensive, like she's embarrassed or something.

They both turn and look at me, but I just stand there and shrug. I mean, what am I supposed to do? Apologize for not being an "IT" girl?

"Mom, I've got a ton of homework, so I'm gonna go upstairs," I say, ignoring the disappointed look in her eyes, because it's nothing new, I'm always disappointing her. "Nice meeting you, Mrs. Wood."

"You too! I'll tell Kristi you said hi," she singsongs.

"You do that," I say, heading for the stairs.

Then my mom goes, "Rio, why is your hair wet?"

But I just keep climbing, ignoring the question.

Nine

The next day in Art I'm still feeling really embarrassed about the very unfortunate *Girls Gone Wild* incident in Jas's kitchen. But he's acting totally normal toward me, so I guess if he can pretend it never happened, then I can, too.

I've decided to do my art project on beauty. But not beauty like you're probably thinking. Not in the usual way of a heavily made-up pop star or a perfectly cultivated rose. But in how it can be found in the unexpected, like in the curve of a teacup, or the dance of a light object caught in the wind.

So I tell Ms. Tate, and after she approves and is walking back to her desk, Jas looks up from sketching and goes, "You're beautiful."

Just like that.

Then he goes right back to his project and doesn't say anything else for the rest of class.

"You're beautiful. You're beautiful. You're beautiful. You're beautiful. You're beautiful. You're beautiful. You're beautiful. You're beautiful. You're beautiful. Yo—"

It's like a mantra in my head. All through Calculus, all through Economics, on the field at lunch when we all just quietly doze in the sun. It keeps running through my head, over and over again, like on continuous play.

He looked up and said, "You're beautiful." And then he looked down again.

But what exactly did he mean? Was it just an observation? Was he just being nice?

Or does he *like me* like me?

When I got home later that day I ran into my room and threw my books down onto—*my bed?*

There's a bed in my room. Which I know is not supposed to be strange because, after all it's a *bedroom,* but where did it come from?

I turn around and yell, "Mom?"

But she's standing in the doorway, laughing. "Do you like it?" she asks.

"Oh, my god, I love it!" And I do. It's like the coolest room ever and I can't believe how she picked it all out, and got it so right, without any input from me.

Everything is simple clean lines, and it all goes together perfectly without being too matched. (I don't like it when things look all matchy-matchy.) She got me a new platform bed and it's covered in this really pretty kiwi-green comforter with all these sequined and beaded throw pillows scattered around. There's a dark wood desk for my computer, floating shelves for my books, two night tables, a really cool large dresser, and these beaded hanging lamps that I had found in a catalog and circled. She even had some of my favorite photos matted and placed in these beautiful silver frames.

"It's so cool," I say, bouncing on my new bed, then getting up to run my hand over my new desk.

"But how—" I start.

"I've been very busy this week. It's not all yogalates you know." She smiles.

"Thanks, Mom," I say, vowing to be nicer to her from now on. Really.

"Mine is supposed to arrive tomorrow. Let's hope it gets here before your dad gets home."

"Dad's coming home?" I ask excitedly. "I thought it was going to be another week."

"It's just for the weekend. He has to go back on Monday."

"Cool." I start unpacking my books and stacking them on top of my new desk.

"I'll start dinner," she says, turning to leave.

"Mom?"

"Yeah?" she pauses, looking at me.

"What does it mean when a guy tells you you're beautiful, but then he doesn't really say anything else to you for the rest of the day?" I mean, let's face it, if anyone's used to being told she's beautiful it's my mom.

"It means you *are* beautiful, Rio." Then she smiles and walks away.

These are the awesome things that happened today (Friday):

1. Kristi was absent from English, which meant I could relax because no one was staring at me.
2. My dad is due in at John Wayne Airport (I swear that's what they call it. There's even a statute of "The Duke" next to the baggage claim carousel).
3. Jas asked me out on a date. (!!!!!!!!!!!!!!!!!)

This is how number three came about. We were sitting on the grass at lunch, and when the bell rang Mason got up to make a quick phone call before her next class, and Jas looked at me and said, "So what are you doing this weekend?"

And I shrugged and said, "Well my dad's getting in today, so I'll probably just hang with my family."

And he went, "Well do you want to do something Saturday night?"

And as I picked up my trash, I was thinking: *This is it! He's going to ask me to Winter Formal at the very last minute!*

So I said, "Yeah, okay."

And then he *smiled* and said, "Let's do dinner. I'll pick you up at seven."

And I go, "Cool."

Then we started walking to class. And I was in front, and he was in back.

And I tripped.

So I looked down to see what I tripped on, but of course there was nothing there. It was just me being my usual clumsy self.

But that's not the point. The point is I'm going on a date with Jas.

So I'm in the Range Rover with my mom on the way to the airport, and I go, "Do you think we could go shopping tomorrow?"

"You want to go shopping with me?" She looks all surprised and happy, like that was the nicest thing I've ever said to her. Which sadly, it may be.

"Yeah," I say.

And then she goes, "Rio! Are you going to Winter Formal?"

Great. I don't want to disappoint her, but if I lie, I'll be showing up for dinner in an evening gown. "No. I'm just having dinner with a friend and I wanted something new to wear."

"Oh," she says, hiding her disappointment, but not entirely. "Is this the same friend that told you you were beautiful?"

I nod, and look out the window, because I'm starting to feel embarrassed.

"So, what's his name?" she asks.

"Um, Jas," I say, hoping she won't remember the last time she heard that name.

But she does.

"Isn't that your detention friend?"

"Don't call him that," I say, mentally scolding myself for trying to open up to her. *God, I should have known better.*

"I don't know about this, Rio." She looks in the rearview mirror as she merges into the arrivals lane.

"Fine. You don't have to take me shopping, but I already said yes to the date." I fold my arms across my chest and shoot daggers at her from behind my sunglasses.

"There's your father," she says between clenched teeth. "We'll discuss this later."

She pulls up to the curb and jumps out to hug my dad, and I climb into the backseat where I sulk until he notices me.

"Hey, kiddo, did you miss me?" he asks, reaching back for an awkward hug.

"Yeah, Dad, I missed you," I say, hugging him with one arm.

We have dinner at this place called Roy's, and like the minute my mom gets up to use the bathroom I pounce. "Dad, someone asked me out for tomorrow night, but Mom doesn't want me to go because you're home. But I kind of want to go, since I'm just starting to make friends here, and you and I can hang out during the day all day tomorrow and again on Sunday."

"Go! Have fun! Don't miss out on account of your old man." He smiles and squeezes my shoulder.

That's what I was hoping he'd say.

So when my mom comes back to the table, my dad looks at her and says, "I told Rio to go ahead and hang out with her friends tomorrow night."

She looks at me and narrows her eyes into tight, angry slits.

"I figured we could find some way to entertain ourselves," he says.

And then she looks at him and smiles. And he winks at her.

Gross.

But totally worth it.

On Saturday afternoon while my mom and dad were looking at linens in some specialty shop in South Coast Plaza (which is like the most amazing mall *in the universe*), I was wandering on my own looking for something to wear for my big date with Jas.

Not that Jas seems like the kind of guy who cares hugely about clothes, and not that my closet's not already full of things that my mom buys for me and sticks in there, I just kind of wanted something new to mark the occasion.

So as I'm about to go in some store called Ron Herman that has a very cool window display, I bump straight into Katrina Wood and her Mini Me, Kristi. I'm not kidding. They're both wearing low-slung jeans, with pastel thongs (sandals, not underwear!) that match their pastel pedicures and little velour Juicy Couture hoodie tops (that match the thongs and the pedicures), and they both have long dark hair, flat-ironed into submission.

"Hi, Rio!" they both say like they're actually happy to see me.

"Oh, hey."

"What are you doing here?" Mrs. Wood asks, while her daughter stands there and stares at me just like in English.

"I'm just shopping around. My parents are looking at stuff for the house."

"Are you going tonight?" Kristi asks.

"Where?" I ask nervously, wondering how she could possibly know about Jas and me.

"Winter Formal!"

I can tell she wants to add *"Duh?"* to the end of that statement, but doesn't because of her mom.

"Oh, no. I'm not going."

I don't think I sounded depressed when I said it, but Kristi and Katrina exchange sad looks, then Mama Wood goes, "Oh, honey. You got a late start. You'll be going next year, you'll see." Then she smiles tenderly and gives me a little pat on the arm. Gag.

When I'm finally rid of them, I go inside the store and browse through this rack of amazing ninety-dollar T-shirts. I mean, at first you might think they look like every other T-shirt in the world, but on these hangers and under these lights, you somehow start believing they're worth it. So I grab a white one and a black one, then I walk around, collecting other stuff like tank tops, jeans, and cargo pants.

And when my arms are nearly full, and I'm heading for the dressing rooms, I pass this section filled with all this stuff that girls like Kristi wear. You know, like little miniskirts and beaded, silky girly tops. I look around to see if anyone's watching (not that they would care), then I grab some of that and take it all into the dressing room.

I try on the girly stuff first.

And when I'm standing in front of the three-way mirror in this frayed denim mini (not unlike the one I already own, but refuse to wear), and this tiny pink halter top that covers *only* the areas required by law, I barely recognize myself. I guess I'm so used to hiding under baggy sweatshirts and jeans that I had no idea this was even possible. I mean, this may sound crazy, but I look like a blond version of Kristi!

I release my hair from its usual ponytail and flip it so it falls wild and wavy around my face, then I reach into my purse, grab my lip balm, and cake it on until my lips are thick and glowy. I turn and gaze at myself, adjusting the mirrors so I can see every angle. And then, I admit, I start posing and dancing around with an imaginary headset, lip-synching just like Britney.

I look seductively into the mirror and jump and kick and spin around and around until I'm dizzy, and just as I'm catching my breath I notice a sign on the dressing-room wall:

THIS DRESSING ROOM IS UNDER SURVEILLANCE

Under surveillance?

Ohmygod! Am I being watched?

I frantically look behind the mirrors, up at the ceiling, and even under the little bench piled high with clothes, anxiously searching for the hidden camera that may have captured a moment that *can never be made public!*

But just because I don't find one doesn't mean it's not there, so I quickly pull off the skirt and top, placing them carefully back on their hangers (just in case I really *am* being observed). Then I pull my hair back into a ponytail and calmly try on the kind of clothes I'm more used to wearing.

———

Dressed in a new pair of cargo pants, a white tank top, some little beaded flats that look like Moroccan slippers, gold dangly earrings with little red stones, and a denim jacket in case it gets cold, I'm sitting on the edge of my bed waiting for Jas, because I don't want to go downstairs and be interrogated by my mom.

I mean, I was really hoping that my parents would just go out to dinner or something so I'd be spared the introductions. But my mom decided to stay home and cook. And I know she's doing it just to spite me.

So the second the bell rings I come charging out of my room, and down the stairs at a potentially leg-breaking speed. "I'll get it!" I shout.

But my mom, who's already downstairs, and therefore has a major head start on me, walks calmly out of the kitchen, reaches for the door handle, looks pointedly at me, and says, "*I'll* get it."

Great.

When she opens the door, Jas is standing there smiling and looking like a total hottie in his crisp, dark denim jeans, cool vintage T-shirt, black leather jacket, and hair still slightly wet from the shower.

"Hi, Mrs. Jones," he says. "I'm Jas." He shakes her hand.

"Won't you come in?" My mom holds the door open and smiles.

Oh, God, here we go.

She leads him into the living room where my dad is busy watching a very exciting program on C-SPAN, and after all the introductions are made my dad asks where the "young man" is taking me.

"We're having dinner at one of my dad's restaurants," Jas says, smiling patiently.

And after a never-ending conversation about *that,* I go, "Um, we should be going now."

Then my mom says something about a curfew, which I swear she just made up right then since I wasn't even aware that I had one. So I make sure I get in one really good eye roll directed right at her, that she sees but my dad misses. And then, mercifully, we're out the door and in Jas's car.

"Sorry about that," I say. "My parents are so lame."

"Most parents are lame," he says, starting the engine.

"But your dad seems really cool." I catch a glimpse of his profile and think how lucky I am to be going out with him.

"He has his moments."

Then right as he's pulling out of the driveway, he goes, "Listen. Mason was going to meet us there but there's been a change of plans so we're gonna pick her up, okay?"

Mason?

Mason is going on our date?

Ohmygod! They really are boyfriend and girlfriend, and I am a total idiot!

But all I say is, "Okay."

Ten

So after picking up Mason, we head back toward the coast to Mirapois, which is the name of Jas's dad's restaurant in Laguna Beach. And I'm now sitting in the backseat since I figured the two lovebirds should be together, right?

They have the stereo cranked up really loud and we're all singing along to some White Stripes CD. But I'm the only one faking it. Partly because I don't really know the words, and partly because what I really feel like doing is hurling myself out of this car, just to see if anyone notices.

When we get to the restaurant there's this tall guy with bleached blond hair and black framed glasses standing near the door, and when he sees Mason he comes over and hugs her.

And then he kisses her.

On the lips.

And Jas just stands there.

Huh?

When they break apart Mason's lipstick is all smeared, and there's even some on her teeth, but she's all smiling and happy and she goes, "Rio, this is my boyfriend, Zane."

And he goes, "Hey, you're the girl from New York, right?"

And I go, "Yeah." I shake his hand and then I look at everyone and I try to get a handle on this latest turn of events.

There are four of us.

And Mason just called Zane her boyfriend.

So does that mean I'm back to being Jas's date?

It turns out that Zane is two years older than us and he goes to Cal Arts, which is some art school in L.A. He and Mason have been dating for like a year, but she pretty much only sees him on weekends because of the distance.

When we get to our table, Mason sits next to Zane so that leaves me next to Jas, and after we order everyone is all quiet, so I go, "You know, up until now, I totally thought you guys were a couple." I point at Jas and Mason. "I guess because you're together a lot with film club and the zine and stuff. I mean, *not* that you're romantic or anything." (I want to make that clear so Zane doesn't think something and get all jealous.)

Jas and Mason look at each other and bust out laughing, and Zane smiles, and looking back on it, it does seem pretty lame and even slightly paranoid.

So we're all eating and Zane, Mason, and Jas are talking about that movie *Eternal Sunshine of the* blah, blah, blah. But I'm just sitting there cutting and chewing, partly because I haven't seen the movie, and partly because all of my attention is now centered on the fact that Jas's shoe is touching mine and I wonder if he realizes it.

And if he *does,* then what exactly does it *mean?* Is it like foreplay— like first we rub feet and then later . . .

Okay, I know it sounds stupid since (as far as I know) the side of the foot is not exactly an erogenous zone, but it's not like I can explain that to my thrashing heart and sweaty palms.

"So what do you think?"

Everyone's looking at me.

"What? Oh, I don't know, I've never seen that movie," I say, carefully placing my fork on my empty plate and trying to fake like I've been listening the whole time.

"I was asking if you wanted dessert." Jas gives me a strange look.

"Oh. No. I'm good," I say, immediately followed by nervous, retarded laughter. *Oh, god.*

So while Mason and Zane decide to share a bowl of assorted sorbets, Jas goes, "Come on. Let's take a walk."

And as I get up from the table Jas grabs my hand, wraps his fingers around mine, and leads me through the restaurant and back into the kitchen where he introduces me to the head chef.

It's total chaos back here, and I'm all worried about being in the way, but Jas just pulls me toward this big silver pot on a stove and goes, "You have got to try this." He holds a spoon full of thick red sauce to my lips.

I swallow the sauce, look into his eyes, and go, "Mmm." Which is my totally pathetic attempt at flirting, which makes me blush, and leaves me feeling like a total cheeseball.

"Good, huh?" he says, pouring us each a glass of wine.

"What's this?" I ask, sipping cautiously since I'm really not used to drinking wine in restaurants, or anywhere else for that matter.

"Silver Oaks cabernet." He swirls his wine and looks around the frenzied kitchen. "This is my dream," he says, smiling.

"But I thought your dad already owned this place," I say, taking another sip.

"He does. What I mean is I want to be a chef."

"You do?"

"Yeah, I love this life. I grew up in it. And if you think about it, food is just another art form, another medium." He smiles. "Just think, I could wake up every morning and surf, paint, and sculpt all afternoon, then head for my restaurant in the evening where I whip up one culinary masterpiece after another. A perfect life!" He clinks his glass against mine.

He's smiling, and his topaz eyes are shining, and his teeth are so white and straight, and his bottom lip has this tiny glistening drop of red wine resting right in the center, and I'm so tempted to lick it off that I distract myself by nervously gulping down the rest of my wine. Which was really stupid because now I'm left with nothing but a dorky smile, a headrush, and an empty glass.

"Want some more?" he asks.

I shake my head no and watch him finish his. Then he puts his hand on the small of my back and goes, "Let's go see if they've ditched us yet."

Sure enough, when we get back to the table Zane is standing and Mason is grabbing her purse.

"I knew you were gonna run out on us." Jas laughs.

"We're taking off. We haven't seen each other for two weeks," Mason says, leaning into Zane. "What are you guys gonna do?"

I look at Jas wondering if he's planned something else, something romantic. But he just shrugs and goes, "Whatever Rio wants."

If he only knew!

We end up wandering through some of the art galleries across from Main Beach, which is the beach they always show on postcards and stuff. During the day it's always supercrowded with body boarders and volleyball players, but at night people like to just hang on the benches and listen to the ocean.

As we're walking into this big gallery called Artist Hut, our hands accidentally bump together, and Jas leaves his like that, warm and lingering against mine. And right when I think he's going to hold my hand for real, he points at this painting and goes, "Can you believe that?"

Hanging on the wall in front of us is this huge canvas depicting the most dreadful rendition of a New York City skyline I've ever seen. The city lights are symbolized by tiny Day-Glo–colored boxes, and the buildings and the sky have such liberal doses of black and charcoal paint that it looks like one of those Tijuana velvet paintings from the seventies. The plaque next to it says the piece is titled, *NYC 24/7*. As a native New Yorker, I'm totally offended.

"Oh, my god, it's awful!" I whisper.

And then Jas starts cracking up. So I start cracking up. And we're laughing so hard we're doubled-over, hanging on to each other. And every time we try to stop, we look at each other and start up again. But then this lady who works there (who obviously doesn't see the humor), comes charging toward us. So Jas grabs my hand and we run out the door and all the way across the street to Main Beach.

We collapse on this bench near the big white lifeguard tower, and as our laughter subsides, I can hear the sound of the waves crashing before us.

"That was the worst!" Jas says, shaking his head.

"Well, maybe if you distanced yourself from the troubled kids you
[ar]em so fond of, the more popular kids would give you a chance. You
[kn]ow, Rio, water seeks its own level."

She looks at me and I roll my eyes, but I do it when I'm looking at
[th]e ground again so that she can't really see it.

"Why don't you wear some of those nice clothes I buy you? Make
[an] effort, and see what happens," she says gently, but persuasively.

"Can I go now?"

"Yes. But, Rio, I don't want you hanging with those kids anymore.
[D]o you understand?"

I just nod my head and take the stairs two at a time.

I nod and pull my jacket tighter around me.

"Cold?" he asks.

"A little," I say.

"Here have some of this. It will warm you up." He offers me a tiny
flask he pulled from his jacket pocket.

I take a sip and immediately recognize the smooth taste of the
cabernet we had earlier in the kitchen, so then I take another. And I'm
so not used to drinking that it immediately goes to my head. "Thanks,"
I say, smiling and leaning into him just a bit.

He puts his arm around my shoulder and rubs up and down, like
he's trying to make me warm. Then he takes his other hand and gently
tucks my hair behind my ear.

His face is close to mine, and he's looking right at me, and I can't
help thinking: *This is it! This is the exact moment when he kisses me!*

And it's kind of embarrassing to admit, but I've never really kissed
a guy before and I'm almost seventeen.

I told you I was a geek.

I mean, a long time ago Paige and I practiced on Hud, so if the opportunity ever arose we wouldn't look completely retarded. But I've
never kissed someone that I really wanted to kiss—like Jas.

So I look into his eyes.

Then I close mine.

And I don't know if it's the wine or just extreme nervousness, but
I hear myself say, "Oh, Jas, I've been waiting for this *all night.*"

Then I open my mouth ever so slightly, and wait.

But nothing happens.

Then Jas says, "Hey." And he sounds a little surprised.

And when I open my eyes this completely gorgeous creature, clad
in an outfit very similar to the one I was lip-synching in earlier, goes,
"I just got off work, and stopped by the restaurant. They said you
might be here."

Then she leans in and kisses the lips that just seconds ago I thought
I was going to be kissing.

And then she looks at me and says, "Hi. You must be Rio. I'm
Monique, Jas's girlfriend."

*E*leven

Can you imagine anything more humiliating than being in the back-seat of a politically correct car watching your almost-boyfriend get touchy-feely with someone who's so gorgeous and so exotic it's like she's from another planet?

And all of this in hot, eager anticipation of the moment when they get to drop *you* off?

Can you?

Well, I can't.

And believe me, I should know. 'Cause I was the sole ticket-holder to the "Monique gets to touch Jas wherever she wants" show.

And it was awful.

So when he pulls into my driveway I leap (yes, *I leap*) out of the car, and mumbling something sounding vaguely like, "Thanksgoodnight," I run through the front door with barely a shred of dignity, only to be confronted with a Breathalyzer.

Well, kind of.

My mom is standing there in the silky robe she wears when my dad's home and she goes, "Rio? How was your evening?"

"Okay," I say, heading for the stairs, not really wanting to play show-and-tell right now.

But she misreads that as my wanting to hide something. After all,

according to her I was out with a notorious Newport Beac[h]
ber. "Come here," she says. "Into the light where I can see

Into the light? She's watching too many "Law and O[rder]
when my dad's away.

But I step into the light. And my eyes are all red, and
is smeared, and I know this because after my leap from th[e]
into silent tears, and then I wiped my face as I came throu[gh]
And even though I can't actually see myself, I only have t[o]
to know what she sees. But she's reading it all wrong.

"Where did you go tonight?" she asks.

"I told you, Jas's dad's restaurant." I look at the grou[nd]
know makes me look even more guilty, but if I look direc[tly]
cry. And I don't want her to see me do that and know th[at]
Because the real truth is much worse than what she's th[inking]
real truth is that I'm a big geek, and a total dork, and I've [made a com]-
plete fool of myself.

So you can see how I'd rather just have her think I'[m in]-
volved in some adolescent shenanigans.

"Have you been drinking?" she whispers, looking ne[rvously]
stairs where I assume my father is sleeping off his jet lag.

"Yes," I say. I mean, why bother lying at this point?

"How much did you have?" she demands.

"I don't know. One? Two glasses of wine?"

"Any drugs?" She eyes me suspiciously.

"No, okay? Now can I please just go upstairs?" I look a[t her]
then back at the ground.

"Rio, I'm going to be honest with you. I don't like you [hanging]
with those kids. I think they'll lead you down the wrong pa[th]

Oh, god. *Wah wah wah.* In my head I make her voice sou[nd like the]
parents on the Charlie Brown Christmas special.

"And I don't know why you reject perfectly nice girls [like Kristi]
Wood," she continues.

"Because girls like Kristi Wood aren't exactly interested [in hanging]
with *me*. They're a pretty tight, exclusive group," I say, my voi[ce reaching]
dangerously high levels that could possibly disturb my fathe[r].

Twelve

If you think that when I got to my room I threw myself on my bed (without washing my face or brushing my teeth), and just lay there and cried until I passed out like a big pathetic loser—well, you'd be right.

So you can only imagine how scary I look when my dad wakes me on Sunday morning.

"Rise and shine, kiddo," he says.

And as I roll over and open one eye, I briefly catch the fleeting expression of horror on his face. So I know it's bad because he's a criminal-defense litigator, he's used to seeing some ugly stuff.

He quickly recovers and clearing his throat, he says, "I thought we could run over to Roger's Gardens after breakfast, it's supposed to be the best plant nursery around."

In an attempt to spare him from further shocking images, I've taken my comforter and thrown it over my face, so through a thick layer of goose down and a duvet cover with a really high thread count, I say, "I'll be down in a minute."

And he says, "Take your time."

When he's gone I roll out of bed and go into my bathroom. And when I look in the mirror I totally admire his self-restraint. A lesser person would have screamed.

Because what stares back at me is truly awful. My eyes are not only bloodshot, but puffed out to twice their normal size. And the ring of smeared black mascara that circles them looks like a police outline of a crime scene.

Which in a way, it is.

So I stand there and torture myself by staring at my own scary reflection. And I think: *Dumbass! Yes,* you *standing there with the smeared makeup.* You *the one who said, "Oh, Jas, I've been waiting for this all night!" And then closed your eyes to receive a kiss that never came. How will you ever face him? Do you think he's laughing? Of course, he's laughing. He's probably laughing this very moment,* with Monique! *And there's absolutely nothing you can do about it because the words are* out there *and you can't take them back! All you can do now is get your pathetic, dumbass self into the shower and try to salvage some crumb of dignity. It won't be easy, but you better do it. Because if you don't, then you're a bigger dumbass than even* you *think!*

So my dad's driving down the Pacific Coast Highway and I'm getting glimpses of the ocean between the clusters of gated communities with their giant McMansions and tiny, little yards, and I'm feeling really happy that it's just us, and that my mom's not here. Because when I'm feeling this bad about myself I usually don't want to be around her. But my dad understands, because he's a geek, too.

It's like, if my house was a high school then my mom would be the prom queen, my dad would be the brainiac, and I would be the big weirdo art geek.

And my mom would refuse to eat lunch with either of us.

When he turns onto MacArthur Boulevard he says, "So, kiddo, you don't have to tell me if you don't want, but from the looks of you this morning you either had too much fun last night or not nearly enough."

And because it's just us, I answer truthfully. "It was the latter," I say, doing a double take as we drive past a bakery that's just for dogs.

"Wanna talk about it?"

I peer at him through the sunglasses he suggested I wear to hide the evidence that lingered long after I showered, and I know that if I want to get this off my chest, now's my only chance, since by tomorrow he'll be back on a plane to New York. And even though I've always bypassed my mom and gone straight to him with all of my problems, it feels kind of weird now. I mean, before it was always about stuff at school like grades, and projects, and friends. It was never about a guy. And I'm just way too embarrassed to talk to him about stuff like that.

So I look over and just as I'm about to lie and say I'm okay, he looks at me and smiles. And I break down and tell him everything.

Well, almost everything. I mean, I leave out the more humiliating moments that are really damaging to me. You know, like detention and falling down and the infamous "wardrobe malfunction" in Jas's kitchen. But he gets the gist.

"Sounds like you really like this boy," he says.

I shrug.

"Do you want me to go after him? Get an arrest warrant issued?" He smiles.

"What? For reckless disregard and endangerment of my poor teenage heart?" I say, laughing.

"I'm sure we can find a statute for it." He looks at me.

"Nah. I've decided not to press charges. I'm moving on."

"You sure?" he asks, parking the Range Rover and opening the door.

"Definitely. Now, let's go look at some plants." And when I get out of the car I give him a big smile.

But I'm not sure I've convinced either one of us.

So we ended up with four small palm trees, two hanging fuchsias, a couple pots of different decorative grasses, six trays of annuals, several curly bamboo stalks for my room, and a climbing rosebush for my mom.

It's getting pretty late in the afternoon and we're still in the backyard planting and planning for what we'll buy next time, when my mom comes out and goes, "I just don't get your attraction to dirt." Then she smiles and sets down a tray of iced teas.

"It's not dirt," my dad tells her. "It's nature."

"And just what does a city boy like you know about nature?" She vamps, shaking her blond shoulder-length hair, and approaching him with her old runway walk, with hips leading and swiveling.

Oh, god, they're flirting again. Gross.

I watch my dad, with his face all tan from a day in the sun, and his gray-streaked hair messed-up and matted with sweat, and I guess I never really noticed before, but he's actually pretty handsome. I mean, he's just my dad you know, so it's not like I'm used to looking at him objectively.

Well, his clothes are all covered in dirt, but he spreads his arms wide and chases after my mom, trying to hug her. So she squeals and darts around the patio in her little kitten-heeled shoes, pretending like she's running away. But of course she lets herself get caught. Then they hug and kiss and laugh and even though it totally grosses me out, I guess in a way it's kind of nice. I mean, at least they're not screaming at each other like Hud's parents used to.

And then it hits me: My dad's a brainiac geek, but who did he marry?

Another brainiac? No!

An art geek? *No!*

He married the prom queen!!!!!!

Ohmygod. Even the smart ones want the one that's not so smart. And if you don't believe me then here's the proof:

Exhibit A: My dad and my mom.
Exhibit B: Jas and Monique.

Okay, I don't really *know* that Monique's not smart, but what I do know is that the first thing a guy's gonna think when she walks into a room *isn't* "nice brain."

I quickly wash my hands under the hose, kick off my shoes because they're all full of mud, and make a run for the house.

My parents both turn and look at me, and in perfect unison they go, "Where are you going?"

"My room. I have work to do!" I yell, running through the open French doors.

Thirteen

The next morning when I'm walking down the stairs so my mom can drop me off before she takes my dad to the airport, she sees me and goes, "Are you really wearing that to school?" She looks shocked.

Damn. I knew I went too far. I never know when to stop. "Should I change?" I ask, suddenly dreading her professional critique.

"No, you look amazing!"

"I do? Really?" I ask, wondering if she's just saying that.

"I can't believe you've never worn that skirt before. You're lucky you got my legs," she says, as my father walks into the room.

"Don't you have uniforms at this school?" he asks, in mock dismay.

"Nope, they let us wear whatever we want."

"Well, he won't know what hit him," he whispers, as we walk out the door.

"That's the plan," I say, catching a fleeting glimpse of my Burberry plaid miniskirt, my favorite black motorcycle boots, and tight black turtleneck sweater as I pass by the mirror on my way out.

When I get to English I'm really nervous. All the bravado I felt in the Range Rover is long gone, and I'm wishing I'd just stayed in the safety zone of my usual jeans, ponytail, no makeup, and contraband sweatshirt.

When Kristi sits next to me she does a complete double take. "Nice skirt," she says, eyeing it with approval.

"Thanks," I say. Then risking an actual conversation I go, "How was the dance?"

"Boring. But, you know." She rolls her eyes.

And I nod my head and roll my eyes too, like I really do know. Even though I have no idea what she's talking about.

Then like the complete dork that I am, I spend the next fifteen minutes trying to think of something else to say. Because if I can just come up with something good, then maybe she'll invite me to hang at her locker after class. And we can stand around, laughing at an inside joke, while all the hot guys flirt with us. And then maybe Jas will walk by, see me surrounded by hotties, and—

So when Mrs. Abbott calls on me and asks, "Rio, can you tell us what it means when the characters in Hemingway's *The Sun Also Rises* are referred to as 'the lost generation'?" I'm caught completely off guard.

And in an attempt to stall for time I go, "Um, sorry? What was the question?" As I quickly scan the back of the book looking for the answer.

So Mrs. Abbott repeats it. And when she's done I go, "They're referring to the post–World War I generation, and their moral bankruptcy, godlessness, and lack of illusions," I say, paraphrasing what I just read.

And she goes, "Why do you say that?"

And I go, "Because that's what it says on the back of the book."

Then everyone starts laughing. And Kristi looks over at me and smiles.

And even though Mrs. Abbott doesn't think it's one bit funny, I have to admit, it was totally worth it.

When class is over I'm still feeling pretty good about making everyone laugh. I'm walking right behind Kristi and when we start to veer off in separate directions, she turns and goes, "Ciao, Brazil."

And I go, *"Ciao, Kristi!"* Then I give her this big smile and wave, even though she's long gone and no longer looking at me. But I just continue to stand there, like a dog hanging out a car window, grinning into air.

I walk into Art just as the bell is ringing. And if I'm gonna be honest, then I have to admit that I timed it like that on purpose so that Jas could look up and see the *new me*. You know, kind of like the much anticipated, climactic moment in one of those makeover shows.

And then what?

He forgets about the stupid, "Oh, Jas, I've been waiting . . ." comment?

He falls in love?

Drops Monique?

'Cause that's not what happened.

What happened was he didn't even look up. He just kept right on sketching and when my chair made that scraping noise against the concrete floor, he mumbled, "Hey, Rio."

"*Hey, Jas!*" I say, all overanimated.

And with all of my might I think: *Look up! Look up! Look at me!*

But nothing happens.

So after sitting there for a while, straining to be noticed, I give up and go over to the wall where my smock is hanging. And when I'm all wrapped and tied and completely covered up, Mason comes rushing through the door yelling, "Sorry I'm late!" Then she sits next to me and throws her bag down all dramatic. And that's when Jas decides to look up and smile at both of us.

Oh, *now* he sees me. Now that I'm all covered up in this paint-splattered nun's habit.

I give up.

Really.

It's so not worth it.

So I turn to Mason and say, "Zane seems really nice." And I smile. Because I'd really like to get to know her better, I think we have a lot in common.

"Really? You think so?" she says in a sarcastic tone that I can't really figure out.

"Well, yeah," I say, nodding and smiling like a bobblehead.

"Well, that's nice. 'Cause we broke up." She looks away and her eyes get all teary.

And as I watch her get up and go over to her easel, I wonder why I can never seem to say the right thing to her. But the truth is, if I'd been paying attention I would have noticed that she looked upset, and that her eyes were all red like she'd been crying. But *no,* I was too busy thinking about *me* in my Burberry miniskirt. Pathetic.

So I turn to Jas and say, "I guess I kind of blew that, huh?"

And he looks at me briefly and shrugs. "You didn't know." Then he looks down again.

"Well, Monique seemed really nice. Or did you break up, too?" I ask, followed by ridiculous nervous laughter. *Way to go, Rio.*

Jas stops sketching and looks at me, but there's something different in his eyes this time, and I don't know what it means. Then he says, "No, we didn't break up, we're still together."

Well, I know what *that* means. So I grab my bag, and walk casually into the darkroom. And once the door is firmly closed behind me, I sink down to the floor and sit there with my head in my hands, wondering if you can actually die of humiliation.

Oh, god, did I really believe that wearing a three-hundred-dollar skirt would change my life? Because all it really did was make me a well-dressed geek. I mean, let's face it, a change of clothes cannot erase that humiliating "date" with Jas, or the stupid thing I just said to Mason. It's like underneath the Burberry, I'm still the same stupid dork. Or more like, the same stupid *friendless* dork! Since there's no way I can hang with Jas now—not after Saturday night. And Mason, well, I really doubt she'll miss all my stupid comments.

So where does that leave me? I mean, I tried being all friendly with Kristi, and while she was nice, she obviously doesn't hang with retards like me. God, I'm on my second week of school, and it may as well be the first day. I haven't made any progress.

$\mathscr{F}$ourteen

After Art we have a ten-minute break, so I go back to my locker and spin the dial because I have nowhere else to go and it gives me something to do between classes.

When I swing the door open I find this piece of notebook paper that's been folded over and over, like a million times, into a tight little triangle and it has my name written on it in big letters with a smiley face over the *i* and big round flower petals around the *o*. And even though it doesn't look scary from the outside, I'm still a little nervous when I open it since I know it's not from Mason or Jas, and the only other person it could be from is Kristi, and I'm not even sure if she likes me.

But when it's completely open I read:

> *Hi Rio!*
> *We eat lunch @ the table under the big tree if U*
> *want 2 sit with us!*
>
> *Kristi!*

Her *i*'s are dotted with hearts.

At lunch I walk right past the field where I used to eat with Jas and Mason and head for the table with the big tree. But the truth is there's like a bunch of trees, and they're all pretty much the same size, so then I start wondering if Kristi's playing some kind of messed-up game. You know, like some hateful cheerleader version of *Punk'd*. Because sometimes popular kids do things like that. Well, at least the ones you see in movies.

But then I hear someone yell, "Hey, Brazil, over here!" And I see Kristi smiling and waving. And I feel totally relieved that the invite was legit.

"You guys, this is Rio," she says. "Rio, this is Kayla." She points to the girl in a shrunken, pink corduroy blazer with brown eyes and blond streaks. "And this is Jennifer, but we call her Jen Jen." She nods at the redhead across from her wearing a leopard-print cardigan.

"Hey," I say, smiling nervously and sitting next to Kristi.

"Rio's in my English class. And, you guys, she showed up like way late on the first day and I thought Mrs. Abbott was gonna *bust!*"

Everybody starts laughing, but probably not because it's funny, but because Kristi is the boss.

"Mrs. Abbott? Gag. Isn't she the lamest?" Kayla says, rolling her eyes.

"Totally." I nod, even though I don't really think she's all that lame. But if I'm gonna hang with the cool kids, I've got to be agreeable. As well as stop making fun of them in my head.

As well as stop using phrases like "cool kids."

"So what's with your name being Rio?" Jen Jen asks.

"Jen!" Kristi says, giving her a look. And then to me, "Ignore her, she is *so rude!*"

"Well, excuse me, but it's not like it's *normal*," Jen Jen says in her own defense. "I mean, were you like, *born* there or something?" She makes a face as she bites into her apple.

"No. It's, it's just after a song my mom liked back in the eighties," I say, wishing for the millionth time I had a middle name I could fall back on.

"Oh, my god, that is *so cool*. Your mom must be really cool!" Kayla says, looking at me in awe.

I think about my mom and just shrug.

"I'm serious. My mom was like *born* listening to old lady music."
She rolls her eyes.

Kristi nods. "If my mom named me after one of her favorite songs
from the eighties you'd all be eating lunch with 'Funky Town' right
now!"

"Oh, my god, remember how our moms used to blast that while
they did step-aerobics when we were little?" Jen Jen says, running her
fingers through her long red hair and taking a sip of her Diet Coke.

"Ew!" Kristi shivers. "That was *so* embarrassing!"

Everyone cracks up, including me. And it's not as fake as you'd
think.

"So is your mom like a famous model or what?" Kristi asks, and
everyone goes silent waiting for the answer.

"Well, she's not, like, *famous*. I mean, not anymore." I nervously tear
off a piece of my sandwich. "She used to model in magazines and stuff,
but that was a long time ago, before I was even born."

"But didn't she take part in a *Vogue* retrospective?" Jen Jen asks.

"What?" I look at all of them. *How could they possibly know about that?*

"We Googled your family," Kristi says. "Apparently your dad's
really famous, too."

"He's a *lawyer*," I say. "Sometimes he does commentary on *Larry King*
or Court TV or something."

They GOOGLED me????

"But we read that he's the one that represented that old guy actor
who butchered his wife," Kayla says.

"And he *was* innocent," I say, sounding all defensive. *God, this is getting really weird.*

"So what are you doing after school?" Kayla asks.

"Um, I don't know. Homework I guess." I cover my mouth with my
hand since I just took a bite of my sandwich.

"Detention's over, I take it?" Kristi says, tapping her French-
manicured finger against her Diet Coke can and eyeing me closely.

I just nod, because I'm swallowing.

"Well, we're going to the mall and you totally have to come with
us," Jen Jen says.

"Oh, okay," I say, finishing my sandwich.

"Cool. Well, we have to go to the gym to set up for the pep rally, but meet us in the parking lot after school," Kayla says, getting up from the table.

"It'll be totally fun." Jen Jen smiles.

"I can't believe you ate that entire sandwich," Kristi says, shaking her head as she walks away.

Fifteen

So instead of going to the usual malls, we went to the Lab, which is like this alternative mall in Costa Mesa, that's also called the anti-mall. And we're in this record store because Kristi, Kayla, and Jen Jen want me to show them the CD with the song that I'm named after. It makes me feel totally lame, but I don't want to seem like a bitch, so I find it and hand it to them and then they flirt with the guy who works there and make him play it.

(It's worth noting that while the alterna girl who also works there is rolling her eyes at us, *the guy* can't stop smiling. And he turns all red, and he gets all nervous, and his hands are all shaky, as he takes off the hip alterna CD they had playing, and replaces it with the Duran Duran *Rio* CD, track one. Which just goes to prove my earlier point about prom queens and how even the cool, smart guys get sucked in. So if I need to later, I will refer to this moment as Exhibit C.)

By the second chorus they know most of the words, since it mostly just repeats itself.

So they're singing really loud, and it's kind of embarrassing, so I walk out of the store, and across the way to Urban Outfitters. And it makes me kind of excited to see something familiar since we have that store in New York, too. But then I remember that Mason works here, and I start to leave because I'm not supercomfortable running into her, but she sees me, and goes, "Hey, Rio."

So I go over to the register where she's ringing someone up and I go, "Hey, cool coat." She has on this incredible little leopard jacket, which has like three-quarter-length sleeves, and this one big red rhinestone button at the top where the collar part is. I mean, it's *amazing* and I've never seen her wear it before.

"Thanks," she says. And when her customer leaves she goes, "What happened to you at lunch?"

"Oh, I, I ate somewhere else," I say, avoiding her eyes.

"Why?"

"Well, I felt kind of bad, saying that about Zane."

"What? 'Cause you said he was nice?"

I shrug.

"Listen, I'm sorry if I made you feel bad. We talked a little while ago and we're gonna try to work it out. It's just really hard with him living in L.A. and stuff." She bites down on her lip and hesitates like she's about to say more but then she just goes, "So I heard you met Monique." She eyes me closely.

"Yeah, and she's *really* nice!" I say, with a big fake smile to match my big fake statement.

"You think?" She looks skeptical.

"Totally," I say, nodding vigorously. Again, bobblehead.

"That's weird."

"Why?" I ask, picking up a rhinestone ring and slipping it on my finger.

"Well, it kind of seems like you like Jas." She's looking right at me.

"I don't like Jas! Why would you think I like Jas?" I ask frantically. Oh, god, my father would not approve of my defense-litigation technique.

"Sorry." She shrugs. "My wrong." She starts scooping up a pile of receipts, but I can tell she doesn't believe me.

And of course I just can't let it go. "Why?" I ask. "Does Jas think I like him? I mean, did he say something to you? What did he say?" I'm clearly out of control, but I just can't stop.

Then the second she starts to answer, Kristi yells, "Brazil! I can't believe you walked out on us while we were totally serenading you!"

I turn to see my three new friends standing in the doorway.

"Um, I should go," I say, slipping off the ring and dropping it back in the little ceramic bowl by the register.

"Yeah, I guess you should," Mason says, raising an eyebrow at them.

I catch up with Kristi, Kayla, and Jen Jen in this outside courtyard, which is also called the "Living Room," and they're all standing there, hands on hips, totally glaring at me. *Jeez, are they really this upset 'cause I bailed on their little karaoke session?*

"Hey," I say, nervously facing them.

"Hey," says Kristi, while Kayla and Jen Jen look at the ground.

"What's going on?" I ask.

"Well," Kristi says, "I know you're new and all, and I'm not sure how to say this, but you probably don't want to be all friendly with Mason." She gives me a hard look.

"Why? She seems really nice." I mean, what could she possibly mean by that?

"Well, you've only known her for like a week, and we've known her for, like, *ever*. And let me tell you that she's totally weird and disturbed."

"Weird, how?" I ask, shifting my bag to my other shoulder, and looking at Kayla and Jen Jen who are very busy studying their cuticles.

"Just spooky, fucking freaky weird, okay?" Kristi says, rolling her eyes. "She wears weirdo used clothes, and sometimes I catch her—" she stops and looks around. "Watching us," she whispers. "And it totally creeps me out."

"Watching *you guys*?" I ask, 'cause to be honest I find that hard to believe.

"*Yes?*" she says, rolling her eyes. "She's like a—what do you call those people that watch you all the time? Stalker?"

"Voyeur," I say.

"Well, she's a stalker-voyeur," Kristi says, crossing her arms and narrowing her eyes.

"She's like a total lesbo, too," Kayla says, making a face and shivering.

"You guys are wrong. I know for a fact that she has a boyfriend. She's not gay. But who cares if she was?" I add.

"That's disgusting." Jen Jen gives me a harsh look, as Kristi and Kayla shake their heads.

They're all lined up like a Juicy Couture firing squad, giving me this awful death stare. And deep down inside I know I should just walk away, and totally blow them off, because what they're saying is clearly wrong.

But instead, I just stand there. Because being friends with them is a really big deal. It guarantees a date for every dance, plans for every weekend, and the envy of everyone who doesn't belong. I mean, if someone as perfect as Kristi wants to hang with me, then it must mean I have the potential to be perfect, too.

"Listen," Kristi says, smiling. "I'm just telling you this for your own good. It's hard to know who to hang with when you're brand-new. We're just trying to help you make the right choices before it's too late." Then she puts her arm around my shoulder and says, "Now let's bail out of this psycho place and try on some makeup at the *real mall*."

Sixteen

So after getting full-on makeovers at Sephora, Kristi pulls into my drive-way and goes, "Are your parents home?"

I shake my head. "My dad's in New York, and my mom's probably with your mom at that yogalates studio."

"Good, 'cause I'm dying to check out your house." She opens her car door and gets out.

"Okay." I shrug. "But it's not like there's much to see. It's mostly not decorated still."

"That's okay," she says, rushing in front of me.

When I unlock the door she pushes ahead and walks deep into the empty living room. "Wow, how many square feet is this?" she asks, looking up at the ceiling.

Square feet? Is she kidding? But all I say is, "I don't know."

"How many bedrooms?" asks Kayla.

"Um, five?"

"How many baths?" asks Jen Jen.

"Um, six and a half?" I say, not entirely sure what half a bath is, but I overheard my mom mention it to someone else.

"This is really nice." Kristi nods approvingly as she walks into the kitchen. "Sub-Zero fridge," she says, running her hand over the front.

Okay, this is bizarre. Do kids in Newport really care this much about real estate?

"Let's see your room," Jen Jen says.

"It's upstairs," I say, motioning for them to follow.

"Wait." Kristi looks at me. "Is there anything to drink?"

"Well, there's some bottled water, and iced tea in the fridge." I shrug.

"No, dummy. I mean, you know, *to drink?*"

"Like what?" I ask, watching her roll her eyes and open the fridge she was crushing on a moment ago.

"Like this," she says, holding up a bottle of champagne and smiling.

"Oh, I don't know. We probably shouldn't drink that," I say, thinking how my mom's gonna kill me when she finds out.

"Please. They'll never even notice." She pops the cork and takes a swig from the bottle.

"Um, I can get us some glasses," I offer. *God, I'm so lame.*

"Nah, too much cleanup. Come on, let's go check out your room," she says, leading the way upstairs.

So we're in my room and Kristi and I are lounging on my bed, Jen Jen is propped on some floor pillows near the window, and Kayla is spinning around in my desk chair and we're all taking turns chugging from the bottle of champagne.

I'm feeling kind of tipsy 'cause it's been a while since my last meal, and I'm not really used to drinking, but I'm trying to act all normal (well, cooler than my *usual* normal), since I'm really nervous about doing something stupid. Because even though they're being really nice to me now, it still kinda feels like this is an audition and I'm just one dorky moment away from hearing, "Cut! Next!"

So I'm not really saying much because I'm just trying to concentrate on making sure I laugh at all the right moments, when Kristi reaches over to my nightstand, and grabs the silver-framed picture of me, Paige, and Hud that was taken on my last day at my old school. We're all in our school uniforms and Paige and Hud are on either side of me and they're smiling, and I've got my arms around both of them and my eyes are kind of squinted closed because I was cracking up. I mean, even though it was my last day with them, I was still just happy to be there.

But Kristi takes one look at it, shakes her head, and goes, "Oh, my god! Geek alert! Don't tell me that was your boyfriend!" She holds the picture up so Kayla and Jen Jen can see it and everyone starts cracking up.

I just sit there, nervously rubbing my arm, while everyone laughs at my two best friends. "You guys don't know them," I say, sounding more lame than forceful. "They're actually really nice, cool people."

"Nice? Maybe. Cool? Doubtful, Brazil, very doubtful," Kristi says, placing the picture back on my nightstand, facedown. Then she looks at me and goes, "So if that's your idea of hot, I can't even imagine who you like at school."

And without thinking twice I say, "Jas Klein is totally smokin'!" But while I'm nodding and smiling I notice everybody's just sitting there, staring at me. So I take a small sip of champagne, and go, "Well kinda."

And then Kristi, having completely lost her patience, shakes her head, sighs loudly, and says, "Listen Rio. I know you don't get the whole social-ranking system, but let me just inform you that *everyone* knows Jas Klein is a total stoner and a big loser, and we can't allow you to like him. I'm sorry, and I know that at first it might sound harsh, but that's just the way it is, and it's not like it's my fault." She looks at Jen Jen and Kayla for confirmation and they both nod. "We work really hard to set good examples for the rest of the school," she continues. "We're involved in every single activity that *matters*. And just because we're totally sweet to *everyone* doesn't mean we're actually *friends* with all of them." She leans toward me and rests her hand on mine. "We really like you and we all agree you definitely have potential." She pauses and they all smile at me. "But if you're gonna insist on hanging with stoners and dykes, then you can't hang with us. I mean, you need to be aware of how your actions affect the group. That is, if you want to be part of our group."

They're all looking at me, waiting for a response, but I just sit there, staring at the carpet. Because even though I'm being given a second chance to pass on their friendship, the truth is that I do want to hang with them. I mean, even though they're kind of phony, and definitely not nice to everyone like she just said, they *are* the leaders of the school—they know all the cool people and do all the cool stuff, and

I really want a piece of that, too. Partly because I've never had a shot at it before. But mostly because I don't want to go back to being a nobody.

It's like, before at my old school, I didn't really care about being a big geek because I had two great friends, and we stuck together no matter what. I mean, yeah, there were definitely bad times like when the cool girls would "accidentally" spike the volleyball smack into my head during PE, or the time when Paige and I were voted number two and three on the "Ugliest Girls" list that was circulated around the entire eighth-grade class, or the countless times Hud had his hair "washed" in the school toilets. But even though I try not to think about that stuff, the truth is I couldn't stand living through it again. And Kristi's friendship insures that moments like those will never, ever happen to me. And without Paige and Hud to back me, it's pretty much an offer I can't refuse.

So if you hate me for my next statement, just imagine how *I* feel when I go, "Well, I think that Jeff Cole guy is cute." I'm referring to the jock that threw the orange at us that day.

"We call him JC, and you're right, he's a total hottie," says Kayla, nodding.

"Total," says Jen Jen.

"And he's great in bed." Kristi looks right at me.

"Really?" I'm trying to act all casual, like I'm so used to having conversations like this.

"Just kidding," she says, rolling her eyes.

"Well you did make out with him," Jen Jen says, flipping through my pathetic CD collection.

"So?" Kristi says, getting up and opening the door to my walk-in closet. "Kayla's the one that blew him."

"Uh, hel-*lo?* That was like, a long time ago. When he was my boyfriend." Kayla rolls her eyes, and inspects the ends of her blond-streaked hair.

"Oh, my god, I totally remember that party!" Jen Jen says, giving up on my CDs and cranking the radio instead.

"Do you guys have a lot of parties?" I ask, just to say something so they won't forget I'm still here.

"Yeah, my mom and stepdaddy number two go away a lot," Kristi says. "Because they trust me." She laughs.

"Suckers," Jen Jen says, getting up and dancing to an Outkast song in front of my full-length mirror.

"So you want to hook up with JC?" Kristi asks, taking my 7 jeans off the hanger and checking the size label. "'Cause I can arrange it."

"No!" I say, a little louder than I would have liked. "I mean, no. Don't say anything. If it's gonna happen, then it will just happen, right? I mean, he probably doesn't even like me." I suddenly feel really nauseous.

"Please. Why wouldn't he like you? You're one of us now," Kristi says, while Kayla and Jen Jen smile.

"Listen," I say, clutching my stomach, "I didn't say I wanted to, you know, hook up. I just said he was cute, that's all."

"Are you a virgin?" Kristi asks, turning away from my closet and staring at me.

My head feels all light and weird, and I know that this would probably be a really good time to lie. But I'm not sure I can fake my way through it, and I'm feeling pretty sick, so I just kind of shrug.

"Oh, my god!" Kristi shrieks. "I bet you've never even hooked up, have you?" She comes over, sits on the edge of the bed, and stares at me.

"What about in New York? Didn't you guys hook up and stuff? I thought New York was supposed to be pretty wild," Jen Jen says.

I shrug. "I didn't really like anyone enough for that." I take a sip from the bottle of water I keep on my nightstand, hoping it will make me feel better.

"Get real," Kristi says. "You don't have to *like* them, you just have to think they're hot. Listen, I can totally set you up. My parents go out of town like every few weeks, and we just hang at my house and do whatever with whoever."

"You mean you guys like, *all have sex together?*" I ask incredulously. Because *that* I want no part of.

"No, dummy. We mostly just hook up."

"But don't you want just one boyfriend?" I ask. "Like, just one special guy to share everything with?"

"Why would I want just one boyfriend? How boring is that?" She rolls her eyes. "Lighten up. If people were meant to be together forever, then everybody wouldn't be getting divorced."

"My parents are still together," I say.

"Wait," she says. "They'll get over it."

I don't know if it's the thought of my parents splitting up, fear of hooking up, or the fact that I am seriously messed-up on champagne. But suddenly, I jump up and bolt straight into my bathroom, where I barely make it to the toilet before I start vomiting over and over and over again.

And while Kayla rushes over to hold my hair back, Jen Jen grabs a washcloth, runs it under the tap, then holds it against my forehead while I continue being sick. And right when I'm thinking how totally sweet they are for taking care of me like this, and how lucky I am to have such nice friends, Kristi goes, "God, Rio, that is seriously disgusting. But it's probably for the best 'cause you really eat a lot."

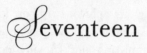

Seventeen

That night as I was trying to fall asleep, I realized it was the first day since I'd left New York that I hadn't e-mailed Paige or Hud. And the truth is, I really wasn't interested in getting out of bed to see if they e-mailed me. It wasn't because I was exhausted, messed-up, and feeling empty from vomiting. It was because I knew Paige would never understand why I was suddenly so determined to be accepted by the kind of people we always used to make fun of.

But since we moved to Newport Beach everything is different. And it makes me want to be different too. Because it's one thing to be a geek when you're in good company. It's another when you're out there on your own.

The next morning I'm standing in front of my closet feeling completely panicked about what I'm going to wear. It's like, now that I'm hanging with Kristi and Company, I can't exactly just throw my hair into a ponytail and run out the door in jeans and a dorky sweatshirt like I used to. Now I have to think about my image, and how it will reflect on the group.

And believe me, I'm not making this up, because right before they left, Kristi laid down the rules when she said, "Listen, Rio. Today you looked really cute in your little Burberry skirt, and on your first day you were fine in that pink Juicy outfit. But all the days in between were pretty brutal. And I happen to know you have cute clothes because I went through your closet. So, like, try to wear some of them, okay?"

And there were other rules, too:
1. Drugs: Drinking is okay. But smoking pot is bad because it makes you hungry in a way that can't be suppressed, and most other drugs are only for hard-core losers.
2. Attitude: Always smile and be supersweet to everyone—even the dorks, because dorks totally look up to us so we have to set a good example.
3. Sex: It's okay to flirt and/or hook up with jocks, preps, and rich, older college guys, but never act like a skank in public unless you're totally drunk and can't help it.
4. Dress Code: *Always* dress cute because it gives other people something to aspire to, and it shows you have good self-esteem. But *never* repeat an outfit more than twice in one month. (Kristi suggested I get a journal so I can keep track.)
5. Image: Try not to eat so much, because it will totally catch up with you, and then you'll get *fat*, and you won't have *any* friends. (I wondered if she'd ever heard of Oprah.)

It's a lot to remember, and I'm not used to following rules, because even my parents don't really set them for me. But I do like the idea of belonging to something, especially something everyone wants to be part of. I know that on the surface my new friends seem like the exact opposite of Paige and Hud, and I guess they are. But Paige and Hud aren't really in my life anymore, and the sooner I get used to that, the better.

So, finally dressed in a white linen miniskirt, a celery-green tank top, a turquoise Juicy Couture hoodie, and some beige Rainbow flip-flops (since it's supposed to be seventy-five degrees today even though there's probably a blizzard in New York), I'm grabbing my books off my desk, when I notice my " ape   Crew" sweatshirt shoved in the trash can. Which is exactly where Kristi made me put it right after I was done throwing up.

"You *so* have to get rid of this," she said, holding it up by the tag, like it was contagious or something.

"Oh, that?" I said, taking it from her and tossing it in the trash like I wasn't really attached to it.

But now I'm not so sure. And I know if I leave it there I'll definitely never see it again, 'cause my mom hates it even more than Kristi, so there's no doubt she'll have the maid make it disappear at the first opportunity. I'm not even sure why I want to keep it, because it's not like it has any sentimental value. It's just a stupid sweatshirt, and I'm being completely irrational. But I pull it out anyway and stash it under my bed. Then I head downstairs and wait.

My mom comes into the kitchen, dressed in a lime-green Juicy Couture leisure suit that she totally swiped from my closet. She looks at her bling-crusted Cartier watch, and goes, "We should get going because I have to be back in time to let the maids in."

"I don't need a ride," I tell her, taking a sip of my coffee and trying to ignore the fact that my stomach is begging for something more.

"Oh? Then how are you getting there?" she asks, looking at me suspiciously.

"Kristi's picking me up." I casually take another sip and wait for her reaction.

"Kristi Wood?" she asks carefully, but I can tell she's holding back some major excitement, just in case she heard wrong.

"Yeah," I say, placing my mug in the sink, and turning to face her.

"Rio, that's wonderful!" She smiles, excitement in full bloom now. "See, I told you that if you dressed up and put yourself out there, they'd come around. Didn't I tell you?"

"Yeah, Mom, you told me," I say, looking through the tiny Louis Vuitton purse I swiped from her closet. I'm applying my new Stila lip gloss when I hear Kristi's horn. "Okay, see ya," I say, grabbing my stuff and double-checking my outfit in the mirror by the door, praying it's okay.

When I look up I see my mom's reflection, and she's standing right behind me. She brushes her hand over my hair (which I'm wearing long and flowy instead of my usual ponytail), and she goes, "You look amazing."

And as I'm walking out the door I realize that's like the second time she's ever said that to me.

Eighteen

Everything at school is different now. After just a few days of hanging with Kristi, Kayla, and Jen Jen, all the cute guys flirt with me, and people who I don't even know, know me. It's almost like being a celebrity or something, and now I get why everyone wants it so bad.

It's because it makes you feel so good.

But it's weird in Art. I mean, now that I no longer hang with Mason and Jas, and I'm involved in things they're not part of, it's like we don't really have the same interests anymore, and there's definitely some awkward moments. I could be wrong, but the other day I was doodling in my notebook, and when I looked up I caught Jas staring at me. And even after I smiled, and made a face, he still kept staring. So I looked away.

I know, you probably think the staring should make me happy, like mission accomplished, right? Because originally I was hoping that my makeover would get his attention—and obviously it has.

But it was almost like that stare contained something other than admiration. Like maybe even the *opposite* of admiration. And that's something I really don't want to know about.

And that's why I looked away.

After school if we don't go to the mall, then we usually all go to Kristi's and hang in her room. Sometimes we drink, but mostly we just play around on her computer, making up fake screen names, and sending nasty e-mails to people we don't like, and stuff. I know that probably sounds really mean, but it's not like I'm doing it, too. I mean, I mostly just sit there and watch them do it.

But on this one day, we were all in her room and Kristi said, "You guys, check it out." She was pointing at her computer, and cracking up.

On the screen was this picture of Mason. It was black and white and kind of blurry, and she looked all frozen and stiffly posed, like it was taken from the yearbook or something. Next to the picture were the numbers 2.5.

"Oh, my god, two point five? How embarrassing." Kayla laughed.

"What is that?" I asked, moving toward the screen to get a closer look.

"It's just this site where you submit your picture so people can rate how hot you are," Jen Jen explained.

"Look, someone rated her a zero!" Kristi was laughing so hard she was doubled-over. "She should just crawl into a hole and die!"

"Why would she put her picture on there?" I asked, totally not getting it.

Kristi rolled her eyes. "She didn't, Einstein. *I did.*"

I peered at the screen again. "That's pretty mean," I said, immediately regretting it, since last time I stuck up for Mason, it didn't go over so well.

Kayla and Jen Jen looked down at the ground, but Kristi just laughed and said, "You know what, Brazil? You're absolutely right. That *was* really mean. 'Cause this is a site for *straight people.* I should have put her on a *lesbo* site, then she might have scored higher."

Then they all bust out laughing, like it was the funniest thing ever. So I started laughing, too. I mean, it's not like Mason tries to be nice to us. She barely even talks to me anymore, it's like she thinks she's too arty and deep for me now. And if you think about it, that's just total snobbery.

Well, today it's just Kristi and me, since for some reason she didn't invite Jen Jen and Kayla. And it was really weird 'cause when we were all walking toward the student lot after school, Kayla said, "Jen and I will follow you guys, okay?"

And as Kristi slid into the driver's seat she said, "Not today."

"Oh. Do you guys have plans?" Kayla asked, her eyes full of suspicion.

"I'm just gonna drop Rio off. I'll call you later," Kristi said, starting her engine, and waving good-bye.

But she didn't drop me off. Instead, she drives straight to her house, parks in her six-car garage, opens the door, and says, "Come."

Part of me really wants to know why she lied to Jen Jen and Kayla like that, but the other part is determined not to get all bogged-down in the details. It's like, we all spend so much time competing for Kristi's attention, that I have to admit it feels really awesome to be chosen. It's like winning a silver medal or something. (I mean, you can't win gold, because that already belongs to Kristi.)

I'm wearing one of her bikinis and we're relaxing in the Jacuzzi. My eyes are closed and I'm loving the feeling of the hot water bubbling all around me, when Kristi goes, "You know, I didn't quite know what to make of you when you walked into English that day. But you turned out to be pretty cool."

I open my eyes and she's looking right at me, smiling. "Thanks," I say, reaching for my water bottle.

"It's really nice to hang with someone new for a change," she continues. "I mean, don't get me wrong, I love Jen and Kayla, and I've known them *forever*, but sometimes, I don't know, I guess, you and I have more in common, you know?"

She looks right at me waiting for me to agree, but I'm not exactly sure what she means, since most of the time hanging with her feels like a balance beam routine, like I'm always in danger of a really humiliating, unscheduled dismount.

"Jen and Kayla are cute and all, and they really do a lot with what they've got. But you and I are way better-looking, right?" She takes a sip of her Diet Coke and stares at me, but I'm not sure what to say to that, so I just kind of nod in semiagreement.

She places her Coke on the edge and rolls her eyes. "Oh, please. It's just us, so why can't we admit the truth? It's not like they can hear us. Face it, Rio, everyone at school wishes they were us."

"I'm not so sure about the seniors. They seem pretty happy with themselves," I say, taking another sip of water.

"Get real. Why do you think they're so bitchy? It's because their guys are always checking us out and they feel threatened. I'm telling you, next year that school is *ours*. You and I will totally own it." She smiles.

"It kind of seems like you already do," I say.

"True." She shrugs. "Anyway, I'm just really glad you decided to move here, because I finally feel like I have someone I can totally relate to. It's like Jen and Kayla are kind of limited in *every* way, don't you think?"

I know I probably shouldn't say anything bad about them because they're my friends too, but I can't explain how great it feels to hear Kristi say all these nice things to me. I mean, she thinks we're on the same level! And she's totally *confiding* in me! I know for a fact she doesn't do that with just *anyone*. So I go, "Well, they're not in any AP classes, and they're all wrapped up in cheerleading and stuff." I stop in a panic. *Oh, god, Kristi's a cheerleader. Why did I say that? And who cares about AP classes?*

But she just laughs. "Totally. You should have seen them at cheerleading camp last summer, they were all practicing and asking questions, and paying attention." She rolls her eyes. "I had to hang with some girls from another school, just to have a little fun. Anyway, don't tell them you were here today, 'cause they'll get all jealous and I so don't have time for that. Deal?" She looks at me.

"Deal."

As we're climbing out of the Jacuzzi and reaching for our towels, some old guy I've never seen before walks into the backyard and goes, "Hey, Kris, who's this?"

His gray hair is all puffed up and folded over like he's trying to hide some major baldage, and he's looking at me in a way that totally gives me the creeps. I mean, gag, he's probably older than my dad.

I wrap my towel completely around me, while Kristi glares at him and motions for me to follow her.

"Does she have a name?" He's right behind us.

"None of your business," she says, picking up the pace.

"You can't talk to me like that, you little ingrate." He sounds seriously mad.

"I just did!" she shouts, walking into the house and locking the door behind her.

I follow her upstairs to her room and when we're inside I ask, "Who was that?"

"Stepdaddy number two," she says, dropping her wet towel on the middle of the floor along with her wet bathing suit.

I turn away and undress in segments. Like first I take off my top and immediately replace it with my bra, and I try to do it fast since I'm not supercomfortable being naked in front of other people. But my skin is still kind of damp in spots so my bra kind of drags and scrapes as I yank it around, and it hurts, but I pretend like it doesn't.

And when I'm trying to pull up my underpants with my towel still wrapped around my waist (which is definitely more difficult than it sounds), I can hear him banging on the sliding glass door downstairs. "Aren't you going to let him in?" I ask.

"No," she says, slipping into a red silk robe, and tying the sash tight around her waist. "The other doors are unlocked. He'll figure it out."

"You must really hate him," I say, changing back into my school clothes, and sitting on the edge of her bed.

But she just shrugs. "He's an ass, but he's my mom's problem, not mine. He's like my second stepdad in the last six years." She sits on the chair across from her bed and looks at me. "But it's not like he has any authority over me. I do whatever the hell I want, and there's nothing he can do about it." She reaches into the drawer of her nightstand, and pulls out a tiny glass vial. "Want some?" she offers.

"What is that?" I ask, squinting.

"Coke." She shrugs, like it's no big deal.

"You mean, *cocaine?*" I say, my voice sounding louder than I planned but she doesn't seem to care.

"Well, it ain't the kind you drink but you still need a straw!" she says, chopping and sweeping it into a perfect little runway. "So are we sharing?" She looks at me briefly, then sticks a tiny straw up her nose and leans down.

I shake my head no and try not to stare, but I can't help it. I've only seen coke in movies, never in real life. "You just keep it in that drawer?" I ask, feeling really uncomfortable and completely out of my element.

"Where am I supposed to keep it?" She sits up, rubbing her nose and blinking rapidly.

"But what if they find it?" I ask.

"They have no business coming in here. And believe me, they don't want to find it. They're in complete denial and that's how they like it. As long as I don't interfere in their life, they don't interfere in mine." She starts chopping and sweeping again, carving out another line. Then she looks at me and goes, "I need you to do something for me."

"What?" I ask, feeling panicked that she's gonna make me do it, like to prove my loyalty or something, even though I know how ridiculous that sounds.

"Don't mention this to Jen and Kayla, okay? I mean, it's *so* not a big deal but still, they'd totally freak. This will just be our little secret. Deal?" she asks, looking at me, waiting.

"Deal," I whisper, watching her lean down again.

When she's finished, she wipes her index finger across the mirror, collecting the white powdery remnants and rubbing it into her gums. Then she gathers all her stuff and sticks it back in her drawer so quickly that it almost seems like it didn't happen.

"So where's your real dad?" I ask, desperate to say something.

"My parents split like ten years ago and my dad lives on Lido Isle." She looks at me and shrugs.

"Oh, that sounds exotic and faraway. I mean, you probably don't get to see him much, huh?"

"Please. It's like ten minutes from here." She laughs. "And believe me, there's nothing exotic about it. It's just a little island full of rich people, just like everywhere else in Newport. But you're right, I don't get to see him as much as I used to because my stepmom's a total bitch. We totally had it out last Thanksgiving, and if she thinks she's gonna inherit the family fortune, she better think again."

I watch her go over to her giant walk-in closet, and brush her hand across a row of dresses hanging from white padded hangers, pulling out a dark pink silky one. She looks in the mirror, holding the dress against her, and after studying her reflection for a while she shifts her gaze to me and goes, "I've had two stepdads and two stepmoms. My first stepmom used to *baby-sit* me when I was little. Can you believe that?" She looks at me and shakes her head. "You know, you're really lucky Rio, 'cause your parents are still together and stuff."

We look at each other for a moment and I feel really bad for her. And I'm just about to say something to try to make her feel better, when her cell rings. She drops the dress on the floor, and flipping her phone open, goes, "Drew, hey. Listen, hang on a sec." Then she looks at me and whispers, "I'm hooking up with Drew tonight, so I kind of have to get ready."

I know when I'm being asked to leave. So I lean down to pick up my wet towel but she says, "Don't worry about it. The maid will get it."

And just as I'm leaving she goes, "Hey, Brazil, wait."

She tosses something to me, and I close my hand around it. When I open my palm there's a small pill lying there. "What's this?"

"Take it when you want to chill." Then she waves and says, "Bye!"

I drop the pill in my pocket and as I'm making my way downstairs I think about all the stuff that Kristi just shared with me. I mean, I knew her original parents were divorced and stuff, but it's weird how someone can seem like everything is so perfect on the outside, when really the inside is just a big, complicated mess. But it's really cool how she trusted me enough to tell me all that. I mean, Kayla and Jen Jen might already know that stuff, but only because they've been around forever. I know it because she chose me to confide in.

And even though it was totally shocking and kind of disturbing to see her doing coke, it's not like she pressured me to do it too. And it just feels so awesome to know that someone like Kristi actually trusts me with all her secrets.

When I pass the living room I see her stepdad sitting on the couch, watching TV, and drinking a beer, and he gives me such a creepy smile that I scooch out of there as fast as I can, running all the way down the long driveway 'til I get to the street.

I'm all winded and out of breath (yes, just from that—pathetic, I know), when I hear someone go, "Rio!"

I look across the street and see Jas standing next to his car like he's about to go somewhere (like maybe on a date with Monique).

"Hey," I say, smiling and waving, and continuing down the street.

"Come here." He motions with his hand.

But I don't really want to talk to Jas. Okay, maybe I kind of do, but it's better if I don't. So I point at my watch, like I really have to be somewhere, but he just goes, "Come on," and keeps waving.

So I look both ways, and then I cross the street until I'm standing right in front of him. He has his keys in his hand, so for sure he's going somewhere, but he's acting all relaxed like he's not in any hurry. "What's up?" He smiles. But I refuse to let it affect me like it used to.

I just shrug. "Not much. I was just over at Kristi's. Doing homework and stuff," I say, wondering why I just lied about what we were doing.

"So I guess you guys hang out a lot now, huh?" He leans against his car and squints at me.

"Yeah." I shrug and look down toward the end of the block so I won't have to look at him. Crossing the street was a bad idea and I'm starting to feel really uncomfortable.

"Isn't your birthday coming up?" he asks.

He remembered my birthday? Does that mean something?

"I remembered, 'cause I'm exactly three months older than you."

Oh.

"Do you have any plans?" he asks.

"Not really."

"You should do something memorable. You gotta really celebrate all your birthdays 'cause you never know how many you'll get," he says.

We stand there looking at each other, and I wonder if he feels that way because he lost his mom early on. "What'd you do for yours?" I ask.

"We went hot-air ballooning in Napa." He smiles.

Notice the use of *"we."* And you know me, I just have to torture myself, so I go, "That sounds like fun. Who'd you go with?" But I ask it all casual, like I couldn't care less who he sailed over the vineyards with.

He looks at me and hesitates. "I went with Monique."

Well, there you have it! The answer I was anticipating. I mean, I can just imagine the gloriously beautiful Monique clutching Jas's strong, taut arms as the big pink heart-shaped balloon (fueled on nothing but high-octane teenage lust) sailed high above endless acres of plump, juicy Napa Valley grapes.

But I just go, "Oh."

And then I nod.

Then I give him a really big fake smile and say, "Well, I should be going. My mom's expecting me." And then I look at my watch, because I just lied, which makes it difficult for me to look at him. I mean, my mom *is* expecting me. But only *eventually*. Not at this exact moment like I made it sound.

"I'll give you a ride," he says. "Hop in."

But I shake my head. "Thanks, but I really want to walk." And I say that because I cannot explain to him that I can't be near him for two reasons—both of which are equally despicable.

1. Because my friends won't allow it and
2. because I can't get *over* him if I'm *around* him.

When I turn to walk away he goes, "See ya." And it sounds like a question.

But I just wave without looking and continue down the street.

Nineteen

By the time I got home the dining room was finally decorated, and my mom was sitting at the brand-new, extra-long dining-room table having a glass of wine with an obvious admirer. He was also obviously gay, so it wasn't like I had anything to worry about.

"You must be Rio!" he says, setting down his chardonnay and pressing his hands together in a prayerlike position. "And you look just like your mom! Lucky you!"

In my mind, I roll my eyes and stick out my tongue. But in real life I just go, "Oh," followed by a tiny fake laugh.

"What do you think?" my mom asks, basking in the glow of new furniture and a new gay admirer to replace those she left behind in New York.

"Really nice." I drop my bag onto the table and look around the room. "Is this supposed to be like, Italy or something?" I ask, noticing the fancy, etched oversized mirror hanging on the opposite wall, and the colored-glass chandelier suspended from the ceiling.

"It's Venetian! And it was Michael's idea. You know, I was going to go traditional, but Michael said that was boring. So then I thought Tuscany! But he said everyone in Newport Coast did Tuscany and it's over. So then he came up with this. He's a genius," my mother gushes.

"Please. All I did was order. Your mother has a wonderful eye for decorating," he gushes back.

I lean against the shiny black table and smile politely.

"You've got to get her into modeling!" he whispers loudly.

"That's what I keep telling her, but she says she doesn't want to." My mother looks at me with great disappointment.

"But it's every girl's dream!" He's staring at me with his fingers resting against the neck of his tight black turtleneck sweater and it's making me really uncomfortable, so I grab my bag and just as I'm about to leave the room he goes, "I know a genius photographer that would absolutely worship her."

"What's his name?" my mom asks. Just because she's no longer in the biz doesn't mean she stopped reading the credits.

"Mario Saldana. He's very in demand."

"Oh, he does great work!" my mom says, turning to look at me excitedly.

"I can set something up," Michael, the decorator-coconspirator, singsongs. "What do you think?"

I'm standing in front of them and they're looking at me with so much hope, and excitement, that it makes me want to shout, "No! Quit gaping at me and leave me alone!"

But I'm not doing very well with the whole peer pressure thing lately. And I know that if I say anything remotely like that, then I'll be in for *at least* half an hour of pleading and cajoling. So instead, I just shrug and say, "Maybe."

Michael claps his hands together, and my mom's eyes go wide with false hope. Then she looks at her new best friend and gives a silent nod to proceed to the next step. And before I can change my mind, he pulls out his cell phone and places the call.

But it's not like I'm gonna stick around to listen to that, so I grab my backpack and head upstairs to my room. Leaving them alone to plan my future together.

I immediately go over to my computer and check my e-mail. There's one from Paige and one from Kristi. I read Kristi's first:

Rio—
I saw U talking 2 loser Jas. I thought we already discussed this.

Lucky 4 U no1 else saw. So I won't tell K & J. But U really need 2 B
more careful. Have a GR8 nite!
C U 2morrow!!!!!!
Kristi

I don't respond. Not that night or even the next morning when
Kristi picks me up. I just get in her car, ask her about her date with
Drew, and for the next twenty minutes that's all she talks about.

I get to Art pretty late because I was in the office asking (actually,
begging would be more accurate), if I could switch to another elective
because I don't want to sit across from Jas anymore. And it's not as
simple as moving to another table, since it's a small class and he's a big
presence (well, at least in my mind). So I figured I would ask (beg), to
switch to just about anything else.

And that's how I found myself sitting across from Mrs. Rove, the
very serious, very conservative, somewhat scary Sea Crest High guidance counselor.

"Are you having some sort of problem with Ms. Tate?" she asked,
gripping the edge of her dark wood desk and leaning forward with
barely suppressed excitement, like she'd been planning a right-wing
coup on the pierced and frizzy-haired art teacher for years now.

"No! No! Not at all! Ms. Tate is great!" I said, which believe me, did
not score any points with Mrs. Rove. "I was just, um, curious about
other electives." *Jeez, what a dumbass answer. I should have rehearsed this
better.* I cross and uncross my legs, and stare at the thin gold chain
hanging up, over, and out of her red turtleneck sweater.

"Well, Rio, I'm sorry, but unless you're having a legitimate
problem—" she stops and peers at me, giving me one last chance to
fess up. When I don't, she sighs and continues, "Well, you can't just go
switching electives out of *sheer curiosity*. Here at Sea Crest, we honor
commitment." She gives me a stern look.

"Okay," I said, rising from my seat, anxious to get out of there.

"How are you doing in your other classes?" she asked, reaching up
to pat her obedient brown bob.

"Fine." I shrugged.

"Good. And Rio, give it a chance. Art's not entirely horrible. You might even find the experience will be good for you."

I nodded like I couldn't agree more. Then I got the hell out of there.

The first thing I do when I walk in the room is scope for Jas. But in a subtle way, you know, just kind of glancing around. But I don't see him anywhere. So I go over to our table, grab my notebook, and start doodling in it like I'm thinking about my project, when really I'm just making these crappy, meaningless doodles. And every now and then I look up to check on Ms. Tate, but she's so immersed in her own abstract painting that she doesn't really notice that I'm totally wasting class time on nothing.

By the time I've filled two entire pages with random markings, Jas walks in, and nods at Ms. Tate. And she just smiles and nods at him.

And I'm thinking: *That's just the sort of thing that would really irritate Mrs. Rove. That complete lack of order, discipline, and commitment in this classroom. Not to mention the ability to just come and go as you please.*

Which are all the things I like best about it.

Jas is walking straight toward me and I start to get all nervous until I realize that he's actually just walking toward his table, and not necessarily *toward me*. But I close my folder anyway and shove it in my bag, and just as I start to get up, he goes, "Rio. Here. Happy birthday."

He's holding this big silver-wrapped package, and I just stand there staring at it like a total retard. And after a few moments of *that*, I get a grip on myself and take it from him.

"Aren't you going to open it?" he asks.

"Oh, right now?" I look at him briefly, then back at the gift. I'm starting to sweat.

"Well, I know today's not your birthday, but I finished it early and I wanted to give it to you," he says, smiling eagerly.

So I remove the blue ribbon, and I'm guiding my stub of a fingernail very carefully under a strip of tape, when he goes, "Remember when you were a little kid, and your parents gave you your birthday gift, and you couldn't wait to get at it?"

I look right into his eyes and smile.

"That's how all presents should be opened."

So I poke my finger right through the paper, making a big gaping hole, and then I rip it all the way down the front, uncovering the most amazing replica of the Duran Duran *Rio* album cover.

Only the girl is *me*.

And I know she's me because she has honey-blond hair and green eyes, like I do.

Ohmygod!

I just stand there staring at it. And I know I have to say something but I don't trust my voice because my throat is all tight and awful-feeling. And I don't trust my heart because it will make me say something stupid and embarrassing.

So when he goes, "Do you like it?"

I go, "Um, yeah. It's incredible." And as I'm looking at him the bell rings.

Then he leans toward me like he's going to hug me, and even though I desperately want him to, I also really wish he wouldn't since I'm all sweaty, nervous, and pretty much an emotional wreck. Not to mention that the last time he moved toward me like this it didn't end so well. So I grasp the painting against my chest, and it makes the hug all bumpy and awkward. And when he pulls away, I wrap the torn paper back around it, and head to my next class.

Twenty

The painting is too big for my locker, but luckily it fits in this black canvas tote that I sometimes use to carry my camera, film, and other art supplies. So at lunch when I sit next to Kayla, I slide the bag off my shoulder and set it on the empty space next to me.

And Jen Jen looks over and goes, "What's that?"

But before I can even answer, Kristi goes, "That's her new lunch bag." Then she starts laughing.

Very funny. You know, it really bugs me how she's always commenting on how much I supposedly eat. I mean, I always thought I ate like a normal person, but according to her (she who lives solely on coke—both Diet and Colombian), I'm well on my way to being a total heifer.

But I just roll my eyes, and say, "It's just some art supplies." Knowing that they'll immediately lose interest, since they're not into art.

Sure enough, Kristi starts talking about last night's date/hookup with Drew and how hot it was, and what he wore, and what she wore, and how cute they were together, and blah blah blah. But I just totally tune her out since I already had to listen to this story on the way to school, and then again in like a zillion text messages she sent during English.

And I'm relieved to have this little mental break, because I'm completely obsessed with the painting in my bag. It's like I just can't stop thinking about it, and wondering what it means. For Jas to spend his free time making something like that must mean that he likes me, right? But if he *really* liked me wouldn't he break up with Monique and ask me out? And if by some chance that did happen, would I even go? I mean, I pretty much promised my friends that I wouldn't like Jas anymore. And I *don't!* I mean, not really, not like I used to. Anyway, he probably does stuff like that for all of his friends because that's just the kind of person he is. Which is still kind of weird since it's not like we're really friends anymore. But maybe he started it back when we were friends, and just decided to finish it so he could cross it off his list, or whatever. Yeah, that must be it. I'm sure it doesn't really mean anything to him, so it really shouldn't mean anything to me.

"Hel-*lo?* Is anyone home?" Kristi's glaring at me.

"I'm sorry, I spaced," I say.

"I asked if you're coming to the mall with us after school?" She does an exaggerated eye roll. *Well, so much for yesterday when I was her new best friend.*

"Oh, I can't," I lie. "I have to help my mom with something." I smile at them, hoping they'll buy it, because the truth is, I've got to get this picture home, since I know Kristi will totally flip if she sees it. And even though I shouldn't care about things like that, we all know that I do.

When I get home from school, my mom's not there, and since I know Kristi and Company won't be coming by, I take the painting out of my bag and prop it on my desk against the wall. And then I sit there and stare at it.

For longer than I care to admit.

I must have fallen asleep because later, when I open my eyes my room is much darker, and I can hear my mom banging around in the kitchen. So I change into some sweats, pull my hair back into a pony-tail, and go downstairs to join her.

"Oh, good, you're up." She turns and smiles. "I just grilled some tuna, are you hungry?"

My head feels foggy with sleep so I just nod and take a seat in the

Venetian room, since the kitchen table is being custom-made in Thailand so it will fit in perfectly with her and Michael's burgeoning "Asian kitchen" theme. I wonder how many people in Bangkok have Sub-Zero fridges?

She sets down our plates and takes the seat across from me. "Your father called, but you were asleep."

"When's he coming home?" I ask.

"He'll be home for your birthday this weekend." She cuts into her tuna.

"Cool." I nod, taking a bite of mine. My mom's a pretty decent cook.

"You know, Rio, I hate to admit it, but with the move, and the decorating, and all the work involved in getting settled in, I'm afraid your birthday completely slipped my mind."

Can you believe she just said that?

I mean, she has *one* kid. That's just *one kid's* birthday to remember and it *slips her mind*. But I don't say that, instead I just shrug and take a bite of my salad.

"So while you were sleeping I called your friend Kristi, and we decided to throw a party for you."

What?

She's smiling excitedly, and nodding, like I'm supposed to get all excited too. But unfortunately I'm on the opposite end of excitement. I don't want some stupid party. And I definitely don't want her calling my friends. So now I'm wishing my birthday had just stayed forgotten.

"You called *Kristi?*" I ask incredulously.

"She thought it was a great idea. She's putting together a guest list."

"But why didn't you just ask me?" I set down my fork and glare at her.

"Because you were sleeping," she says, taking a sip of chardonnay.

"I took a *nap,* Mom. It wasn't intended to be some Disney fairy-tale hundred-year snooze. Besides, I don't want a party."

"What are you talking about? Of course, you want a party!"

"Mom, I just said that I *don't.*"

"Rio." She shakes her head in exasperation. "It's perfect timing. Think about it. You're new in town, you're making all these wonderful friends, it will be a chance to get everyone together and sort of seal your place."

"So this isn't really about my birthday, then is it?" I say, getting increasingly angry. "This is like some kind of campaign you dreamed up. So I can rise among the social ranks into a position of power."

"Why do you always have to be so difficult? It's just a party. It's supposed to be fun." She shakes her head. "Anyway, we don't have much time to plan it, so Kristi's going to call me back with the guest list later this evening. Would you like to look it over?"

"No thanks," I say, pushing away from the table and my plate that's still half-full. "I'm sure you and Kristi can handle it." Then I go upstairs to my room and e-mail Paige.

Okay, I admit, I haven't e-mailed Paige in over a week, even though she still e-mails me like every other day. And I feel kind of guilty about it, especially since I'm only e-mailing her now so I can vent. But I can't help it. I just really need to communicate with someone *normal*. And at the moment she's the only normal person I have access to.

So when I see she's online I write:

How R U? Sorry it's been sooooo long. Blah blah blah.

And after we go back and forth with polite small talk, I spill the beans. I tell her about the picture Jas made, about my mom calling my friends while I'm asleep, and about my new friends being really cool, and really popular, but also kind of controlling. Though I leave out the stuff about the drugs and drinking since you have to be careful with what you put in writing.

And then I wait for her reply.

But when it comes, it totally pisses me off because she writes some crap about being true to myself, and all kinds of touchy-feely nonsense that I don't really feel like reading right now.

Because who is she to say that to me?

She's not the one that was forced to move all the way across the *world* and start over in some *foreign place* where practically everyone's rich, and beautiful, and perfect. And they all play by these insane social rules that you can't figure out until you break one and are banished forever!

So after reading her sanctimonious little message, I just simply don't respond. I just sit there and let her message me two more times, before I make up some lie about having a ton of homework to do and having to sign off.

Then I take that pill Kristi gave me the other day. Because if I ever needed help chilling, it's right now. And right as I'm falling asleep I hear the phone ring. And I know it's Kristi calling with the guest list, but I don't care. I just let sleep take me away until morning.

Twenty-one

The next morning when Kristi picks me up she's all excited, talking about my party, how totally cool my mom is, and how awesome it's all gonna be even though it's totally last minute. I don't do much except nod and go along, partly because my head feels completely sand-bagged from that pill I took, and partly because I've made the decision to just let it go. I mean, my mom working alone is bad enough. But my mom paired with Kristi is a force I just don't have the energy to fight.

"Um, what was that pill you gave me the other day?" I ask, leaning my head against the neck rest, and totally interrupting her.

"Just Valium. Why? Did you take it?" Her eyes light up.

"Yeah, but I'm not sure if I liked it."

"What do you mean?" She looks at me closely.

"Well, my head feels a little funny. And like, it totally knocked me out."

"That's the point. I've got more. My mom has a cabinet full of stuff from her shrink and all of her surgeries."

She looks over and sees the expression on my face. "*Plastic* surgeries. You didn't really think her nose and boobs were real, did you?" She laughs.

I just shrug.

"Anyway, your mom even promised that she'll only be there for the very beginning then she'll bail so we can have fun. I've arranged it so that your parents are going to dinner with my mom and stepdad. And trust me, the guest list is totally A-list, *and* since it's your birthday, you get first crack at all the guys!"

She's looking at me and I know I'm supposed to be superexcited by that, so I give her a big smile that hopefully resembles someone who is.

And then all through English she sends me like a zillion text messages about the party. By the sixth one I am so totally over it, I feel like turning it off. But I don't, because you just don't ignore Kristi. So I keep that fake smile firmly plastered on my face, and send little messages back, while Mrs. Abbott drones on and on about Hemingway's spare, masculine, journalistic style.

When I get to Art (late, again, and yes, on purpose), Ms. Tate is in the middle of a slide presentation. And right between projections she stops lecturing and says, "Rio, welcome. Starting tomorrow could you please make an effort to get here on time?"

Wow, I guess even the laid-back Ms. Tate has her limits. I mumble an apology, slink toward my desk, and sit next to Mason who glances at me briefly, then focuses her attention back on the screen.

So I look at Jas, trying to determine if there's anything different between us since he gave me that picture. But he just nods and smiles and looks back at the screen.

And I hate to admit it, but I don't look at the screen. I just open my notebook and doodle more crap.

When I get home from school my mom's not there, so on my way to my room I stop by the kitchen to grab something to eat. But when I pass the downstairs guest room I do a double take. She can't be serious.

I push the door all the way open and gape at the fake potted palms, the double-layered mosquito nets, and the dust ruffles resembling gigantic grass hula skirts, and I can only wonder whose "genius" idea this was—my mom's or Michael's? I mean, it looks just like a room you might find in a cheesy Caribbean hotel, or a Disney theme park.

Jeez, I'm starting to feel like I need a passport just to move from room to room.

I close the door so I won't have to look at it again and go upstairs to my room, which is like the only normal place in this house. Then I drop my books right in front of—*the picture Jas made!*

Ohmygod! What if my mom saw it?

I meant to hide it this morning, before I left for school, but I was so messed-up from that stupid Valium I forgot. I quickly grab it and shove it under my bed, covering it up with my " ape   Crew" sweat-shirt. Then I sit at my desk and take some deep cleansing breaths and pray she didn't see it.

So imagine my surprise the next day, when my mom drops me off, and all the important juniors, and even a few seniors are waving around their very own postcard-sized version of Jas's painting.

"Hey, Brazil! Check it out!" Kristi says, running toward me, waving one in the air.

I grab it, flip it over, and quickly scan the back. I'm completely hor-rified when I realize it's an invitation to my party.

"Where'd you get this?" I ask, with barely concealed panic.

"Your mom had them made! Aren't they awesome? Oh, my god, everyone's coming, including Drew and some of his hot friends. It's gonna be *so great!*"

I just stand there feeling completely ill, and when I look up, I see Jas. *Oh, god.*

But Kristi sees him, too, and as he walks by she goes, "Hey Jas, *nice work.*" Then she hands him one so he can see it all up close and per-sonal.

I just stand there watching him trace his finger over the front, be-fore he flips it over and reads the back. When he's done he hands it back to Kristi, but his eyes are on me.

I know I should say something, anything. But I just continue to stand there like a total retard. Then the first period bell rings and Kristi looks at Jas and goes, "Ciao, loser!" Then she puts her arm through mine and drags me all the way across the quad.

And I don't try to stop her, and I don't look back. Not even once.

I want to ditch Art.

And I seriously consider it, until I see Ms. Tate in the hall and she says, "So, how's your project coming along?"

"Oh. Um, okay."

"Good." She nods. "I'm very interested in seeing your interpretation of Beauty."

"Uh, yeah," I mumble, reluctantly following her into the classroom and wondering if I should hold my breath and try to faint or something, since at this point I'd rather be rushed to the emergency room than face Jas. But awful as I may feel, I can't just faint on cue. So I suck it up and head for my seat.

The second I sit down Mason goes, "Hey, what's up?"

And I go, "Um, nothing." And then I shrug. And then I smile. But she just looks at me, and then at Jas (who I'm still afraid to look at), then she gets up and goes over to her easel.

I can feel Jas staring at me, and I know I have to say something, so I take a deep breath and go, "Look, I'm sorry. I didn't know my mom was going to do that. She swiped it out of my room without asking. And you have to believe me, because I never would have allowed it." When I finally glance at him, I feel even worse, because he's looking at me like I'm some horrible person.

"So you bootleg my work, and I don't even get an invite?" he says.

Okay, I'm just gonna go with the truth. I mean, I owe him that. So I say, "Jas, I'm really sorry but I can't invite you."

"Why? Concerned about fire codes?"

"No." I shake my head. "I can't invite you because my mom and Kristi are planning the party, and my mom thinks you're a bad influence."

"What? Why?" He leans toward me, waiting for an answer.

"Well," I say, my eyes glued to the scarred wood tabletop. "Because I was with you when I got detention."

"Yeah, and I picked you up to go to dinner a few days later. She didn't seem to have a problem with me then."

Okay, technically that's true. But I can't exactly tell him how I came home that night totally freaked-out and red-faced because I discovered he had a girlfriend just seconds after throwing myself at him. And how my mom totally misread it—and I let her. So I just say, "Well, she waited up for me, and she knew I'd been drinking, so she said I couldn't hang with you guys anymore."

"Drinking? Rio, you had like *one* glass of wine. You were fine when we dropped you off. I don't get it."

I just shrug, and continue to stare at the table, but I can feel him looking at me.

"Well, I guess that explains it."

"Explains what?" I ask, looking up.

"Why you just stopped hanging with us. But I wonder. If your mom thinks *I'm* a bad influence, how'd you get *Kristi* past her?"

"What's that supposed to mean?" I ask defensively.

"Come on, Rio, you've been hanging with her long enough to know what I'm referring to." He narrows his eyes.

And did he just smirk?

I lean all the way back in my chair, and cross my arms in front of me. "Well, I'm sorry *Jas*, but I *don't* know what you're referring to. And before you say anything else you might regret, you should know that Kristi Wood is one of my best friends. I mean, it's not like she ever *misled* me or *lied* to me." I lock eyes with him.

"So far, I have no regrets," he says, smiling.

Smiling? Does he think this is funny?

"Well, it's really none of your business who I'm friends with, is it?" I continue. "And it's not really your place to *judge* them, since you don't even *know* them. I mean, it's not like you don't have your own *friends* to keep you warm and busy."

Oh, god! Oh, no! Did I say "warm"?

I'm back to looking at the table. "So, just handle your business and stay out of mine." *Kind of harsh, but it should get the point across.*

"You're right. It's not my concern," he says, getting up. "And I'm sorry for any problems I might have caused you with your mom.

But, Rio, don't think for a second I don't know all about your friends."

I can feel him looking at me, then he turns and walks away.

And after sitting there for a while, just breathing in and out and staring at the table, I grab my camera and tell Ms. Tate I'm going to do some outdoor photographs. She gives me a hall pass and I don't return until after the bell rings.

After school Kristi, Kayla, and Jen Jen come home with me and we go into the kitchen, where my mom is waiting at the brand-new intricately carved table that came all the way from Far East Asia just to live in our house. She's set out a big pitcher of iced tea and a bowl of weird-looking fruit that may or may not be edible, but it blends in perfectly with her Thai kitchen theme, and that's all that really matters. And all of this is taking place so we can sit around, chug iced tea, and hammer out the final details of my stupid, fucking party.

"What d' you think of the invites?" my mom asks excitedly as I walk into the kitchen.

"Well, I kind of wish you'd asked me first," I say, dropping my bag on the counter.

"I wanted to surprise you! I found that painting in your room and thought it would be perfect! Who painted that by the way?"

She doesn't know?

I just assumed she did since Kristi did. But I just look at her carefully and say, "Um, someone from my art class." Then I avoid Kristi's eyes, even though I can feel them burning into me. "They did it for a project and then they gave it to me," I lie.

"Well, I hope they don't mind, but it was just too good to pass up!"

I just shrug. Then I sit there slumped at the table for like the next hour watching my mom and my friends debate important issues like catering (not like they eat), and a band vs. a DJ vs. CD's. And I know I should be grateful and excited that they all want to do this for me, but I can't stop thinking about that horrible fight with Jas, and the way he sounded right before he walked away.

There was something so final about it.

———

When they finally leave (with all the big decisions having been made with absolutely no input from me), I go upstairs to my room and on my desk I find a big square envelope with a New York stamp. I open it excitedly, wondering if it's from Paige or Hud, and when I read the cover I realize it's from both.

They sent one of those cards that you find in the "from all of us" section at the Hallmark store and they each wrote a little note in it and enclosed a picture. At first when I look at the picture I just think, "Oh, that's cute." Then I set it down and start to reread the card.

But then it hits me.

So I pick it up again. They're at Winter Formal. Which is really no big deal because if they wanted to go then of course they would go with each other, being best friends and all. But there's something about the way Hud is holding Paige, and something about the way Paige is leaning into Hud, that makes me feel really angry because it looks like they're a couple. *And how can they be a couple when we're all supposed to be JUST FRIENDS?* I mean, how long has this been going on? Were they just waiting for me to leave so they could hook up?

Ohmygod—was I just a third wheel with Paige and Hud, too?

I don't even bother with the computer. I just pick up the phone and punch in the numbers. And when she answers I go, "I got your card."

"Oh, good," she says. "I was hoping it would get there on time."

Then without even making an attempt at small talk or beating around the bush, I go, "Did you and Hud hook up?"

And she goes, "Well, we're dating now, yeah." And she sounds really uncomfortable when she says that.

"Are you guys serious?"

"Well, kind of. Yeah."

I don't know why, but hearing her say that makes me feel even angrier. And my voice is kind of shaky when I ask, "So exactly how long has this been going on?"

"Uh, a couple weeks after you left," she says quietly.

"Why didn't you tell me?" I demand. "I mean, you e-mail me like every day!"

"Well, I wanted to." She hesitates. "But your messages always sound like you're having kind of a rough time. And I don't know. I just—"

"Well, don't go feeling sorry for me," I say, totally cutting her off. "Because my life is *great!*" I kick over my trash bin for emphasis, watching wads of paper and water bottles scatter across the carpet.

"I'm happy to hear that," she says softly.

"And just so you know, I'm having a major party this weekend, and like *everyone* from the junior class will be there. Even some of the hot senior guys are coming. It's going to be really big, really major," I say, crushing an Evian bottle under my foot.

"That sounds fun. I wish we could be there," she says.

We!

"Well, listen," I say, feeling completely irrational and out of control, but unable to stop. "I have to go."

"Are you mad at me?" she asks, sounding so genuinely caring that it totally infuriates me.

"*No!* I'm really very happy for you, Paige. I'm happy for *both* of you. But I'm extremely busy right now, so I have to go!"

"Okay, well, have fun at your party."

"Oh, I will."

"Okay, well, bye," she says.

"Ciao!" I say, and then I push the off button really, really hard.

But it's hardly the same as slamming it.

$\mathscr{T}$wenty-two

Okay, so here's a list of the people I am no longer talking to:

1. Paige
2. Hud
3. Mason
4. Jas

And here's a list of the people I am talking to:

1. My mom
2. My dad
3. Kristi
4. Kayla
5. Jen Jen
6. All the juniors and seniors on the invite list
7. All the juniors and seniors that *weren't* on the invite list, but who are totally sucking up to me hoping for a zero-hour reprieve

So on the night of the party, I come downstairs in this amazing green BCBG halter dress that my mom bought for me on a recent shopping trip to Fashion Island (which isn't really an island, just an upscale, outdoor *shopping experience*).

My mom's on the phone and when she sees me she goes, "Oh, here she is now." Then she hands me the phone and whispers, "Honey, it's your dad."

"What?" I give her a confused look as I take the receiver because he's supposed to be walking through the door, not calling me. "Dad?"

"Hey, kiddo, happy birthday!"

"Where are you?" I ask, hoping he's just fooling around, like calling me from the driveway or something.

"I'm at the studio," he says. "I finished late, missed my flight, and now I'm about to tape a *Larry King* segment. I'm sorry, honey. I wish I could be there, I hear your mom has quite the party planned."

I feel like crying. But that will ruin the makeup my mom spent the last hour applying, so I tell him it's okay, even though it's really not. And then I go, "But when are you coming home?"

"Well, I've got to be back in court on Monday morning, so probably not until next weekend. But listen, we'll do something great, something to make up for it. I promise. But meanwhile, try to take a little time out from your party to watch your old man on *Larry King*. I just might surprise you."

When I hang up, my mom gives me her "it's just you and me so let's try to get along and not maim each other" smile, and I just shrug. Then the doorbell rings, and it's Kristi, Kayla, and Jen Jen, all three of them dressed in two-hundred-dollar jeans and high-heeled, stiletto sandals with a vintage-looking beaded cardigan (Kayla), a white ribbed tank top and black sequined capelet (Jen Jen), and a red silky halter top (Kristi).

We all sit on the couch and watch my dad yak with Larry, and when the segment is almost over and my friends are nearly bored to tears (because once the initial charm of my dad being on TV wore off, we were left with nothing more than insomnia-curing legal speak), Larry goes, "So, Griffin, I hear it's your daughter's birthday today."

My dad looks at Larry and then directly into the camera and goes, "That's right, Rio's just turned seventeen, and I've got a lot to make up for since I'm spending it here with you, Larry."

And then they both chuckle.

Then Larry looks into the camera and tells me to have a happy birthday.

And my friends look at me with their mouths wide open.

And while it's nice that they're impressed, I still feel totally gypped. 'Cause even though this isn't the first birthday of mine that he's missed, it's definitely the one where I'm really missing him.

I look at my mom sitting on the couch, laughing with my friends, and it's like she fits in easier, and with less effort than I do. Then she looks at me and smiles, and it's obvious how proud she is that I'm part of all this. And it makes me want to feel happy and proud, too.

Within a half hour the house is filled with like forty of my closest friends, and apparently, according to Kristi, there're some seniors who may or may not show up. I guess that's not really a ton of people when you think about it, but she was very strict with the guest list.

Kristi's floating around, acting like this is her party and she's the hostess (which I guess in a way she is). But I don't really mind since it allows me just to hang back and observe, and I'm really more comfortable with that anyway.

I go into the living room (which, by the way, has now been fully decorated to resemble something one might find in the Taj Mahal section at Disney's Epcot World Showcase), and I find my mom perched on top of a silky, beaded floor pillow, showing off numerous scrapbooks of her glory days when she was an almost-supermodel. God, I can't believe her! I mean, can't I have just *one thing* that belongs to me? Isn't it enough that she leaves voice-mail messages for my friends?

So I walk right up to her and go, "Uh, Mom, you're totally gonna be late for dinner. You really need to wrap it up." Then I give her a look.

And she goes, "Oh, right." Then she gives me a look.

But it's not as harsh as the one I gave her. Then she gets up from her little cushion, grabs her purse and car keys, and says good night.

Kristi runs to the window and when my mom's car is safely out of view she grabs the Louis Vuitton duffle bag she brought, unzips it, and pulls out several bottles of vodka, champagne, and beer, and sets up bar on the coffee table.

"Happy birthday!" she yells, popping the cork on a champagne bottle and holding it up high so the bubbles run down her arm.

She drinks from the bottle then hands it to me, and the second I'm done she takes it back, puts her arm through mine and goes, "Come on, I've got something for you." She leads me down the hall and into the big guest bathroom near the stairs, then she pulls me inside and locks the door behind us.

"What's the big secret?" I ask, wondering what she could possibly have that can only be given to me in a bathroom.

She sets her brand-new black Balenciaga bag on the counter and pulls out a little glass vial of coke. "Happy birthday!" she says, handing it to me.

Instinctively I reach for it, but once it's in my hand I start to feel really uncomfortable. I mean, if she wants to do coke, that's her business, and her secret is safe with me, but there's no way I can partake in this. I set it on the marble counter and look at her. "Um, Kristi—" I start.

"It's supposed to be really good stuff," she says, grabbing it and tapping it out against a little handheld mirror. "But I haven't tried it yet, I thought we could do it together. You know, just us. Kayla and Jen Jen can't know."

I just stand there not saying anything because even though I've totally made up my mind that I'm not gonna do it, there's still this tiny part of me that's whispering, *Why not?* I mean, I've watched Kristi do it, and it's not like it made her all crazy or anything. And it's not like one line's gonna make me an addict.

"I bet you're really disappointed that your dad totally ditched your birthday, huh?" she asks, sculpting a perfect white line.

"I'm used to it." I shrug. But she's right, I really am kind of angry.

"And your mom showing everyone her swimsuit photos." She shakes her head and cringes. "Kinda harsh."

I just shrug. But she's right, it is pretty sick and wrong.

"I read this great line recently, about how your friends are the family you choose." She looks at me and smiles. "I'm really glad we're friends, Rio." Then she leans down and inhales.

And when she comes back up her eyes are wide and sparkling, and her skin is flushed slightly pink, and she looks so happy and perfect, that I think: *What the hell? I mean, it is my birthday. And I'll only do a little bit. And no one will ever find out since it's our secret . . .*

"Exactly how do you do this?" I ask, moving toward the mirror.

Within two hours most of the alcohol is gone, but there's still plenty of food. Everyone's just sort of scattered all over doing whatever, and some guy I've never seen before has plugged in his iPod, and all this really great music is blasting through the house.

I admit, after doing those two lines of coke I'm feeling pretty hyper and aware, and almost kind of powerful, and I'm just wandering around and around until I end up standing outside the little cabana next to our pool.

It's pretty dim, but there are candles flickering inside so I can just make out the shapes of people moving around in there, and I'm cupping my hands against the glass to get a better view when someone comes up from behind and hugs me. I have no idea who it is, but the hug feels nice so I just close my eyes and let it unfold.

And then he says, "Happy birthday."

And I think:

Oh, my god, Jas?

So I turn around and JC is standing there smiling. His light-brown hair is gelled perfectly in place, and his eyes look bloodshot and sleepy, but he's still cute in the way most girls agree on. But I can't hide my disappointment when I say, "Oh, it's you."

He's all ego though, so he just laughs. "After you," he says, opening the cabana door.

We go inside and there are these random couples everywhere, and JC grabs my hand, leads me to the couch, and pulls me down next to him. And when my eyes adjust to the dim light I realize those random couples are my friends.

Then he leans in really close, touches my face, and says, "You are so hot."

And I wonder if he means I have a fever.

Then he kisses me.

And even though I don't have much experience, and my head is feeling pretty messed-up, I'm still kind of disappointed that my first real kiss is turning out to be not so great. But I don't stop him, because I'm seventeen now, and it's about time I hooked up with someone.

So we're making out and he's way more into it than I am, because mostly I'm just wondering how far I'll let him go. I mean, yeah, JC is cute and popular and all the girls like him, but still, this is nothing like I hoped it would be. And just as I'm thinking we should probably stop, he takes my hand and puts it right on his crotch.

"Oh, my god! What are you doing?" I say, moving my hand and backing away from him.

But he just laughs in that overconfident, lazy way and goes, "Relax, it's no big deal."

"It is to me," I say, not caring how uptight I sound.

"Look around," he whispers, sliding closer to me. "Everyone's doing it."

So I look around, and he's right, everyone is doing it. But that doesn't mean I have to. "Forget it," I tell him, getting up to leave.

"Okay, okay. It's your call," he says, lifting his hands in surrender and following me back into the house.

Twenty-three

The next morning Kristi, Kayla, Jen Jen, and I are dressed in cute, cotton good-girl pj's and we're drinking fresh-squeezed orange juice and eating the blueberry pancakes my mom made. And we're telling her how great the party was.

Or rather, they're telling her. My head is pounding so bad I'm surprised blood isn't pouring out of my eyeballs. I guess I don't have the same tolerance for bodily abuse as my friends.

I also lack the keen organizational skills of Kristi. A half hour before my mom was due back, she kicked out all but a few chosen people who she made help with the cleanup. But we didn't overclean. We didn't want it to look *suspiciously clean*. Oh, no, with Kristi's guidance, we removed only the really severe evidence, and kept the stuff that depicted wholesome fun. And by the time my mom walked in the front door the house was looking pretty decent and most of the guests were gone.

"So, I noticed a lot of cute boys last night," my mom singsongs, as she joins us at the table clutching her coffee mug.

Everybody giggles on cue. Well, everyone but me, because it hurts to laugh.

"Do any of you have a boyfriend?" she asks.

Kristi shakes her head. "No. That would just interfere with our other activities. I mean, we go on group dates and stuff like that, but nothing serious. We just don't have time for that right now." She smiles at my mom, and Kayla and Jen Jen nod in agreement.

"Wow. You girls are so disciplined and together. I was nothing like that at your age," she says wistfully.

"Weren't you modeling in Paris?" Jen Jen asks, reaching for her orange juice.

"I was just fourteen when I left home, and I certainly didn't have the good sense that you girls do. I'm afraid I got a little caught up in it all." She shakes her head at the memory.

"Did you meet a lot of famous people?" Kristi asks, rearranging the food on her plate so it looks like she's eating.

"Oh, yes, plenty." Then she takes a sip of her coffee and goes, "You know, talking to you girls, makes me feel so much better about Rio."

I look up, startled.

"What do you mean?" Kristi asks.

"Well, she probably didn't mention it because she's so modest, but we're setting up a test shoot with Mario Saldana. I'm getting her that for her birthday."

Everyone is looking at me in shock. But no one's as shocked as me.

"I thought the shopping spree at Fashion Island was my gift," I say.

"No, honey, you *needed* those clothes. A gift is supposed to be something you don't necessarily *need*."

"Is it also supposed to be something you don't necessarily *want*?" I ask.

"Oh, Rio, we'll discuss this later," she says, frowning at me and getting up from the table.

Kristi, Kayla, and Jen Jen left shortly after breakfast as they all had to get ready to go to church. Yeah, that's right, *church*.

But before they left Kristi asked, "Do you really want to be a model?"

And I said, "No. *My mom* really wants me to be a model."

Then Kayla goes, "Rio, you should totally do it."

And Jen Jen goes, "Totally. You're definitely tall enough, and pretty enough."

And then they smiled at me—but just the two of them.

Kristi just stared.

———

On Monday I rode to school with Kayla and Jen Jen because Kristi had a tooth-whitening appointment with her dentist. And like the minute we got out of the car JC was all over me acting like we're boyfriend and girlfriend or something, which is kind of weird 'cause I thought the whole point of hooking up was so you could ignore each other afterward and not act all committed.

So when I find him waiting for me at my locker after English, I'm thinking I really need to have a talk with him and explain how I just want to be friends. But then he puts his arm around me and goes, "Where to?"

And I go, "I have Art now."

And he goes, "I'll walk you."

Then right when I'm about to say, "No, don't walk me," I change my mind. I let him walk me to class, with his arm around me the whole time. And I even let him kiss me right in front of the door, for as long as it takes for Jas to walk up and say, "Uh, excuse me."

Then we break apart and JC goes, "Sorry, bro."

And I giggle, and wipe my mouth, and go, "See you at lunch, JC!" loud enough for Jas to hear.

Then I walk inside the classroom and sit at my desk. And when I glance over at Jas (just to see his reaction), his eyes are so full of disapproval that it really pisses me off. Because it wasn't that long ago when I was forced to sit in the backseat and watch Monique's hands go on a scavenger hunt in Jas's pants! And it's not like he tried to stop it or anything. So excuse me for trying to have a little fun of my own. I mean, what gives him the right to judge me?

$\mathcal{T}$wenty-four

I'm JC's girlfriend. Don't ask me why or how, because I'm still not sure what happened. It seems that in a world of random hook ups meant to go nowhere, I ended up with a boyfriend. And since I've never had a boyfriend before I decided to just ride it out for the experience.

And even though JC isn't really my type (I mean he kinda has that all-American Nick Lachey look when I mostly go for that dark, smoldering Johnny Depp thing), everyone else thinks he's completely hot.

So I guess I should feel lucky.

But our conversations aren't exactly thrilling. I mean, we really don't have much to talk about (unless you count the day we discovered we use the same hair products), and it seems like all he wants to do is make out, watch sports, play sports, and talk about sports he's watched and played. Which, quite frankly, gets a little boring.

And even though the making out part isn't so bad, I totally draw the line at "real" sex because no way am I doing *that* with *him*. I mean, it's not like he doesn't try (like every single time we're alone), but I refuse to give in. I'm holding out for love.

Still, I'd be lying if I said I didn't like the attention I get from being his girlfriend.

Because I do.

It just feels really great to be part of something that everyone wishes they were part of. It's like VIP status all the time. It's like the ultimate backstage pass.

On the outside we're like the perfect couple. I mean, the whole school thinks we're adorable, and JC is constantly talking about how great we look together. And just the other day Jen Jen said we were single-handedly making a totally archaic idea like going steady cool again. And Kayla said that if we're still together in late spring we'll definitely get voted "Cutest Junior Class Couple."

But Kristi just rolled her eyes.

And even though it really bugged me when she did that, there's this part of me that totally agreed. Not to be mean, but JC isn't exactly the sharpest knife in the drawer. It's like, earlier, when I was making my point about smart guys and prom queens—well now I feel like I'm caught in this weird reversal where *I'm* the brainiac and *he's* the prom queen, like *I'm* Nick and *he's* Jessica, like *I'm* Exhibit D. And it's really starting to bug me.

But my days are so full now with all of the important school activities, that I had no choice but to drop out of the art show. I mean, I just don't have time for that anymore with all the clubs, games, and parties I have to attend.

So one day I just walked right up to Ms. Tate's desk and told her that I was sorry, but I just didn't have time to help out, but that of course I would still hand in my assignment. She gave me kind of a sad look, but whatever.

Then I walked over to another table and took a seat. I don't know why I didn't think I could do that before, because it was so easy. So now I don't have to look at Jas and Mason unless I accidentally look at the other side of the room. And believe me, I only made that mistake once.

In addition to everything else, my relationship with my mom is way better. We go shopping more, and instead of fighting her all the time, now I listen to her advice on clothes and stuff. And because of it, Jen Jen said that if I keep it up, then for sure I'll get voted "Best Dressed" when we're seniors.

It's weird too because a lot of girls at school, including Jen Jen and Kayla, have started to dress like me. They even copy my hair, bleaching theirs blond and wearing it all long and wavy, and for Kayla that means extra highlights and getting up even earlier to use a curling iron. At first it really annoyed me, but then my mom said, "Imitation is the sincerest form of flattery." So I should be flattered.

And I am.

But it still kind of bugs me.

I guess you could say that my life is going really, really great. I hardly ever think about Paige and Hud, or that stupid crush I had on Jas. I mean, why would I? That seems like such a long time ago, like it happened to another person or something.

Looking back, it all just seems so juvenile.

After school, I'm being a dutiful girlfriend, and sitting in the bleachers pretending like I'm watching JC's basketball practice (but really I'm just zoning-out), and when Tyler (who is like *the* mega-hot senior guy) runs by, he smiles and winks at me.

And it gets me thinking: *Hmmmmmm.*

Then Kristi turns and punches me in the arm and goes, "Did he just wink at you?"

"He most certainly did." I smile.

"Well, doesn't he know you're dating JC?"

I just shrug.

She continues staring at me with narrowed eyes.

But I ignore her.

After practice we all go back to Kristi's and lay out by the pool (even though it's only March and it's still snowing in New York). I'm all shiny with oil and lying faceup on this beige padded lounge chair, and I just want to close my eyes, relax, and enjoy the last half hour of sun.

But then JC comes over and goes, "Hey, come swim with me."

"Not now," I say, keeping my eyes firmly shut, hoping he'll go away.

But he ignores that, and starts pulling on my foot, "Come on. The pool's heated," he says.

"You're blocking my rays and disturbing my peace." I open one eye and look at him. But when I see his hurt expression, I smile to soften the blow.

Well, that was a mistake. Because he leans down, picks me up off my towel, and throws me smack into the deep end. Then he jumps in after me. And while we're both underwater he starts groping me. And when I open my eyes and look at him, hair standing on end, eyes stinging from chlorine, I can't help thinking how bored I am, and how I'd much rather be with Tyler. I mean, I'm really getting tired of our dumb conversations and the way he hangs all over me.

So when my head pops out of the water right after his, I kiss him quickly on the cheek and swim away as fast as I can. But he catches right up to me. And just as I'm grabbing onto the edge, he forces me to turn around so he can kiss me for real. When he's done, he looks right at me and says, "I love you."

But I don't say anything. I just duck back underwater and swim to the other side without once taking a breath.

Later, we're up in Kristi's room, and it's just the girls since she made the guys leave before her mom and stepdad came home. I'm lying on the chaise next to her window when I go, "You guys, JC told me he loved me."

Kayla's eyes go wide. "When?"

"In the pool."

And Jen Jen goes, "Oh, my god, that is so totally sweet."

I just shrug and look at the ceiling.

Kristi looks at me closely. "Well, what did you say?"

Then I tell them how I didn't respond.

Kayla and Jen Jen just look at me with their mouths hanging open, but Kristi goes, "It was probably the beer talking. He tossed one back when you were changing. I wouldn't worry about it. I'm sure he doesn't really love you."

And when we look at each other, part of me hopes she's right. But the other part is kind of pissed at her response.

Twenty-five

The next day I'm walking home from school. Can you believe it? The most popular girl in the junior class (okay, after Kristi) is walking. I mean, Kristi, Kayla, and Jen Jen all had individual family obligations, JC left school early 'cause he's spending the weekend at his dad's place in Palm Springs, and my mom is in L.A. being photographed by Mario Saldana.

It was supposed to be me, but I just couldn't go through with it. It's like, despite all the other changes in my life, the one thing that remains the same is that I don't want to be a model. So I told her I wasn't ready, which didn't really make her back off. So then I spoke in a language that she could understand. I told her I was feeling too fat to be photographed.

"Well, you don't just cancel an appointment with Mario Saldana!" she said. "He is very much in demand. Michael did us a huge favor by setting this up!"

But I just shrugged and said, "So why don't you go instead?"

And right after she scowled at me, her eyes lit up. Then she picked up the phone.

Apparently they're collaborating on a possible comeback.

Great.

So I've only covered about a block since the bell rang (because it's hard to walk fast when you're busy feeling sorry for yourself), when this black SUV with dark tinted windows pulls up next to me.

I don't recognize the car so I pick up the pace, hoping it's not some pervert intending on making me the next Amber Alert, when I hear someone go, "Hey, slow down."

And when I look over I see purposely messy blondish brown hair, big blue eyes, and like the sexiest smile ever. It's Tyler. So I don't just slow down, I stop.

"Where you going?" He smiles.

"Home."

Then he leans all the way across the seat and opens the door. "Get in, I'll take you."

I don't even hesitate. I just slide in next to him.

"Why are you walking?" he asks, pulling away from the curb.

"Everyone's busy, and I don't have my license yet," I say, staring at his gorgeousness while wishing he'd turn down that stupid Eminem CD.

"You're kidding? How old are you?"

"Seventeen." I bite my lower lip and rub my arm, 'cause I'm feeling kind of nervous.

"Don't you at least have a permit?"

I shake my head.

"Have you ever driven?"

I shrug.

"Wanna learn?"

"Okay," I say, assuming he means sometime in the distant future.

But he pulls over right then and goes, "Ready for your first lesson?"

By the time he dropped me off (after teaching me the basics and letting me drive for a block or two, he wisely took over again), I was convinced it was time to break up with JC.

And after he leaned over and kissed me good-bye, I was positive.

"See you Monday?" he asks, his face still close to mine.

I'm so overwhelmed I don't trust my own voice. I just bite down on my lower lip and nod. Then I get out of the car, run into the house, and try to instant message Kristi, Kayla, and Jen Jen. But they're not online. So I call. But they don't answer. So I send a group e-mail.

Then I lie back on my bed and try to close my eyes, and replay everything that happened with Tyler. But I'm so full of energy that I can't lie still. So I keep trying to call my friends, over and over and over again, but no one answers.

And then right when I give up, the phone rings. So I pick it up and go, *"Hello!"*

But it's only JC. "Do you miss me?"

"Um, yeah, sure," I say.

"That didn't sound very convincing," he says, laughing nervously.

But I don't say anything. I just sit there, trying to think of a good excuse to get off the phone. Because talking to him makes me feel guilty.

"Rio? Are you there?"

"Um, yeah. But my mom needs me to help her with something so I have to go." Then I hang up before he can say anything else.

By the time my mom does come home I'm exhausted. I took all that guilt-fueled nervous energy and put it into finishing my homework, organizing all of my drawers, and rearranging my entire closet. And now as she sits on the edge of my bed going on and on about her stupid photo shoot, I can barely keep my eyes open.

She leans across the duvet, pats me on the knee and goes, "Poor baby, you're really overbooking yourself these days, aren't you?"

I just nod.

And after that I can't remember.

My dad got home really early on Saturday morning, having taken the red-eye from New York. Usually when he does that, he heads straight upstairs for a nap since he says he can never really sleep on the plane. But this time when I came downstairs for breakfast he was sitting at the kitchen table, drinking coffee, and reading the paper while my mom was upstairs showering.

"Hey, kiddo," he says.

"Hey," I say, feeling groggy.

"I thought we could go over to Roger's Gardens today and pick up some more plants for the back." He smiles.

I pour myself a cup of coffee and go, "I can't. I've got a paper I've got to finish by Monday."

"We'll only be gone for an hour or two," he says, trying to convince me.

"Yeah, well, I really gotta get this done." I feel kinda bad about not wanting to hang out with him like I used to but it's not my fault he's never here when I need him.

I hop onto the counter, and I'm sitting there drinking my coffee when he goes, "So how's your art project coming along?"

"Okay." I shrug.

"Just okay? I thought you were really excited about it. I thought this art show was some kind of big deal?" He looks at me closely.

"Well, it turns out it's really not that big a deal," I tell him. "It's actually pretty small-time. So while I'm still turning in a project for a grade, I'm not submitting anything for the show. And I'm not helping to organize it either. I'm just superbusy with bigger things."

He looks at me and nods. But there's something more in his eyes that I don't really want to see. So I quickly finish my coffee, place the mug in the dishwasher, and go back upstairs to my room.

On Sunday night, after I finish my paper, I go to Kristi's. Kayla and Jen Jen are already there, and I'm really starting to regret that e-mail I sent, because now that two days have passed, the thrill of being kissed by Tyler has pretty much worn off.

Yeah, I still think he's totally hot, but the fact is I already have a boyfriend. And even though it was just one kiss, I know JC would be totally crushed if he ever found out. I mean, he told me he loves me! But I just don't love him, and I know we should probably break up before things go any farther, but I don't really know how to do it without hurting him.

Anyway, I was really hoping my friends would just forget all about it, so we could talk about other stuff, but they're totally grilling me. So I'm trying to make it sound awesome (because I want to impress them), while also trying to downplay the significance (which is not as easy as it sounds).

"Oh, my god, I can't believe you kissed him!" Jen Jen says. "He's *so incredibly hot!*"

"What are you gonna do about JC?" Kayla asks.

"Nothing." I shrug. "I mean, it's not like I'm going out with Tyler or anything, it was just one kiss."

"But you said he said, 'see you Monday,'" Jen Jen says.

"Well, yeah. We go to the same school, right?" I pick up the latest issue of *Lucky* magazine and start flipping through it, desperate to change the subject.

"I think JC has a right to know," Kristi says, casually inspecting her cuticles.

"Why?" I ask.

"Because he's your boyfriend." She looks at me.

"Listen," I say. "It was just one kiss. It's really no big deal." I look back at the glossy page, and try to focus on "Fifty Great Handbags!"

"That's not what you said in your e-mail."

"I was caught up in the moment!" *God, why won't she just let it go?*

"Well, I still think you owe it to him."

"I can't believe you're saying this." I drop the magazine and shake my head. "You, of all people!"

"What's that supposed to mean?" She gives me her infamous death stare.

"You're like this firm believer in the random hookup!"

"This isn't about *me*. It's about *you*. And JC happens to be your boyfriend who told you he loves you," she says firmly.

"Yeah, and you're the one that said he probably didn't mean it!" I glare at her. She's really starting to piss me off.

"I don't recall saying that. And if I did then I was probably just joking, and you took it seriously."

"You weren't joking. You guys heard her say that, right?" I look at Jen Jen and Kayla, but their eyes are fixated on the ground.

I shake my head and go, "Just let me handle it, okay?"

"Whatever. It's not like it's any of my business." She rolls her eyes and shrugs.

The next morning I'm kind of dreading the ride to school with Kristi, because I don't want her to get all judgmental about the JC-Tyler situation.

But she doesn't even mention it. Instead she just goes on and on about how Drew called her after we left, and how she snuck him into her house and they totally hooked up right there in her room.

"Jeez, how many times have you guys hooked up now?" I ask.

"I lost count." She shrugs.

"Are you guys, like, dating?"

She pulls into the student lot and goes, "He totally asked me to commit, but I'm just not ready to get myself all tied down like you. So I said we should just keep things the way they are." Then she looks at my purse and goes, "Oh, my god, where did you get that?"

I smile and hold up my new Louis Vuitton bag. "My mom scored it for me."

"Give me that," she says snatching it. "That is so Louis Faux-ton."

"No, it's real. Look inside."

She unzips and scopes it out, and after using my Stila lip gloss, she hands it back and goes, "I thought there was a waiting list."

"My mom got it from Mario. They used it on a shoot and she got to keep it."

"Nice."

When I get out of the car I look for JC, because he's usually in the parking lot tossing a football around with the other jocks while waiting for me. But he's not here. And even though I'm not really anxious to see him, it still feels kind of weird.

By lunch, I still haven't seen him so I ask Kristi if she has.

"Yeah," she says, drinking from her can of Diet Coke. "He's right over there. Are you guys in a fight or something?"

I don't answer, because I really don't know the answer to that. What

I do know is that when one of his friends sees me staring, he nudges JC. And then JC looks at me, then quickly looks away.

And it makes me wonder if we are in a fight. And if so, why? I mean, there's no way he could know about me kissing Tyler because the only people who know about that are my best friends, and they would never tell. So it must be something else. Only I can't imagine what.

I know I said I want to break up with him, and that's still true. But the fact that he won't talk to me kind of bothers me, especially when it might be my fault.

So determined to get to the bottom of this, I get up from the table and approach him. But when he sees me coming, he walks away. And I'm left standing there, staring after him like a total reject.

When I get back to my table, Kristi looks at me and goes, "Wow, looks like you guys are in a fight. I wonder if he found out about you and Tyler?" Then she smiles and takes another sip of her Diet Coke.

After school I'm walking to the student lot with Kayla, who promised to give me a ride home (since my boyfriend won't talk to me and everyone else is too busy for me—which doesn't make me feel very popular), when Tyler walks up and goes, "Ready for your next lesson?"

I glance at Kayla and she looks all alarmed and gives me this not-so-subtle head shake.

But I just ignore all that and go, "Okay."

And Kayla says, "Um, Rio, are you sure you don't want to go *with me?*" Still shaking her head.

But I just look at her and go, "Yeah, I'm sure. I'll call you later, okay?"

Then I turn my back on her disapproval and follow Tyler to his shiny, black Cadillac Escalade. I mean, if my boyfriend refuses to acknowledge me, then I'm free to do whatever I want, right?

Tyler hands me the keys to his SUV and goes, "You drive."

"Are you sure?" I ask, hesitating.

"It's insured." He smiles.

I drive all the way home. And this thing is so seriously large and expensive that it makes me majorly nervous. I try to go slow and steady, but my hands are all shaky and even kind of sweaty, so when

I stop in front of my house, I discreetly wipe the wheel with the sleeve of my pink velvet shrunken blazer so he won't be grossed out when he goes to touch it later.

Then I go, "How'd I do?"

"Excellent," he says. "You're a natural."

We sit there smiling at each other, and I can feel my stomach growing all tight and nervous. Then he looks over at my house and asks, "Is anyone home?"

I look at the driveway, scanning for my mom's car. "Yeah, my mom's home," I say, even though her car's not there. But I just don't trust myself to be completely alone with him in a house with five bedrooms and no chaperones.

"Bummer." He shrugs.

And when I look at him again, I wonder if I did the right thing, because there isn't one girl in my entire school who wouldn't trade places with me now. Thinking about that makes me want him even more.

He pushes a button on his stereo and the song switches from middle-class, white-boy rap to something softer, less angry. And as he moves toward me I can hear the leather on his letterman's jacket rubbing across the seat.

And then he's kissing me, and one of his hands is buried in my hair, while the other is slowly, carefully sliding its way down my shoulder, down my arm, and then over to my left breast.

Then right as he's angling his hand up under my double-layered Abercrombie & Fitch tank tops, I hear someone go, "Hey, Rio!"

I immediately pull away, and cover my mouth with my hand. And when I turn I see JC, sitting in his dad's Porsche, parked right next to us.

"Oh, shit," I mumble.

"Dude, what are you doing?" Tyler asks, totally annoyed at the interruption.

But JC just ignores him, and yells, "Hey, fuck you, Rio!" And his voice is really harsh and he looks really upset, like he's gonna cry or something.

"JC, wait!" I say, feeling really bad, but not exactly sure what to do about it.

But Tyler's already on the street and he's approaching JC like he means business. "Dude, get a grip man, don't talk to her like that!"

"Stay out of it, bro, this is between Rio and me." JC slams his door, then he looks at me and yells, "I can't fucking believe you. I can't believe you used me like that!"

"I didn't use you!" I shout from the driver's seat. "You wouldn't even talk to me, and Tyler was just giving me a ride home." Okay, it's not exactly the truth, but it's not a complete lie, either.

He's heading toward the SUV and he looks really upset. And I feel really bad knowing I'm the reason.

Then Tyler steps in front of him and holding up his hand, goes, "Dude, relax. We can work it out, okay?"

But JC knocks Tyler's hand out of the way, like he's batting a fly, and he looks at me and goes, "Kristi warned me about you, but I didn't believe her." Then he rushes right at me and I jump onto the passenger seat, trying to get as far from him as possible.

Tyler grabs him by the shoulder and says, "Dude, I'm serious, leave her alone." Then he pushes JC so hard he loses his balance and nearly falls.

And from inside the SUV I watch his face get even redder.

JC looks at Tyler, eyes narrowed, jaw clenched, hands shaking. And even though I'm totally against violence of any kind, I have to admit part of me is thinking: *Ohmygod! Are they gonna fight? Over me?*

Because how cool would that be!

I place my hands over my eyes, fingers slightly parted so I can see through the cracks, part of me anticipating the first swing, and the other part dreading it, since I really don't want anyone to get hurt.

But then JC suddenly stops and looks at Tyler, then back at me. Then he shakes his head and goes, "Fuck it, bro, she's not worth it. You can have her." Like I'm his property or something.

Then he gets in the Porsche and drives away.

That's it? He gave up just like that?

When Tyler turns and looks at me, I suddenly feel really embarrassed. Especially when he says, "Um, I should probably hit it."

So I go, "Oh, okay." Then I get out of the SUV and watch him get in. And I feel like a total reject. It's like, now that JC has "given" me to Tyler, it's pretty obvious that he can't wait to be rid of me, too.

I'm walking toward my house when he goes, "Hey, come here!"

So I swing around to face him, but he's just dangling my backpack out the window. "You forgot your bag," he says.

So I grab it and head back toward my house, without once looking back.

$\mathcal{T}$wenty-six

The next day the JC-Tyler story is being circulated all over school. And by lunch, I've definitely learned how even though there may be two sides to every story, people like to root for the underdog. Which means half the girls in school have turned on me, and the other half are ignoring me. And I'm not sure which is worse.

Just yesterday when I walked down the hall, all these girls waved and smiled, trying to get my attention. But now it's like the opposite of that. Now they whisper, and point. So by the time lunch rolls around, I'm feeling pretty low.

"Am I still allowed to sit here?" I ask, half-joking and half-fearing what the answer will be.

Kayla and Jen Jen assure me I'm still welcome, but Kristi just shrugs.

I pull half a sandwich out of my lunch cooler and start to unwrap it when Kristi goes, "Well, I see you've still got your appetite."

Ohmygod, it's *half* a sandwich! But I don't react, I just shrug and say, "You know me," then I take a bite, and chew it very slowly, just for her.

She watches me for a moment, not even trying to hide her disgust, then she goes, "So you're today's headline. I knew something was up when you didn't call last night."

"We were on the phone pretty late," Kayla says.

"You talked to Kayla?" Kristi eyes me closely.

"We were on a conference call," Jen Jen says.

"*Without me?*" Kristi asks incredulously.

"You weren't home," I say, even though the truth is no one tried to call her.

"When?" she demands.

We all look at one another, but Kristi sees it. "Just forget it," she says, pouting and looking at me accusingly.

"Relax. I did call you," Jen Jen says. "But you didn't answer your cell."

Kristi sits there, staring at us. "I went for a run," she says, somewhat calmer, but still hostile toward me. *Get in line.*

"So what'd you talk about?" she asks.

"Duh?" Kayla says, and points at me.

"I know *that*," Kristi says, glaring at her. "I meant, what are you going to do?" She gives me a harsh look.

"Nothing." I shrug. "I tried apologizing this morning in the parking lot, but he just walked away, so I guess that's it." I take a bite of my tuna sandwich.

"I heard some girl call you a skank," Kristi tells me.

Ouch, that hurts, but I don't tell her that. "How can I be a skank when I'm a virgin?" I ask, laughing nervously.

"Hmm, let's see, maybe by cheating on your totally sweet boyfriend who's in love with you?" She looks at me. "Anyway, you don't have to worry about it. I told her not to talk about you like that in front of me. I totally stuck up for you." She takes a sip of her Diet Coke.

As I sit there watching her, I remember that time my dad told me about Stockholm Syndrome, which is when a person is taken hostage and they start to act all friendly and supportive of their kidnapper, thinking that if they cooperate and act all nice and sympathetic, they'll remain unharmed. Eventually they can become so isolated that they actually start to fear their rescuer.

And I realize that's exactly what it's like being Kristi's friend.

I mean, obviously I'm not being held hostage, since technically I'm free to walk away at any time. But as long as I hang with her (and act all nice and sympathetic and put up with her abuse), I'm guaranteed popularity (which is the same as remaining unharmed). Whereas if I leave, fight back, or allow myself to be "rescued," then I risk being cast out, shunned, and basically left to die alone. And believe me, like any good hostage-taker, Kristi knows she has all the power.

"What?" she asks, totally annoyed that I'm staring.

"Nothing," I say, shaking my head. "You know, JC mentioned you yesterday." I take another bite of my sandwich.

"What'd he say?" she asks casually.

"He said you warned him about me. Is that true?"

I'm looking right at her, but she doesn't even flinch. She just rolls her eyes and goes, "Get real. Why would I do that? I mean, quite frankly, I always thought JC was cute but a little slow." She taps the side of her head. "But you liked him, so why would I be on his side? Besides, I just told you how I totally stuck up for you when that girl called you a skank. You could at least thank me."

But I don't say thanks. I don't say anything. Because right at that exact moment I see Tyler walking toward me. And I just sit there frozen, watching him get closer and closer until he's standing right next to me.

"Hey." He smiles at me and ignores my friends.

"Hey," I say, as casual as possible.

"Do you have a sec?" he asks.

"Yeah."

I stuff the rest of my sandwich inside my lunch bag, and follow him to another table. He leans against the edge, and goes, "Sorry about yesterday."

I just shrug. Because now that I've been informed people think I'm a skank, I don't really feel like reminiscing.

"I didn't know about you and JC."

"It wasn't serious," I say, looking down at the toe of my new round-toed pumps.

"Wasn't?"

"We broke up." I shrug.

He nods and looks over at my friends (who are totally gawking at us and not even trying to hide it), then back at me. "Are you going to the Moondance?"

Is he asking me out? And if so, is it because he thinks I'm a skank?

"Um, no." I shrug.

"Wanna go with me?"

I look up.

Did he really just say that?

"Well?" He smiles.

"Yeah, okay," I say all casual, even though my heart is thumping so hard I'm sure he can hear it.

He leans in and kisses me, and it's like I can still feel it even when it's over. "I'll call you," he says.

Then the bell rings. But when I get back to my table, my friends are willing to risk a tardy just to hear what happened.

"He asked me to go to the Moondance," I say, gathering my stuff.

"What'd you say?" Kristi asks, eyes narrowed.

"I said yes," I look at her briefly, then throw my trash in the bin.

"So now you're going to the dance with Tyler, and I don't even have a date?" she says, following closely behind me.

"I guess so." I head toward my locker.

"Oh, my god, he is such a total hottie! You are so lucky!" Kayla says.

"What are you gonna wear?" asks Jen Jen. "We totally have to go shopping!"

They're both smiling, like they really are happy for me. But Kristi looks furious.

"I can't fucking believe this," she says. "I can't fucking believe *you* have a date and *I* don't."

She's standing next to my locker with her hands on her hips, totally glaring at me, like it's just so unbelievable that two different guys could like me in the course of a week. It's not my fault no one's asked her yet.

And you know what? I'm starting to get a little tired of her attitude. I'm also starting to feel a little more confident than I did twenty minutes ago. So I say, "What about Drew? You said he was bugging you to commit."

Kayla and Jen Jen look at her in shock. "Is that true?" they ask.

But she ignores them.

Then right as I slam my locker shut I go, "Well, if all else fails, I heard JC is available."

She glares at me, but I walk right past her and head to class.

Twenty-seven

After school I was really looking forward to another "driving lesson" with Tyler, but he was busy with practice so I hopped a ride with Kayla and Jen Jen. We were hanging out upstairs in my room when my mom came home.

"Hi, girls!" she says, barging in after one, barely audible, warning knock.

"Hey, Mrs. Jones!" they say, acting all happy to see her. Which makes me wonder if they really are.

"Where's Kristi?" she asks, actually looking concerned.

We all just kind of look at one another and shrug, since up until now we didn't really notice she was missing. And it's weird how Kristi used to be like the sun and we all rotated around her. But now it's like she's starting to burn out, and we just don't gravitate to her like we used to.

"Did Rio tell you about my Gap ad?" my mom asks, dropping her shopping bags, and making herself comfortable on my bed.

"Oh, my god, really?" Kayla says, like she's eager to hear more.

"It's not *your* Gap ad," I say, rolling my eyes for emphasis. "There's gonna be other models in it, too."

My mom shoots me a look, and continues, "They're using a group of former big names for the fall ad, and I'm flying to New York in a couple weeks for the shoot! It's going to be so fun, just like a reunion!"

I'm studying the intricate weave of my duvet, patiently waiting for this to end. But my friends must look impressed because she goes, "Hey, you girls have great taste. Maybe you can help me decide on a color for the upstairs guest bathroom." She reaches into one of her shopping bags and pulls out like twenty swatches of different shades of ecru, which is just a fancy word for beige.

"I thought you already finished that room," I say, wishing she'd vacate immediately and leave us alone.

"Yeah, but I'm just not thrilled with it. It lacks something." She shakes her head.

"Like restraint?" I give her a cold look that she ignores.

"Come on, tell me what you think," she says, clutching the swatches, and motioning for my friends (but not me!) to follow. And as they're heading down the hall I hear her say, "Right now it has a sort of eco look, but it seems kind of blah. So I was thinking Paris! You know, can-can girls, *Moulin Rouge*—did you see that movie?"

And I'm left, sitting in the middle of my bed, bitter and alone, because my mom is a total friend-poacher.

By eleven o'clock, I'm totally exhausted, and that's just from the constant telephone calls, e-mails, and instant messages that I'm obligated to partake in every night, with all the same people that I hung with all day at school, and for most of the time after.

And it was weird because at one point when all of us were on a conference call, Kristi asked what happened to us after school, and Kayla lied and said she had to go to the dentist, and Jen Jen said she was at her doctor's, so I said I was helping my mom choose a color for the upstairs guest bathroom.

And Kristi just said, "Oh."

Then my cell phone rang, and I was all exited thinking it was Tyler, since he said he'd call. So I try to make my voice sound all low and sexy when I go, "Hello?"

But it was just Paige. "Hey, Rio. God, we haven't talked forever."

"I *know*," I said, trying to sound like I cared even though I was looking in the mirror and rolling my eyes.

"So how've you been?" she asked.

"Perfect. But I'm *so* busy. Can I call you back?"

"Oh, okay. If I'm not home, try me on my cell 'cause I might—"

"I'm sure I'll find you," I said, cutting her off and hanging up. I mean, just because I haven't talked to her forever, doesn't mean I wanted to talk to her then.

But now it's getting late, and Tyler still hasn't called, and I still haven't picked out an outfit for tomorrow, not to mention the homework I haven't touched all week. It's like there's just not enough time in the day to fit it all in, and it makes me wonder how other people do it. People who have jobs and stuff like Mason. But then again Mason doesn't really have a ton of friends like I do, and it's not like she has to keep a log of what she wears from week to week so that she doesn't repeat. I mean, all she cares about is getting into art school, that's her entire focus. I guess it used to be mine, too, but now it doesn't even make the list.

I sit on the edge of my bed, debating whether or not I should do just the tiniest hit of the coke that was left over from my birthday. I mean, just enough to keep me up for one more hour, so I can put an outfit together, and maybe start my paper for English. But it's probably not a good idea, because even though I'm not an addict ('cause I've only done it that one other time), getting high alone is a bad sign. So I decide on a power nap instead. Just ten short minutes and then I'll wake up and tackle everything. I swear.

When my cell rings at midnight I'm thinking it's my alarm, and I keep hitting it, over and over again, trying to locate the snooze button. And by the time I figure it out, it's just about to go into voice mail. I grab it and go, "Hello?" My voice is all groggy and messed-up sounding.

"Did I wake you?"

Ohmygod, it's Tyler! "Um, that's okay," I say, even though he didn't apologize.

Then I start to clear my throat just as he says, "You sound really sexy. I wish I was there."

"Oh," I say, quickly trying to recapture that groggy sound, but it's too late since I already coughed.

"Listen, I won't keep you. Go back to sleep and I'll see you tomorrow."

"Okay," I say, even though I'm wide-awake now.

So I turn off my phone and reach all the way into the back of my nightstand drawer where I've stashed that little vial of coke. I know I just went on and on about getting high alone, but really, it's not like I'm an *addict*.

I pull the drawer all the way out but I still can't find it, so I dump the contents on the ground. And after sifting through travel-sized bottles of lotion, ballpoint pens, a pot of Smith's Rosebud Salve, and some random tissues that look like they've been used (gross), I still can't find it. And then I remember how Kristi finished it last time she was here. And even though I'm pretty wide-awake now and could probably make it without the extra boost, the fact is I kinda want some.

So I call Kristi.

"Hey," she says.

"Did I wake you?"

"No, what's up?"

"I was wondering if you had anything."

"Do you want me to come by?"

"If you don't mind."

I sneak downstairs and enter the code for the gate so she can just drive in without waking anyone. And as she pulls into the driveway, she cuts the engine, and turns off her lights. Then we tiptoe upstairs to my room.

She flops on the end of my bed and empties her purse. "Here," she says, handing it over.

I busy myself getting it all laid out, like I've seen her do. Then I slide it toward her so she can go first.

"You go. I'm good for now."

So I lean down and inhale deeply until the surface is entirely clean. And when I come back up I see her watching me with this strange expression on her face.

"Sorry I got a little bitchy with you today," I say, rubbing my nose. "I know you didn't say anything to JC." Okay, it's not like I truly believe that, but I feel like I have to say something nice since she came all the way over here.

"Whatever." She shrugs. "So what's this all about?"

"It's just that I have so much to do still, and I'll never get it all done if I sleep," I say, lining up some more so she can have some too.

But when I pass it to her, she just shakes her head again. "No, thanks. I should get going." She gets up and heads for the door.

"How much do I owe you?" I ask, leaning down for some more.

"Nothing," she says. "Believe me, it's my pleasure."

When I sit up I catch a glimpse of her face right before she turns to walk out the door. And there's something about her expression, something so *happy*, it makes me regret calling her.

Twenty-eight

When I get to school I'm still headlining, but this time it's all good. It's like, now that everyone knows I'm going to the Moondance with Tyler, all of my earlier skankiness seems to be forgiven (if not forgotten).

In English I got, like, five different text messages from different people, asking me if it was true about Tyler and me. Then the second Mrs. Abbott left the room, all these girls ran over to my desk and were asking if I bought my dress and stuff. And every time I looked at Kristi, she was sitting there with her lips pressed all tight together, glaring at me.

So then this girl who sits behind us asked her who she's going with, and get this, Kristi said, "I haven't decided yet."

Like she has so many guys to choose from. But when she looked at me, I didn't say anything. I just rolled my eyes and kept talking about dresses.

Later on, during the ten-minute break, I was in one of the bathroom stalls when I overheard these two girls talking about Kristi. According to them, she totally freaked in the locker room when she heard Drew was going to the dance with some sophomore girl who isn't even a cheerleader.

"She took off her shoe and flung it across the room! It barely missed my head," said unidentified voice number one.

"What'd you do?" asked voice number two.

"Nothing, but you should have *seen* her! She looked like she was gonna *explode!*"

I don't flush. I just stand there very still, listening.

"She is *so over*. She can't even get a date. Rio gets all the hot guys because she's way prettier, and Kristi can't handle it."

When I'm positive they've left, I vacate the stall. And while washing my hands I stare at my reflection in the mirror and I can't believe how everything has changed so much that I'm actually more popular than Kristi now.

No wonder she's been acting like such a bitch.

After school I go shopping with my mom, and when I asked if Kayla and Jen Jen could come, she said, "If you don't mind, I'd rather it be just us."

That really blew me away. I mean, she usually loves hanging with my friends, but I guess she's looking forward to some kind of mother-daughter bonding session. Which I know is supposed to make me feel all nice and happy, but it's actually kind of disturbing.

Though I have to admit, it's not as bad spending time with her now that we have more in common. I mean, before when I was all into photography she could never understand how someone would prefer to *take* the picture when they supposedly had such great potential to *be* the picture. But now that I'm all into clothes, and dating, and stuff, we have a lot more to talk about since those are the things that interest her.

So this morning when I was drinking my coffee before school she said, "So how's JC? He never comes by anymore."

"We broke up." I shrugged.

And then she got all emotional, like she was gonna jump up and hug me or something. So I quickly moved away, went over to the coffeemaker, and refilled my mug.

Then she said, "Honey, I'm so sorry. Are you okay?"

And I said, "Mom, I'm fine. It's no big deal. Besides I'm dating someone else now."

Her eyes lit up. "You are?"

"Yeah."

"Who?" she asked, like she just might possibly know him.

"His name is Tyler, and he's the hottest guy in school. And we're going to the Moondance."

"We have to go shopping!" she said.

And that's how I ended up in dressing room number three, in the Nordstrom Savvy department. I'm standing in front of the three-way mirror in like the hundredth dress in two different malls, when I go, "Mom, I'm starving, can we please get something to eat?"

She's standing behind me with her mouth all twisted in heavy contemplation, while her hands are busy pulling, tucking, and imaginary hemming.

"If we have this taken in just a smidgen, right here, it will be perfect," she says.

"That's what you said about the others." I roll my eyes and wonder if she'll feel guilty when I've fainted from hunger.

"Let's get this one, too, take them all home, and try them on with different shoes and purses."

"Mom, you already bought me three beautiful dresses," I whine, wondering if extreme hunger causes insanity since I must be crazy to actually complain about that.

"So, we can return them or keep them, it really doesn't matter. What does matter is that you look *perfect,* and have the best night ever!"

I look at our reflection from all three angles, and in each one I can see how happy this is making her.

So I give in. I let her buy me the fourth dress.

Afterward, we stop at this cute little restaurant that's situated halfway between the mall and home. And I'm so hungry by this point I practically maul the bread basket like the second we get to our table.

I've grabbed a generous slice, thoroughly slathered it in butter, and am just about to take one big, dreamy bite when my mom goes, "Do you really think you should eat that?"

I lock eyes with her. "Yes, I really think I should." And then I bite off a huge chunk, much bigger than I normally would, just to annoy her.

While I'm busy trying to break down this massive piece of bread Jas's father walks up and says, "Rio! I thought that was you!"

I slap my hand over my mouth, and I'm nodding, and working my molars like crazy, and when I finally gulp the bread down I go, "Hi, Mr. Klein. This is my mom." And I point at my mother who is smiling so brightly you'd never guess that just a moment ago she was staring at me with complete and total disgust.

"Hi," she says, "I'm Jahne Jones." And as she's shaking his hand she's smiling in anticipation of the response of someone hearing her name for the first time in a long time: *Did you say, Jahne Jones? The Jahne Jones former almost-supermodel?*

But it doesn't come. So her smile grows tighter.

"Rio, how come you never come by anymore?" he asks.

"Oh, um, I guess—" I'm just about to make up some lame excuse when Jas walks up.

"Rio's being kept pretty busy these days." He looks at me.

Those are the first words he's spoken to me since that awful fight, and I can't even tell if his smile is genuine. I feel so awkward and embarrassed that I don't know what to do, so I just look at my mom, hoping she'll say something to smooth this over. But she just sits there, with her smile pulled all tight across her face.

"Well, don't be such a stranger," Mr. Klein says. "Come by anytime." Then he turns to my mom and goes, "I remember you now!"

And just like that, she's all lit up again.

"You and your husband attended the Back Bay Benefit last month. Griffin, right? He outbid me on that Montage Resort weekend package." He laughs. "All for a good cause though. Give him my best, will ya?"

My mother just nods.

"Well, I'm gonna leave you with Jas, but let me know if you need anything else," he says, before heading back into the kitchen.

Jas just stands there, and we're both looking at each other, but neither of us says anything, and it's getting pretty uncomfortable, so my mom goes, "Do you think we could get some water?"

And he goes, "Oh, sure. I'll have someone bring it right over."

I wipe my sweaty palms on the napkin in my lap, and when he's gone, my mother says, "Well, do they *both* work here?"

I roll my eyes. "Mom, Mr. Klein *owns* this restaurant, and several others."

"Why'd we come here?" she whispers, fake-smiling at the busboy as he sets our water glasses on the table.

"You chose it," I say, picking up the menu.

"Well, I'm certainly glad you're not hanging with that Jas character anymore." She looks around the dining room with complete disdain, even though it's actually really nice.

"Mom, stop. You don't know what you're talking about. He's not so bad. Now can we please just order?"

"Fine," she says, picking up her menu. "But if I were you, I'd stick with the salad after that loaf of bread you just ate."

I don't respond to that. Just like I rarely respond when Kristi does that to me.

But when our waitress comes to take our order, I make sure I ask for pasta with extra sauce.

After she clears our plates, the waitress comes back with two small bowls of crème brûlée that she places in front of us. "Excuse me, we did not order this." My mom points at the dessert like it's a big, smelly bowl of dog shit.

"Jas made it," she says. "He wanted you to try it."

"Oh, how nice." She fake-smiles and lifts her spoon like she's actually going to eat some. But the second the waitress leaves she drops the spoon on the white tablecloth, looks at me, and goes, "You're not going to eat that, are you?"

"Mom, lay off," I say, tapping on the caramelized sugar, until it breaks through to the creamy good stuff below.

"That boy is trying to sabotage you," she whispers.

"You think he poisoned it?" I ask, spooning it into my mouth and swallowing.

"Worse, he's trying to make you *fat*." She nods, having totally convinced herself.

"Why would he bother?"

"Trust me," she says, still nodding, but offering no further evidence.

"Do *you* think I'm fat?" I take another bite.

"No. Not *yet*." She raises her eyebrows at me.

"Then leave me alone."

"What?" she asks, sounding shocked and hurt.

"I mean it. I am so sick of you and Kristi constantly measuring everything I put in my mouth. God, Mom, it's hard enough dealing with all the pressure I have at school to be perfect all the time. I really don't need to get the same crap from you." I push the bowl away, cross my arms, and glare at her.

My mom looks frantically around the restaurant, trying to determine if anyone was privy to my little outburst.

"I'm serious," I say, louder than she would like. "Just leave me alone."

"Are things not going well at school?" she whispers, more upset by that than the way I just spoke to her.

I roll my eyes. "Things are great. Apparently Kristi's out and I'm in. I'm the new 'It' girl."

"Really? You're more popular than Kristi?" she asks carefully, just in case she misheard.

"She doesn't even have a date for the Moondance," I say.

"But it's just a few weeks away!" Her eyes go wide with shock and awe.

I just shrug and look across the room where Jas is laughing and joking with two girls at the bar. One of them reaches out and touches his arm, her hand lingering against his skin.

Then I look back at my mom sitting across from me, looking really happy and proud.

Twenty-nine

When we got home from dinner I went straight to my room and crashed. The coke I'd done the night before had totally caught up with me, and all I wanted was to go to bed and just black out on my life for a while. Then at ten o'clock when my cell phone rang, I woke up just long enough to turn it off.

The next morning I got to school pretty late since I slept through my alarm, and when my mom came into my room all frantic, I told her I wasn't feeling well. Then I figured, if I'm gonna miss first period, then I may as well miss second and third, right? But by lunch, I was wide-awake and feeling much better, so I decided to go.

As my mom drove me to school she kept going on and on about how I might still be sick and that maybe I should stay home and rest until I got better.

"You don't want to be sick for the dance," she said.

"Mom, it's like three weeks away." I rolled my eyes.

"But still."

"I'll see you later." I slammed the car door and headed for the lunch tables, feeling bad about faking sick, but probably not as bad as I should.

Someone comes up behind me and puts his hands around my eyes. "Guess who?" he says.

Okay, maybe he's not the smartest guy in school, but if he'd let go of my face I could confirm that he's still the cutest. "Hey, Tyler."

"You knew." He sounds disappointed. "Where've you been? I tried your cell but it was off."

"I slept late, I wasn't feeling well," I tell him.

"Are you sick?" he asks, quickly dropping the hand he had just been holding.

"No, just tired."

"Oh." He nods, taking my hand again. "Why don't you come hang with us?" He starts pulling me toward the table where the cool seniors sit.

"Well, my friends are kind of waiting for me," I say, looking over at Kristi, Kayla, and Jen Jen as they totally gawk at me.

"I want you to meet everyone," he says, ignoring my protest and wrapping his arm around my waist.

So I go with him. And I spend the entire lunch hanging with the alpha seniors. And every time I look over at my friends, they look away.

After school Tyler doesn't have practice so he offers me another "driving lesson." And after navigating the short drive to my house, we end up inside.

Upstairs.

In my bedroom.

We're on my bed totally making out, and words cannot express how much better it is with Tyler. I mean, JC was like a dumb, needy *little boy*. But Tyler is like a hot, sexy, older *guy*. But I'm still determined to take it slow. Not that it's easy with him being so cute and all, but I really am trying.

My top is somewhere on the floor, but I've got my bra on, so I'm still in control. But then he starts sliding his hands down my jeans. And even though part of me is really tempted, there's just no way I'm letting that happen. Especially since my mom could walk through the front door at any moment.

So I go, "Tyler, no, okay?" Then I grasp his hand and pull it back up into the "safe zone," which is anywhere north of my navel.

"Why?" he mumbles, still kissing me.

"My mom's gonna be home any minute," I say, grabbing his hand again and pulling it back up again.

He stops kissing me. "Is that really why?"

He's looking right at me, waiting for an answer, and I don't know what to say. But then I just close my eyes and tell him the truth. Because being a virgin is nothing to be embarrassed about. *Is it?*

"For real?" He seems pretty shocked. Which makes me wonder if JC has circulated some false rumor about me. But then he goes, "I didn't know there were any left, except for maybe a few of the freshmen."

I just shrug.

Then he pulls me close and whispers, "I wanna be your first."

I just lie there, not saying anything. Then finally I go, "Oh, okay." I mean, I don't really know what to say, since it's not like I'm holding auditions or anything.

Then as luck would have it, I hear my mom open the front door and yell, "Rio! Come down and see what Michael and I picked out for the study!"

I look at Tyler and go, "You're not gonna want to stick around for this, trust me."

I'm totally dating Tyler now, and I'm telling you, it's like the best thing that ever happened to me. I know I used to think that being with a junior jock was pretty cool. But that's only because I had no idea how off-the-charts amazing it is to be with a varsity stud. I mean, Tyler's, like, not only the hottest guy in school, but he's also a star athlete, super-wealthy (his dad owns a bunch of luxury car dealerships), and he just got an early-acceptance football scholarship to USC (which my dad points out is *not* an Ivy League school, even though everyone here in Newport Beach—with their USC vanity plates—seems to think it is).

And it's so cool because now I hang with *all* the seniors, and the girls are starting to be way nicer to me than they were in the beginning. They're always telling me how lucky I am because Tyler is *sooo* amazingly hot, and even though he's hooked up with a lot of girls, apparently I'm the first he ever wanted to be exclusive with. So even though sometimes it feels like we don't have that much in common, it really doesn't seem important like it did with JC.

But unfortunately my complete happiness is causing all this tension with my friends. And Kayla, Jen Jen, and Kristi are getting pretty upset about all the time I spend with the seniors now. Just the other day they actually accused me of putting Tyler first. Which is so not fair since I recently invited them to come to a party with us at some house in Corona del Mar. Not to mention that every now and then I even let them sit with us at lunch. Although, to be honest, most of the time Kristi acts so bitchy toward me, I end up wishing she'd just stayed at her old table.

Look, it's not my fault the dance is less than two weeks away and she still hasn't been asked.

Oh, yeah, and I've finally found a focus for my art project—Tyler! When he offered to help Michael move a bookcase into the study that day, Michael went as crazy over him as he did over me. Okay, maybe he went a little crazier over Tyler because he kept poking at him under the pretense of "assessing his model potential." (Which was pretty much just an excuse to grope him.)

He told Tyler he should get into "the industry," and then Tyler confessed he always wanted to be an actor (which was news to me, I thought he wanted to play pro football). So Michael told him he could set up a shoot with Mario Saldana.

I'm starting to think Michael is Mario's pimp.

But it turns out that Mario is superbooked for like the next six months. And Tyler was so disappointed that I told him I'd do it. At first he laughed, but then I showed him some of my photos, and he agreed.

So now I'm shooting his portfolio, which I'm also going to use for my art project. And it still fits under the category of Beauty, because he really is beautiful.

Sometimes I can't believe how lucky I am and how great my life is. I mean, just the other day I was replacing that picture on my nightstand of me, Paige, and Hud with one of Tyler's headshots. I was just about to crinkle it up and toss it in the bin when something caught my eye. I sat on the edge of my bed and peered at it closely, trying to remember what it felt like to be that smiling girl in the photo. She seemed like such a stranger.

I mean, I may have looked happy then, but that's only because I didn't know any better.

Thirty

So Sunday afternoon we're in my room and Kayla, Jen Jen, and Kristi are helping me choose an outfit for Tyler's USC early-acceptance party, which, by the way, has already started.

"I would go with the cords and the shrunken tweed blazer," Kayla says.

I start to scrunch my nose and make a face, but then I notice she's wearing cords, so I go, "Well, I kind of need something dressier since it's the first time I'm going to meet his parents."

"What about this?" Jen Jen says, holding up a green chiffon handkerchief-hemmed dress.

"Yeah, but I also don't want to be overdressed and look like I'm trying too hard," I say, noticing how the discard pile is starting to outnumber the maybes.

"Uh, hello? You *are* trying too hard," Kristi says, dropping her magazine and rolling her eyes.

When I look at her I remind myself: *She's just jealous. She still doesn't have a date for the dance. Don't react!* Which I have to do more and more these days, just to tolerate her.

"You're gonna meet them for what? Thirty seconds?" She shakes her head. "You act like you're having a private dinner when the fact is, it's a *party,* and they'll be hanging with their friends and Tyler will be hanging with his and you might not even see them."

"You don't know that," I say.

"FYI Rio, I've been to my share of Lido Isle wingdings. My dad lives right down the street, you know." She reaches for her purse, pulls out her lip gloss, and applies another layer while I stand there in my robe, glaring at her. "I'm just saying you shouldn't stress because it's not gonna be the big formal introduction like you think." Then she gets up, reaches into my closet, and says, "Trust me, it's way more important to have your boyfriend think you're hot than to have his parents think you're adorable. Especially since by the time we get there they'll be on their third or fourth drink and they won't know the difference anyway. Now, *this* is what you should wear."

I take Kristi's advice because even though she's kind of a bitch these days, the truth is she really does know her way around. So when I've changed into some cuffed jeans, a sage-green, lace-edged silky camisole, and brown stiletto boots, she says, "Here, take this." She removes the long handknit scarf from her neck and wraps it around mine.

"Are you sure?" I ask. I mean, lately I can never tell if she's trying to save me or sabotage me.

"Positive." She smiles, adjusting her white sequined tank top and denim miniskirt. "It looks better on you anyway."

By the time we get to Tyler's I see everything Kristi said is true. There are so many people I have no idea which of them could possibly be related to Tyler, and from the sounds of the all the laughing and whooping, there's definitely been some major alcohol consumption.

"What'd I tell ya?" Kristi links her arm through mine and laughs. "Just a bunch of rich old drunks with shiny new spouses half their age. I bet Tyler and all the hotties are outside on the yacht. Let's grab some champagne and go find them," she says, picking up a flute and dragging me out the door and onto the dock while Kayla and Jen Jen trail behind.

We spot Tyler on deck talking to some people and Kristi goes, "Parent alert."

"That's his mom?" I whisper, gaping at the platinum blonde in the low-cut jeans, silver stiletto sandals, and tight, black V-necked sweater.

"No, they're not married yet. She's still auditioning." Kristi laughs.

"You know her?" I ask, wondering why she failed to mention that before.

"Yes and no. I mean, I didn't know she was with Tyler's dad, but she's a friend of my stepmom and they go on these power walks every morning. She's learning the tricks of the step-monster trade," she says. "Anyway, you go play nice. We'll catch up later."

I watch them take off in the opposite direction, then Tyler waves me over and goes, "Rio, come meet my dad and his fiancée, Sienna."

I shake hands with his dad, Chip, who looks like Tyler will look in thirty years if he gains thirty pounds and starts wearing lots of gold jewelry and Tommy Bahama Hawaiian shirts, and I give a little wave to Sienna because that's how she greets me. That is, after she looks me up and down a few times. But then again, Sienna doesn't look much older than me, so I shouldn't expect her interest to be very maternal.

"So what colleges have you applied to?" Chip asks, taking a sip of red wine and smiling.

"Oh, I haven't yet. I'm still only a junior," I say, smiling nervously and feeling kind of weird when I sip my champagne right in front of him.

"Gotta keep an eye on the future. Tyler here's been working toward USC since day one." He balls his hand into a fist and digs his knuckles hard into his son's shoulder. "I'm an alumnus and I'm telling you it's the best school out there. You can do anything you want with a degree from USC."

I glance at Sienna who's bored as hell and bouncing an empty champagne flute against her man-made breasts, then I look at Chip and go, "Oh, well my dad sort of has his heart set on Columbia. 'Cause that's where he went."

Chip stops smiling and looks at me like I've said something horrible. And I just stand there like a total reject, knowing it took less than five minutes for me to blow it.

"Well, I better go make sure my house is still in one piece. You kids have fun." He slugs Tyler in the arm and smiles at me. But only with his lips, it never quite makes it to his eyes.

When they're gone I turn to Tyler and say, "Oh, god, your dad hates me."

"Who cares." He shrugs. "Come on, I'll show you around."

After going in and out of several amazingly, overdecorated rooms, we end up in this massive stateroom that's bigger than most New York City apartments. "Jeez," I say, looking around at the cream and gold walls and the painting of frolicking cherubs hanging opposite the bed. "This is really . . . something."

"Isn't it?" Tyler says, settling onto the elaborate gold-embroidered bedspread and holding out his hand for me to join him.

"What if someone comes?" I ask, standing in front of him, hesitating.

"Don't worry, the door's locked," he says, grabbing my hand and pulling me down next to him.

We're lying on the bed totally making out, and even though I love being with Tyler, I can't really relax because I keep thinking about how Chip is gonna hate me even more when he comes barging in and finds me in bed with his son. I mean, even though Tyler swears he locked the door, it's still his dad's boat so I'm sure he has a key.

But Tyler doesn't seem to care about any of that since he's already unwrapped Kristi's scarf from my neck and thrown it to the ground. And now his fingers are heading straight for my zipper.

I open one eye and peer at the door, staring at the big gold handle, hoping it really is locked. Then I do what I always do when Tyler tries to get in my pants. I push his hand away, and get in his.

Usually when it's over, he kisses the top of my head, hugs me tight, and tells me I'm beautiful. But this time he just pulls me up so we are face-to-face and says, "Rio, when do you think you'll be ready for *more?*"

Oh, great. I close my eyes and snuggle into his shoulder so I won't have to make eye contact. Because even though I'm totally into him, the fact is I'm not in love with him. And it may sound lame, but I really wanted to be in love my first time.

He lets out a long, exasperated sigh, and says, "This really isn't working for me anymore. It's getting kind of old."

But I just stay there, hiding in his shoulder, breathing in his musky scent, and not saying anything.

"I'm serious," he says. "Either we're taking the next step, or I'm gonna have to bail."

Okay, I'm pretty sure that was blackmail. And I know I shouldn't fall for it. But there's no way I'm gonna risk getting dumped by Tyler, because being his girlfriend is a really big deal. So I take a deep breath and say, "My parents are going out of town next weekend."

Then he hugs me and kisses the top of my head and says, "Perfect."

After we leave the stateroom Tyler goes to get us more drinks and I head into the living room or salon (or whatever they call it in yacht-speak), where Kristi, Kayla, and Jen Jen are sitting on this cream-colored couch talking with some guys from school. Kayla's sipping a beer and focusing all of her attention on Kevin, who she's liked for awhile now, and Jen Jen, as usual, is flirting with everyone just to increase her chances. But Kristi's just sort of sitting on the sidelines, watching everyone and looking completely bored. And it seems really strange how just a couple months ago she was the center of everyone's attention, but now she can't even get a date.

It's like, from the outside nothing's changed, because she's still tiny and beautiful and totally perfect. But inside she's grown harder, nastier, and bitchier.

And I wonder if it's because of me.

I mean, before I showed up she was the undisputed queen of the junior class. But now it's pretty obvious I'm wearing the crown.

"Where've you been?" she asks, crossing her tan bare legs and taking a sip of champagne.

"Tyler gave me a tour of the yacht." I sit on the chair across from her.

"Did you christen the stateroom?" She laughs.

"How'd you know about the stateroom?"

"It's not my first yacht, Brazil." She rolls her eyes. "So did you?"

"Not exactly. I kept imagining his dad barging in on us. It was kind of a mood-wrecker," I say, picking at a loose thread on the arm of my chair and avoiding her eyes.

"Tyler must be getting really tired of that," she says, raising her perfectly arched brows.

"We're fine. Don't worry about us." I give her a hard look.

"If you say so." She taps the rim of her glass and stares at me. "So how'd it go with his dad?"

"Okay." I shrug. I mean, no way am I telling her how I messed that up.

"You know his mom's like a local celebrity. She was a USC song leader, and a backup dancer in some music video in the eighties. Did you meet her?"

"Is she here? I thought they were divorced?" I say.

"Yeah, she's here. She's inside the house sitting on her little stud muffin's lap. And they're definitely divorced but they try to get along 'for the sake of the children.'" She mimics that last part and rolls her eyes.

"What's this stud muffin story?" I ask, when what I really want to know is how she knows more about Tyler's family than I do.

"She's dating this guy that waits tables at The Bungalow. I totally hooked up with him last summer at this beach bonfire. We smoked a joint and made out for a while. He's pretty cute." She laughs.

"I thought pot was for losers?" I say, remembering how it's on our forbidden list, and wondering if that list is just for us, while she does whatever the hell she wants.

"It was that kind of night." She shrugs, and glances around the room.

"Are you sure it's the same guy?" I watch her finish her champagne and nod.

"Definitely." She smiles.

"Poor Tyler," I say, thinking how embarrassed he must feel.

"Welcome to Newport." She laughs.

Tyler walks up with two glasses of champagne and when he hands me one and keeps the other, Kristi goes, "Hey, thanks. That's real chivalrous of you."

"Oh, sorry," he says. "Here, take it. I haven't touched it."

She reaches for the glass then looks at me and goes, "So where's my scarf?"

"What?" I ask, touching my bare neck. *Oh, no, I lost her scarf. I'll never hear the end of it.* "Um, I don't know. It must be around here somewhere." I look around the room frantically, even though I'm sure it's not here.

"It's probably in the stateroom," Tyler says, rubbing his fingers along my shoulder. "Down that hall, last door on the left," he tells Kristi.

"Can you show me?" she says, standing and not bothering to fix her miniskirt, which is all creased and folded up way extra-high. "I'll follow you." She smiles.

Tyler looks at me and shrugs, then he leads her down the hall.

And as I watch them walk away I get this terrible feeling in my gut. Because something in that smile makes me wonder if I can trust her alone with my boyfriend. But then I feel guilty for thinking like that, because I know I can trust Tyler. Especially now that I've given him something to look forward to.

$\mathcal{T}$hirty-one

I'm really excited because I'm going to lunch with my dad, and it's gonna be just the two of us, since my mom's not invited. In fact she doesn't even know about it, 'cause my dad's been so busy that I was actually forced to call his secretary to set it up.

I was talking to him on the phone when I said, "Dad, when you get back on Tuesday, do you think you could drop by my school and take me to lunch?"

And he said, "That would be great! Call my secretary and see if I'm free."

So I did. And she informed me that he wasn't free on Tuesday, or Wednesday, or even Thursday. So we made it for today, Friday. Which is good, since Kristi's having one of her infamous parties tomorrow night, and I promised Tyler he could spend the night at my house since my parents will be up in L.A.

But now I'm getting kind of nervous about it, because when I originally told him that it felt like the right thing to say to keep him happy and get me through an awkward moment. And after a week of watching Kristi openly flirt with him, hang all over him, and even try to get rides from him (under the guise that her car's in the shop even though there are four more in her driveway), I'm more determined than ever to go through with it. I mean, I really think it's the final act that will totally seal our relationship. And I'm sure that the second it's over I'll be totally in love with him, and I won't have anything to regret.

But even though I'm getting used to the idea of moving forward, growing up, and finally losing my virginity, there's still this part of me that wants to cling to the past and just hang with my dad, like I used to.

So the second the bell rings I run out of class and head for the parking lot. I'm wearing these gray wool pants, suede flats, and a V-necked argyle sweater with a white blouse underneath. It's way more conservative than how I usually dress, but I know my dad likes this outfit and I want everything to go perfect.

He pulls up in my mom's Jag, since she needed the Range Rover for yet another home-decorating expedition, and I climb in beside him and kiss him on the cheek.

"Hey, kiddo, I like your outfit," he says, smiling and pulling away from campus.

"That's why I wore it. Where we going?" I ask.

"I've made reservations at The Ritz. It's over by Fashion Island."

"Sounds good," I say, crossing my fingers and hoping that Jas's dad doesn't own that one, too.

We pull into the parking lot and there are so many Bentleys, Ferraris, and Mercedes that it looks more like a luxury import dealership than a restaurant. My dad tosses the keys to the uniformed valet guy, and when we go inside it takes a moment for my eyes to adjust to the dim lighting. The place is all formal-looking with dark wood walls and a deep burgundy paisley-print carpet. And on the way to our table we pass several booths filled with wealthy businessmen eating and deal-making, while a handful of trophy wife hopefuls giggle a little too loudly at the bar.

My dad must have noticed the same thing I did, 'cause like the minute we're seated we both look at each other and start cracking up, and it makes me feel really connected to him, just like I used to.

We both order cheeseburgers with extra fries instead of fresh fruit, since my mom's not here to judge us, and when the waitress walks away my dad looks at me and goes, "So what's up, kiddo?"

"Can't a girl just want to have lunch with her dad?"

"Sure," he says. "Although I was under the impression it involved something more." He looks at me closely, waiting.

"Seriously," I say, picking at the hem on my napkin. "I just wanted to hang out. I mean, we never really get to do that anymore do we?"

"True," he says, taking a sip of his half–iced tea half-lemonade, which I think is named after some famous golfer, but not Tiger Woods. "So how's school going?"

"Everything's really great." I pause while the waitress sets down our plates. "I mean, I feel really settled in, I like most of my teachers, and I've made some great friends." I smile.

"Sounds like you've got it made." He bites into his cheeseburger, then uses his napkin to wipe a stray crumb in the corner of his mouth.

"I really do," I say, picking up a French fry and making it dance circles in the little bowl of ketchup on my plate. And I want to say something more, something to get his assurance that he'll always love me, no matter what, but then his cell phone rings.

He gives me an apologetic look, flips it open, and says, "Yeah? You're kidding? Just now?"

Then his eyes briefly meet mine and I look down at my plate because I don't want him to see how disappointed I am. I mean, it's not his fault.

"Okay, I'm on my way." He closes his phone. "Rio," he starts.

"It's okay, Dad."

"The jury just came back with a verdict. I'm sorry. Can we have a rain check?"

"Sure."

"How 'bout Sunday? We can have brunch, go to the plant nursery, whatever you want, just you and me."

"Okay."

"Let me get the waitress to wrap these up." He points at our half-eaten burgers.

"That's all right," I say, pushing my plate away. "I've had enough."

During the ten-minute drive back to school I didn't want him to feel bad about having to bail on me, so I mostly spent the time joking around, trying to make him laugh.

But when I get out of the car and watch him drive away, I'm kind of embarrassed to admit this, but my throat goes all tight and I feel like I'm about to cry. I guess it was really stupid to try to recapture that bond with my dad because things are so different now and there's just no going back.

I stand there, squeezing my eyes shut, refusing the tears. And when the moment finally passes I run my hands through my hair, touch up my lip gloss, and head straight for the lunch tables and Tyler, knowing I'll feel better once we're together.

But when I get there, Kristi's sitting right next to him.

"Hey," I say, leaning down to kiss him, and glaring at her. *I mean, who does she think she is, sitting here when I'm not around?*

"What happened to your lunch date?" he asks, moving away from her to make room for me.

"He bailed." I laugh, even though there's nothing funny about it.

"Well here, have some of this," he says, pulling me close and giving me half his sandwich.

I close my eyes and nuzzle into his neck, feeling the warm assurance of his skin. Then I reach for the sandwich, take a bite, and stare at Kristi. And I continue staring at her until she finally gets up and moves away.

Thirty-two

When I wake up on Saturday morning the first thing that pops into my head is: *This is the last morning I'll wake up a virgin.*

I put on my favorite thick, white terry-cloth robe, which my dad got for me on one of his business trips. It has a lion's head on a crown and says "Ritz-Carlton" in blue embroidered script underneath. Then I go downstairs, where my parents are having breakfast.

My dad is hunched over a bowl of cereal, reading the *New York Times* (yes, even though we've moved west he refuses to read the L.A. papers), and my mom is sipping coffee and scrutinizing the glossy society pages of *Orange Coast* magazine—scanning for pictures of all her new best friends.

"Morning," I say heading for the coffeemaker.

This is the last time I'll pour coffee as a virgin.

"Hey, kiddo." My dad winks at me.

"Do you want me to make you some eggs or something?" my mom asks, still not looking up.

"No, thanks," I say, grabbing an orange.

This is the last orange I'll peel as—well, you know.

"Rio, tonight's that benefit in L.A. Are you sure you'll be okay by yourself?" she asks.

"Mom, we've been over this. I'm seventeen. I'm not a baby." I roll my eyes and peel my orange.

"Well, you can have some of your friends over if you want and Tyler, too, but no parties, and no spending the night! Well, your friends can, but *not* Tyler!" She gives me a stern look.

"Jeez, Mom." I shake my head and act as though the thought never occurred to me. *But ohmygod! How did she know???*

She's back to reading her magazine so it's not like she's dwelling on it or anything, but I'm still completely creeped out by her saying that. So I quickly finish my orange, grab my coffee mug, and go to my room, pretending I have homework and stuff, which technically I do, but it's not like I'm actually planning to do it.

I flop on my bed and watch TV for a while. Then I pick up my cell and call Kayla. After four rings she finally answers. "What're you doing?" I ask.

"Getting ready to go to Kristi's."

"Already?" I glance at the clock on my nighstand. "But the party's not 'til way later."

"I know. We're just gonna hang by the pool until her parents leave, then we'll start setting up."

"Is Jen going, too?" I ask, sitting up and gripping the phone even tighter.

"Yeah, we're going together."

"Oh," I say, wondering why no one invited me.

"We were gonna invite you," she says, like she's reading my mind or something. "But we figured you'd be busy with Tyler."

"Oh, well I'm not. I'm just hanging in my room, totally bored," I say, hoping she'll invite me now.

But she just goes, "So are you guys gonna come by *before* or *after?*"

"Before or after what?"

"You *know.*" She laughs.

"Oh, *that.* Well, I think we're gonna leave the party early and then come back here. My parents are staying in L.A. tonight so we'll have the house to ourselves," I whisper.

"Cool. Oh, listen, Jen Jen's here. Gotta run."

"Kayla, wait—" I say, but she already hung up.

I sit on my bed staring at my silent phone, because I can't believe she didn't invite me. It's like ever since I started dating Tyler they've been doing all this stuff without me, and it's so not fair. I mean, just because I hang with the seniors a lot doesn't give them the right to ignore me when I'm alone.

I spend most of the day sequestered in my room, and by the time my parents *finally* leave (it took my mom *forever* to get ready), I only have an hour left to come up with the perfect outfit for losing my virginity. But after trying on nearly every piece of clothing in my closet, it suddenly occurs to me that clothes aren't really the issue tonight. It's really more about what's underneath.

And I'm kinda freaked since Tyler's never seen me naked. I mean, he's seen *parts* of me naked, but never like, "all together in one continuous piece" naked. Somehow I always manage to keep something on. But tonight he's expecting to see *everything at once,* and it's making me feel really self-conscious.

I don't know how other people do it. And I'm not talking about actresses and models and porn stars that get paid to be naked sometimes (well, in the case of a porn star pretty much all the time), but just normal everyday people with husbands and boyfriends and gym memberships where they walk from the shower to the locker with only a towel on their head.

I mean, how do they see themselves naked, and not hate what they see?

Okay, I know I'm supposed to love and accept myself and refuse to fall prey to evil things like fashion magazines and MTV videos and the impossible standards the media puts on women. But honestly, how can you truly not care? It's like, before I moved here I never really thought about how my body looked. I was short and chubby and always hiding in a pair of baggy jeans and a sweatshirt or an ill-fitting school uniform. And getting naked in front of some gorgeous guy never seemed like something that would happen to me. But then, you know, everything changed—my home, my body, my friends, my clothes—*everything!* And now I'm supposed to put myself on *full display* in front of my boyfriend who's completely perfect, and I'm panicked. I mean, what if he expects me to be perfect, too?

I'm starting to wonder if maybe I should have listened to Kristi and my mom when they tried to warn me about eating so much. Because, what if they're right? It's like, just now I turned to the side to check out my profile, and I swear, my stomach doesn't look near as flat as it used to, and it seems like my butt is in direct competition with J. Lo's. And believe me, three husbands and gazillions of dollars aside, that's *not* a look that's exactly coveted in my neighborhood.

But even worse, what if Tyler notices and gets all grossed out or something?

I'm glaring at myself and poking at the flabby parts when I hear him drive through the open gate.

I throw on a faded denim mini, a pink cami (that matches my new pink lace bra and matching thong), a green BCBG wrap sweater, and some gold Chanel ballet shoes that belong to my mom.

I'm swiping her little pink Dior handbag just as he rings the bell. But before I go downstairs, I run back in my room, unscrew the lightbulb in the lamp next to my bed, and bury it in the trash. That way when we come back after the party, the room will be so dark he can't see all my imperfections.

When I open the door he goes, "You look hot." Then he comes inside and kisses me.

"Thanks," I say, anxious to get out of here, so I can delay the inevitable for as long as possible.

"What's the hurry? Are your parents home?" he asks, looking worried.

I shake my head.

"Then let's hang awhile." He pulls me toward him.

I let him kiss me, but then he starts really getting into it and I can totally tell he's gonna try to blow off the party, and there's no way I'm letting that happen. So I push away. "We *have* to go. I told Kristi, we'd help set up." (Okay, maybe I lied, but he doesn't need to know that.) Then

I smile and say, "But I promise we can bail early." (Knowing that once he gets around his friends and a keg of beer, he won't want to leave.)

Then I drag him out the front door, all the way to his black Escalade.

The second we walk in the door, Tyler ditches me. Okay, maybe it's not quite that bad, but the fact is he sees a bunch of his friends (and the keg) and heads straight for them without once looking back to see if I'm following.

What'd I tell ya?

But I don't go after him. Instead I go searching for my friends, making my way through the crowded living room, through the sliding-glass doors, and out to the backyard. I say hi to a few people, grab a beer from a big metal can filled with ice and bottles, then I lie back on one of the beige padded lounge chairs by the pool.

I see JC lounging in the Jacuzzi between two girls I vaguely recognize as frosh-soph cheerleaders. They're draped all over him, kissing him, and when he reaches for his beer, he looks right at me.

I want to look away, but it's too late now, so we sit there gazing at each other, and I start remembering how much I hurt him, and I wonder if he still hates me.

Then JC smiles and goes, "Hey, Rio, come 'ere." He waves me over to join them.

And while it's nice to know he's not holding a grudge, I'm definitely not interested in making it a ménage à quatre. So I give a little wave back, then get up and go inside the house.

I wander into the den where I find Kristi and Kayla sitting in a circle playing a game of spin the bottle. But it's definitely not the sixth-grade edition I'm familiar with. In this version an empty champagne bottle is spun and whomever it lands on gets to hook up with the spinner.

Kristi motions for me to join them, but I just shake my head since it's not like I can play this game. I mean, I'm not single like they are. I came here with my boyfriend. So I just stand there watching the next spin, and when Kevin spins on Kayla I'm really happy for her because she's liked him forever. And as I'm watching them go upstairs together, Tyler walks up and whispers, "Wanna play?"

His hand is on my back and he's pushing me toward the circle, so I take a sip of my beer and say, "Okay."

We sit across from each other so we'll have a better shot of getting the bottle to land where we want. And when Drew takes the next spin, it lands right between this girl Heather and me.

I just kind of laugh, and scooch over so it's more on Heather, but Drew goes, "Nice try, Rio. When it lands in the middle you get to choose who to kiss." Then he starts moving toward me.

I look frantically at Tyler but he just shrugs, then I look over at Kristi and she's giving me the death stare. And before I can stop him, Drew is kissing me and trying to shove his tongue down my throat.

I can feel everybody watching, and I'm waiting for Tyler to do something to make him stop, but he just sits there. So I push Drew away, and wipe my mouth with my sleeve. And when I finally look at Tyler, he's just drinking his beer like nothing happened. But when I look at Kristi she's totally glaring at me.

I take a sip of my beer and watch Heather spin, and the bottle goes around and around until it finally lands on Kristi.

Okay, girls don't have to hook up with each other, unless they're into it. And since Heather and Kristi aren't into it they don't.

But they still have to kiss.

So they crawl toward each other, and they're both doing it all sexy like Halle Berry in *Cat Woman*. But I know they're just doing that for the guys 'cause guys *always* want to see stuff like that.

But then Kristi kisses Heather—*with her mouth open!* And she's *not* the first to pull away.

And even though it's such an obviously staged Madonna-Britney moment, it's also kinda strange since Kristi's always calling Mason a lesbo, like that's such a horrible thing to be. Yet now she's making out with Heather.

I'm thinking about all this as Kristi takes her spin. So it's a while before I realize it landed on Tyler.

But I know it's a mistake, since Drew's sitting right next to him, so it's obvious her aim was a little off. I look at Kristi and smile, since now she'll have to spin again, because it's not like she can hook up with my boyfriend.

But Kristi looks right at me as she stands up.

And when I look at Tyler, he just shrugs.

But I know they're just fooling around, so I go, "Okay you guys. *Very funny*. You can sit down now." And then I laugh.

And while I'm laughing they go upstairs together.

Thirty-three

I don't go after them. I just sit there in the circle like a coma victim. I know I should get up, I know I should do *something,* but it's like I'm frozen, and everything around me seems surreal.

And when that stupid bottle eventually lands on me, I look up and see this girl I barely know crawling toward me. So I jump up and run.

"Bitch!" she yells.

I run into the first bathroom I see, lock the door behind me, and slide all the way down to the floor where I sit with my head in my hands for the longest time. And when someone bangs on the door and tries to come in, I yell, "Go away!" Then I reach for a guest towel, bury my face in it, and break into loud, choking tears. When I come up for air, the towel's smeared all black with mascara, so I toss it in the trash, get up, and start pacing.

I can't believe what just happened! I can't believe Kristi actually did that—*right in front of my face!* And the way Tyler acted so casual makes me wonder if they've been hooking up all along, and I've been too stupid to see it. I mean, ever since last weekend on the yacht, she's been hanging all over him, and following him around. And I'm such a total dumbass I just sat back and let it happen, all the while convincing myself he'd wait for me!

I sit on the counter next to the sink and put my face in my hands. God, I'm such a fucking loser I didn't even try to stop them! Yet what was I supposed to do? Chase them down with the garden hose? And what if I were able to stop them? What would I be left with then? A boyfriend and a best friend who hook up right in front of me? I mean, do I really want friends like that?

I turn and look at my reflection in the mirror, I'm a total wreck. My hair's all knotted, my lip gloss is smeared down my chin, and my cheeks are glazed with thick black mascara. I lean over the sink, pump some antibacterial soap into my hand, and wash it all away, desperate to start over.

When I'm finished I just sit there staring at my pale, bare face. And it suddenly occurs to me how all this time I've been so worried about sleeping with Tyler when I'm not in love with him, that I never noticed that Tyler's not in love with me.

I run my fingers through my hair, breaking through clumps of tangles, then I empty my makeup bag, and start from the beginning. When I finally look normal again on the outside, I go pharming through the cabinets looking for something to make me feel normal again on the inside.

But all I find is a small bottle of aspirin (and it really is aspirin, I checked), a brand-new purple-and-white toothbrush still in its box, a black rubber band with a long blond hair attached, and one super tampon.

When I open the door some freshman girls shove past me and give me a dirty look. And it makes me wonder if word's already out about what a joke I am and how my boyfriend's upstairs with someone who used to be my best friend.

I wander into the kitchen where some guys are doing shots, and I ask them to pour me one.

Then another.

And when I ask for a third, one of them goes, "Shit, Rio, take a breather."

So I grab the bottle and pour it myself. And when my glass is empty, I slam it on the black granite counter and leave.

I'm feeling kind of dizzy, but I manage to navigate through the living room, and I know I should just go home, go to bed, and deal with everything tomorrow. But I refuse to leave without confronting Kristi.

Then right as I'm about to go in the backyard, Jen Jen comes in. And I'm so happy to see one of my *real* friends, that I grab her arm and go, "Jen, oh, my god, I have to talk to you."

"Wha?" she says, sounding messed-up and struggling to focus.

"Jen, I'm serious. I really need to talk to you," I say, holding on to her, fearing she might fall over if I don't. I mean, she's way worse off than me.

"Rio, relaxsh," she says, smiling and pulling away.

"Jen, please I really need you," I plead.

"You're always so serioush." And then she yells across the room, "Hey, Parker!"

And I'm starting to get annoyed so I go, "Jen!"

But she walks away and goes, "I'm going to talk to Parker!"

I watch her stagger across the room, but I don't follow. Instead I head for the study, or home office, or library, or whatever they call this room full of books no one reads, the latest Apple computer, and a brown Ralph Lauren leather couch.

I'm hoping I can be alone so I can try to sort out exactly what I'm going to say to Kristi when she surfaces, but Drew and Marc are in there, all bent over a table, doing coke.

I'm standing in the doorway when Drew looks up and goes, "Hey, there's some extra if you want." He motions to the powdery mirror in front of him.

So I join him on the couch, lean down, and Hoover it up, hoping it will clear my head and give me a little twenty-minute boost. Then he hands me the bottle of beer he's been drinking from, so I take a sip. But when I go to hand it back I remember how much Kristi likes him. And the expression on her face when he kissed me. And how she's hooking up with my boyfriend right this very minute.

So I look in his eyes and smile. And when he tries to grab the bottle I pull it back and take another drink. I do that like two or three more times until he finally wrestles it from me.

When he kisses me the first time Marc is sitting there watching.

But when he kisses me the second time, Marc's gone and the door is closed.

Thirty-four

The second I lie down I know I'm in trouble. So I close my eyes hoping that'll make me feel better but it just makes the spinning even worse. I move my right leg off the couch and onto the floor, so I can dig my heel deep into the carpet and make the room stand still, but Drew must think it's an invitation 'cause when I open my eyes again, I see him sliding his pants all the way down and positioning himself between my opened legs.

I try to shake my head no and ask him to stop, because I never meant for this to happen, I was just trying to get back at Kristi. But his mouth is pressing hard against mine, so I can't get the words out. And even though the room is spinning out of control, I'm starting to feel kind of sleepy again, so I close my eyes, for just a minute.

I can feel his hands reaching back to undo my bra and it makes me wonder what happened to my sweater and cami. So I start to feel around on the floor, trying to find them, but he grabs my wrist and holds my arms up high, so now I can't touch anything.

He yanks my bra roughly, up over my head, and I can feel his hand and mouth moving all over my breasts. He's squeezing them kind of hard and it's really starting to hurt, but just as I'm about to tell him that, I feel this wave of nausea. So I close my eyes again, willing it to stop.

And then everything's quiet. And Jas is telling me I'm beautiful, just like he did that day in art class. And it makes me feel so good, and so happy, and so loved, that I'm about to tell him that I've missed him, and that I think he's beautiful too. But then he starts pushing my skirt up around my waist and yanking my panties down to my knees. And he's hurting me.

But when I open my eyes, I see it's not Jas. It's still Drew.

And I know I have to stop him. Because he's not the right one, and it's not supposed to happen like this. So I go, "Stop it." But I don't think he heard me because he keeps yanking on my thong. So I press my legs together as tight as I can and go, "*Stop it!*"

But he won't stop.

So I kick him in the balls.

And then he stops.

I didn't kick him that hard, but he's naked, so I guess it must have hurt, because he screams.

And while he's screaming, I jump off the couch, find my bra, and shove it in my purse. Then I put on my cami, grab my sweater, and make a run for the door.

I look back just as I open it and he's all hunched over, cupping his hands between his legs. "You fucking bitch!" he yells.

But I just slam the door behind me.

I must look pretty bad, because the second I'm out of there a bunch of kids look at me and point. And some of the girls even laugh.

But no one asks if I'm okay.

I run my hands through my hair which is like a big, tangled mess, fold my arms across my chest since I'm no longer wearing a bra, and head straight for the front door, desperate to get out of here and go home.

Kristi's coming down the stairs, and even though I've been waiting all this time to confront her, after everything that just happened it no longer seems important.

But she walks right up to me and goes, "What the hell happened?"

I ignore her, and try to brush past.

"Hel-*lo*? I'm talking to you." She's following right behind me.

I'm about to open the door when I turn and say, "I can't fucking believe you."

"Oh, please." She rolls her eyes, and puts her hand on her hip. "You can't really be upset about that?"

"How long have you guys been hooking up?" I ask, dreading the answer.

She shakes her head. "Get a grip. It's just a game." Then she looks me up and down and goes, "Like you should talk."

"Excuse me?"

"If I remember right you were totally making out with Drew right in front of us!"

"I was not making out with him!" I say, louder than I'd planned.

"Oh, and did you come here braless? Or did someone take it off for you?" She narrows her eyes and smirks.

"You have no idea what just happened," I say, and start to turn away.

"Well, knowing you, nothing happened, because nobody's ever good enough for you. Not even your own boyfriend. Poor Tyler, it was the least I could do."

She's standing there smiling, and she's so beautiful and perfect-looking you'd never guess the horrible things she's capable of. And it makes me feel dizzy and sick to my stomach. But even worse, I feel like the world's biggest sucker for trusting her. "I can't believe I thought you were my friend," I say, reaching for the door handle.

"Get real, I'm the best friend you ever had! Before me you were just some big weirdo with a lame camera, really bad clothes, and loser friends." She shakes her head, and tosses her long dark hair. "I felt sorry for you. And because I'm such a nice person I decided to give you a shot at something better. It's because of *me* that you got to date the two hottest guys in school, and have everyone worship you! I'm the reason you're popular! I *rescued* you!"

I stand there gripping the doorknob knowing that she's right about some things, but wrong about others. But I don't say anything. I just open the door, I've got to get out of here.

"I'm just being honest," she continues. "You know, everyone's really getting tired of how you act like you're better than them. I heard some girls call you a stuck-up bitch."

"Sure they weren't talking about you?" I say, walking out the door.

"Oh, and now you're leaving? You think you're too good for my party?"

I don't speak. I just walk.

"If you leave, I swear you won't have one friend come Monday."

But I just keep walking.

Even when she yells, "You'll be sorry!"

When the door slams behind me, I start running. But halfway down the street I stop, and double-over in nausea. Then I start vomiting, over and over again, until it runs down the sidewalk.

It's splattered all over my clothes, and there's even some in my hair, but I just stand there bent over like the world's biggest dumbass, vomiting and sobbing onto my mom's shoes.

Then a car pulls up beside me, and I hear someone go, "Hey, are you okay?"

I recognize his voice. And it's not Tyler.

But I don't want anyone to see me like this, especially him. So I start walking quickly down the street, wiping my face with my sweater and refusing to look beside me.

"Rio, stop," he says.

But I can't. So I look over briefly and wave at Jas, like everything's okay. And as I'm turning away I get a glimpse of a girl sitting next to him.

So I start running. And I don't stop until I get home.

Thirty-five

When I walk in the door, part of me is relieved that my parents are gone, and part of me wishes they weren't, so they could see what a mess I am, and how fucked up my life is. And then I could stop pretending.

I go to my room, take off my clothes, and throw everything (including my mom's shoes) in the little trash bin next to my desk. Then I reach in my purse, retrieve my bra, and throw that in there, too.

I get in the shower and turn on the water so hot it makes me cringe. Then I fill my palms with shampoo and bath gel, and I lather my hair and my body over and over until the vomit is washed away and my skin is bright and raw.

I pat myself dry with an oversized towel and weave my long, wet hair into a single braid. Then I slip into some old, worn flannel pajamas with faded pictures of strawberries and oranges, and pull on my favorite pair of old gray socks that come all the way up to my knees. Then I climb into bed.

But I can't sleep because my mind is spinning around and around, but it's no longer from the alcohol. It's spinning with thoughts, and pictures, and things I don't want to think about, and I know I'll never get any sleep like this. So I open my desk drawer and grab a Valium that Kristi gave me. Then I place it on my tongue, and go into my bathroom for some water.

I fill up a glass, and just as I'm about to swallow I catch my reflection in the mirror.

And I think: *Who are you?*

Because the pathetic, messed-up girl in the mirror is unrecognizable. She's like a mosaic of what everyone else wanted her to be. And I don't remember there being any broken pieces before. Because I used to be whole.

So I spit into the sink, empty my glass, and watch the water chase the pill down the drain. Then I go back in my room and crawl into bed.

And when my mind finally quiets, I sleep.

When I wake up on Sunday the first thing that pops into my head is: *Was that a dream?*

But then I look at the bin full of smelly vomit clothes and I know it wasn't.

I lie in bed until I hear my parents come home, then I hide the trash in my shower so they won't come in here, see it, and start asking all kinds of questions. And when I climb back in bed I realize I've just chosen to lie again.

"Hey, kiddo, it's after noon and you're still in bed? Are you okay?" My dad asks, poking his head in my room.

"I'm not feeling well," I say, as my mom plops herself down next to me.

"Why? What happened?" she asks, eyes full of scrutiny.

"Nothing happened." I look at my dad then back at her. "I have cramps," I whisper loud enough for him to hear, knowing he'll get embarrassed and leave.

Well, that's one down.

"Maybe you should get up and walk around," my mom says, refusing to follow him. "Yoga really helps me."

"Mom, I'm not doing yoga. My cramps are *really* bad." I roll my eyes and bend into a fetal-like position for emphasis.

"Okay," she says, sounding skeptical as she walks out the door. "I'll be back to check on you later." She says it like a promise, but I know it's a threat.

I ended up staying in bed, faking cramps, until they finally left. That's the problem with lying. Once you start, you pretty much have to take it all the way to the bitter end.

It's not like they didn't try though. I mean, my mom really thought she could lure me out of bed by offering:

1. Brunch at the Ritz-Carlton.
2. A few hours at Salt Creek Beach.
3. Shopping and gallery hopping in downtown Laguna.
4. Disneyland? (I think she was just testing me because it's not in the five-mile radius of this particular field trip.)
5. Ice cream at the Haagen Daz across from Main Beach.
6. Browsing through the Laguna Art Museum.

But I held my ground and refused it all. Then I remained in bed until long after they left. I mean, I was playing the part of a girl with cramps so well, I was reluctant to get out of character.

By dinnertime they were back and I was starving, so I made my way downstairs to join them in the Venetian room.

"How you feeling, kiddo?" my dad asks.

"Okay," I say, filling up the plate my mom had set out for me.

"Cramps are gone?" She gives me that same skeptical look.

I take a bite of corn on the cob and shrug.

"You missed a good exhibit," she says. *"One Hundred Artists See God."*

"Next time you should see *One Hundred Artists See the Devil,*" I say.

"Is there such a thing?" my dad asks.

"Yeah, it's in Santa Ana."

"So what did you do last night?" my mom asks, sipping her wine all casual and nonchalant, but I'm onto her.

"Nothing," I say, cutting my salmon.

"*Nothing?* Why, were you sick last night, too?"

"No. I just wanted a break." I steal a quick peek at her and it's pretty clear she's not buying it.

"So let's see," she says, wineglass suspended in air. "It's a Saturday night, your parents are out of town, and you don't invite *anyone* over. Not even your boyfriend."

I roll my eyes. "Does it look like I had a party?"

"I didn't say you had a *party*." She looks all excited now, like she just got a big break in the case. "*You're* the one that called it *a party*."

Oh, nice work from the prosecution.

I give her the eye roll–head shake combination, then look at my dad and go, "Can you please step in here? I'm in need of a good defense attorney."

So my dad looks at my mom and goes, "If Rio said she didn't have a party, then I'm sure she didn't."

That's it? He gets paid all kinds of money for that?

Then after giving me a long look, my mom takes a bite of her salad. And we all sit there quietly eating our dinners.

But she's still watching me. And it *really* bugs me, so I go, "God, Mom, I have *cramps* okay? You act like you don't believe me or something."

"No one said anything about not believing you, Rio. Though I'm wondering if we should take you to the emergency room. Since if I remember correctly, you already had your period last week." She takes a dainty bite of corn and smiles.

Oh, god, I'm so busted.

"This is *so bogus!*" I yell, dropping my fork and getting up from the table.

"Where are you going?" my father asks.

"Can I be excused? Because I'm *really* not feeling well." I hug myself and bend forward, like I'm in terrible pain or something.

"Go ahead." He nods.

And when he's not looking, I glare at my mother and head for my room.

$\mathcal{T}$hirty-six

Monday morning I was filled with dread. It wasn't until after I'd show-ered and dressed that I realized not one person had called me this whole entire time, and the only e-mail I got was from Paige. And I'm still not answering those.

I went downstairs and poured my usual cup of coffee, and even though I was armed and ready for battle, my mom didn't mention one word about last night's cramps.

But by eight o'clock, when nobody had come to pick me up, and I was still just sitting there in total denial, she said, "Rio, do you need a ride to school?"

I set down my mug, and said, "Yeah, I guess I do."

I got there just as the bell was ringing so I didn't even have time to go to my locker. I just headed straight for English, not sure what to expect when I took my usual seat next to Kristi. I mean, I knew I wasn't capa-ble of pretending that nothing happened, but I wasn't exactly sure what she was capable of.

But when I sat down I noticed her seat was empty, so I took a deep breath, and tried to relax a little. Obviously she's running behind, and even she's not crazy enough to show up late then try to start some-thing right in front of Mrs. Abbott.

I place my pen, notebook, and John Steinbeck's *The Grapes of Wrath* (that I was supposed to start reading over the weekend and didn't), on my desk and wait for something to happen. Mrs. Abbott walks over to her podium, and leaning on it with both elbows, goes, "Kristi, can you please open your book and begin reading from page twelve?"

And I'm thinking: *What?*

The chair next to me is empty and there are no other Kristis in this class. So I look back at Mrs. Abbott, and then I look over to where she's looking. And sitting on the opposite side of the room, as far from me as possible, is Kristi. Her long dark hair is pulled back into a high ponytail, and she's all decked out in her cheerleading sweater and skirt. She looks right at me, but only for a second. Then she starts reading from her open book.

I look down at my desk and listen to Kristi, but I can't concentrate, because it's weird seeing her all the way over there when Mrs. Abbott is all about the seating chart. And since she knew where to find her when she called on her, that means Kristi must have asked permission to move. And it makes me wonder if she gave a reason.

I notice a few girls sneaking glances at me, but it's not in the way they usually do. There are no smiles, or little waves, or anything remotely friendly. They just check out my clothes, then toss their hair over their shoulder and laugh (but quietly so Mrs. Abbott remains completely clueless). It's like all these girls are tossing their hair and laughing at me and I have no idea why. But it reminds me of what Kristi said just as I was leaving her party. I guess I didn't really believe it at the time, but now I wonder if it's true.

After class I go to my locker to switch out some books, but I'm also kind of hoping I'll see Kristi. I mean, it's not like I want to hang with her after all the nasty things she said, but I really don't need her as an enemy either. But no one's around and there's also none of the usual notes in my locker, or text messages on my cell. And it's starting to feel even worse than the first day of school. Because back then the only reason people didn't talk to me was because they didn't know me.

Now they don't talk to me because they do.

———

When I walk into Art my eyes are glued to the floor as I head for my table since I'm determined to avoid all contact with Jas after that totally humiliating moment on the street. I can't even imagine what I would say to him at this point anyway. He's probably totally disgusted by me, and wondering why we were ever friends in the first place. And that's assuming he thinks of me at all.

Thank god, Ms. Tate has another slide show planned. So when she turns out the lights and starts talking about Impressionism, I lay my head on the desk and close my eyes until the bell rings.

By lunch I've decided that despite the fact that everyone seems to be avoiding me, I'm still going to eat lunch with my friends. What happened is just between Kristi and me. I mean, Kayla and Jen Jen weren't even there when Kristi and I fought, so it's not like they can be mad at me, too.

So with lunch bag in hand, I smile and make my approach. And just as I'm about to slide onto the end of the bench, everyone (without even looking at me!) spreads out so quickly, I end up on the ground.

I'm sitting there, flat on my ass, but they just continue laughing and joking like I'm not even there. So I get up, brush myself off, clear my throat, and go, "Hey, you guys."

But they just keep on like that, acting like I don't exist. And it's not like I can force them to see me, so I look over at the senior tables and since Tyler's not there, I decide to sit with them. I mean, I'm still good friends with everyone else.

But when I get there one of the girls looks at me and goes, "Sorry, no sluts allowed." And everyone busts out laughing.

"Excuse me?" I say. My breath feels panicked and cold in my throat.

"This table has a strict no-sluts policy," she says, staring me down.

"What's that supposed to mean?" I stand there hoping no one can see how bad I'm shaking.

"It means you go out with the two hottest, sweetest guys in school and you cheat on both of them. Everyone knows you slept with Drew." She shakes her head, and gives me a nasty look.

"You have no idea what really happened," I say.

"Everyone saw you with half your clothes shoved in your purse."
She looks across the table and points. "Marc was there, you were doing
it right in front of him!"

"That's not true!" I look at Marc, but he just sits there and shrugs.
Then I remember how he saw me flirting with Drew and kissing him.
And how he left before the bad stuff happened. "You don't know what
you're talking about," I say. But I'm losing steam, because now I see it
how they see it, and it's not pretty.

"Everybody's sick of you walking around like some big celebrity,
tossing your long blond hair, and telling all the guys you're a virgin.
What a joke." She gives me a hateful look. "Why don't you go back
where you came from, skank?"

I just stand there, speechless and humiliated.

"You can go now," she says.

So I do. And as I'm walking away people start pointing and laughing, and someone throws something at my head. It hits me, but I just
keep walking.

When I go inside the library a few people look up, but only briefly, and
it's kind of nice to be in a place where no one actually knows me, because the fact is there isn't one person I used to hang with that would
risk being seen in here during lunch because at this time of day the library is strictly geek territory.

I walk toward a table in the very back, throw my bag on the floor,
flop onto this hardwood chair, and lean forward, pressing my forehead
against the cool wood table. I stay like this for a long time, telling myself everything's gonna be okay, even though it's pretty obvious that
it's not.

And then someone goes, "Rio?"

I don't want to look up. But I know if I don't they'll say it again,
only louder. So I slowly raise my head until I see Mason standing there,
wearing some cool, vintage fake-fur capelet, with a rhinestone pin fas-
tened at the top. Her arms are loaded down with books and papers.

"Hey," I say.

"Are you okay?" She looks concerned.

I sit up straighter and yawn like I was just sleepy or something, and go, "Yeah, I was just napping. What's up?"

"I was just doing a little research," she says, sitting on the chair across from me and placing her stuff on the table. I glance at the titles quickly and notice most of them are art books.

"I heard you opted out of the exhibit," she says.

"Yeah, I've just got so much other stuff going on." I run my index finger along the wood grain, unwilling to meet her gaze.

"That's too bad. Your stuff was really good."

I can feel her looking at me, but I don't want to talk about art anymore. So I go, "How's Zane?"

"We broke up. For real this time."

Okay, so why is it that I only seem to experience déjà vu on the most uncomfortable moments of my life, and never the good ones? "Sorry," I say.

She shrugs. "It's okay. He's a really cool guy and we're still friends, but the distance got to be too much, and he's in college now so he should be free to experience that. And it's not like we were gonna get married or anything, so, it's just better this way."

"But you guys seemed really good together," I say, feeling kind of depressed that they couldn't make it work.

"Yeah well, things change. You know that."

I sit there for a moment, not really knowing what else to say, then I glance at her stuff. "What's that?" I ask, pointing to a stack of papers.

"The 'zine. Want one?"

"Sure."

"It's our last one on paper," she says, handing me a copy. "Next month, we'll be on-line. Well, I'm gonna get to class a little early. See you around." She picks up her books and heads for the door.

I look at my watch. I still have some time 'til the bell rings, so I pick up the 'zine and stare at the picture on the front. It's a take on Edvard Munch's most famous painting, *The Scream*. Only this one's more modern and it depicts girls instead of boys, and school lockers instead of a river in Oslo. In the foreground there's this ordinary girl holding her hands up to her ears, and her eyes are closed and her mouth is wide-open because she's screaming. And she looks like she's in so much pain that you wonder what happened. But then you notice the two girls in the background and they're pointing at her and laughing, so you can kind of figure it out. I mean, it reminds me of me, twenty minutes ago.

The picture is so amazing that I just sit there staring at it. Then I notice the signature in the bottom right-hand corner, it's Mason's.

I think about how Kristi, Kayla, and Jen Jen are always making fun of her clothes, and calling her a lesbo and stuff. And even though I didn't always join in, I usually did nothing to stop it. I guess I always thought of Mason as being such a strong, independent person, that it never occurred to me she might actually be hurt by stuff like that. But by the looks of this picture, I guess she is. And now that it's happening to me, I feel even worse about doing nothing to help her.

On the next page there's an article she wrote titled, "R U Guilty?" And it's all about how girls torture one another with gossip and rumors and stuff. It's like the word version of her cover art.

When the bell rings a few minutes later, I ignore it. I just sit there reading until I'm finished.

After school I call my mom and ask her to pick me up. And when she meets me out front by the office she goes, "What's going on, Rio?"

And I go, "Nothing, okay? Jeez." Then I roll my eyes and slump way down in my seat, wishing she'd just leave me alone.

"Well, something's going on. Because this morning I had to drive you to school, and now I was in the middle of redoing the living room when you called. Did you and Tyler have a fight?" She looks at me, face full of alarm.

"No, we didn't have a fight," I say, looking out the window so I won't have to look at her. But it's not really a lie, since Tyler and I haven't even spoken, much less had a fight.

"Well, good," she says, clearly relieved. "Because you've got those four beautiful new dresses for the Moondance next weekend, and we'll need to narrow it down in the next couple days so we can decide what to do with your hair and makeup!"

She says that like it's *sooo* important. But I guess in her mind it is.

"And Rio, I'm going to be really booked for the rest of the week, trying to finish up the house, and get myself in shape for the photo shoot. So you need to make arrangements with your friends to get to and from school. Because this is the last day I'll have time to do this for you."

I just nod and continue looking out the window.

The first thing I do when I go in my room is throw my backpack onto my bed. The second thing I do is check my e-mail. But there's nothing. Not even from Paige.

Determined to handle this before it gets any worse, I message Kayla and Jen Jen. And even though I can see they're on-line they won't respond. So I pick up the phone and call. And when Jen Jen finally answers I go, "Hey, what's up?" As though everything was perfectly normal.

"Oh, hey, Rio," she says, sounding normal, too.

"Um, are you guys mad at me?" I ask, my voice betraying my nervousness.

"What are you talking about?" she says innocently.

"Well, like, you guys never called me all weekend, and then you totally ignored me, and pushed me off the bench at lunch!" My face feels hot and my hands are all sweaty.

"Don't be ridiculous," she says

"Jen, I'm serious, you know you did that. And I just don't get it because even though Kristi's mad at me, that doesn't mean you guys should be. I mean, it's between me and her."

"You're totally delusional." She laughs. "Why would Kristi be mad at you?"

"She said some pretty harsh things when I was leaving the party."

"She was probably drunk."

"Well, yeah, I guess she was drinking and stuff. But still, she seemed pretty serious. And then today in English she sat all the way across the room."

"I wouldn't worry about it. I'm sure it will blow over, and you guys will be friends again."

"Well, I'm not really sure that's what I want," I say.

"What are you talking about?"

"Did she say anything to you? About what happened?" I ask, trying to get a feel for what she knows, because I know she knows something.

"Rio, I really don't want to get in the middle of this, okay?"

"What'd she say?"

"Okay, fine," she sighs. "Kristi's feeling pretty hurt because you hooked up with Drew."

"I did *not* hook up with Drew, she hooked up with Tyler!"

"I'm just telling you what she said."

"Well, it's not like I'm making it up, Jen. There were plenty of people who saw the same thing."

"Well, that's not what I heard."

"What are you talking about?"

"Rio, everyone's saying you were totally trying to hook up with Drew, and that the only reason Kristi kissed Tyler is to get back at you."

"That's not how it happened! That's totally backward!" I'm so upset I'm shaking. "Kristi and Tyler hooked up, and then Drew totally attacked me!"

"He attacked you?" She says, voice full of disbelief.

"Yes."

"Drew?"

"*Yes,* I'm not making this up! God, I even kicked him in the balls to get him to stop!"

"That's not what I heard."

"Well who are you going to believe?" I ask, barely controlling my anger.

"Listen, Rio, you're taking everything way too seriously. It was just a stupid game, and you're getting all bent over nothing."

I just sit there, holding the phone, not sure what to say. Because I know I'm not imagining this, and I know I'm not crazy.

"Listen, I gotta go. See you tomorrow?"

"Okay." And then feeling like a needy loser, I go, "Um, do you think you can give me a ride?"

"Sure," she says. "But I'll be there early because cheerleading tryouts are starting and we're having a meeting."

Then before I can say anything else, she hangs up.

Thirty-seven

The next morning I've been sitting in the kitchen for more than an hour, drinking coffee and waiting for Jen Jen to come pick me up, and I'm getting kind of anxious since she still isn't here.

And for someone who's supposedly so busy they can't drive me to school, my mom somehow finds the time to keep coming downstairs to say, "She's not here yet?" And then she gives me a suspicious look, like it's my fault.

So when my dad comes into the kitchen I ask him what his schedule's like, and he says, "Well, I need to stop by the office on my way to the airport."

"Do you think you can drop me off first?" I ask.

Which causes my mother to look at me and go, "What happened to your ride?"

And I go, "Oh, she just called, she overslept."

"She called? I didn't hear the phone ring." She takes a sip of the green tea Katrina swears will jump-start her metabolism, and peers at me.

"It was a text message," I lie, rolling my eyes. "So Dad, can you take me?"

"Sure," he says, kissing my mom good-bye. "Let's go."

When we've pulled out of the driveway my dad looks at me and goes, "How's it going?"

And I really hate lying to him so I go, "Okay."

"Just okay?" he asks, glancing at me briefly while changing lanes.

"Well, things are kind of messed-up right now." I feel relieved to say it out loud.

"Care to talk about it?"

I start to, and I want to, but I can't. I mean, if he had just been here from the start, when I really needed him, maybe I could have avoided all this, or at least handled things better. But now it's too late, and it's gone too far, and I don't want him to know what a fuckup I am. So I just go, "It'll work itself out."

He looks at me for a moment, then says, "If you change your mind I'm here for you." Then he reaches over and pats me on the knee.

But it's total bullshit, because he's always somewhere else. But I don't say that. I just nod and turn up the radio.

I'm walking across the quad on the way to my locker when I see Tyler hanging out with a bunch of his friends. I haven't actually seen him since the party, and it's weird to think how just last Friday I was going to sleep with him and now I'm not even sure I want to walk past him.

And just as I'm about to avoid them by going the long way around, he shouts, "Hey, Rio!"

I look over and see him smiling and waving, but no way am I going over there. But then he calls my name again, and now everyone's smiling and waving and as I approach them I start to feel lighter, like this horrible burden has been lifted and now everything can go back to being normal again.

So I go, "Hey, what's up?" And then I notice Kristi standing right next to him.

Then Tyler goes, "About the Moondance."

"Yeah?" I look at both of them.

"I'm going with Kristi." He puts his arm around her, and she stands on her toes to kiss him.

I just stand there watching them, with my face frozen into this awful smile. Then someone laughs. And pretty soon they're all laughing.

Then Tyler goes, "Good luck." And they all walk away.

And after a while, I walk away, too.

As I'm heading for my locker I can smell the dog shit before I see it.

And that's because it's *inside*.

On the *outside* in big capital letters it says:

STUCK-UP BITCH!

People are crowded all around, but I push my way through until I'm standing right in front of it, staring in disbelief. And then the bell rings, but no one seems to care, they just continue pointing and laughing. So I take off running, all the way across campus to the administration office.

"Someone put dog shit in my locker!" I say, catching my breath, and causing everyone in the office to look up.

"Excuse me?" one of the secretaries says.

"There is dog shit, *inside* my locker! *Dog shit!* And on the outside someone took a big black marker and wrote 'Stuck-up Bitch!' all over it!"

"Watch your language!" she says, coming around her desk and shaking her head at me.

"I'm just telling you what it *says!*"

"Do you have any idea who would do this?" she asks.

"Yeah, I know of three people."

Fifteen minutes later Kristi, Kayla, Jen Jen, and I are sitting in Principal Chaney's office. They're all grouped together on the couch, and I'm on the crummy wooden chair that's reserved exclusively for juvenile delinquents. And I know this because that's the same chair he made me use the last time I was in here.

"So why is it you're accusing these three?" Principal Chaney asks, as though I'm the one on trial.

"Because they're the only ones that know my combination," I say, crossing my arms and standing my ground.

"And is there anything else?"

What am I supposed to say?

Kristi slept with my boyfriend before I could? They won't let me sit with them at lunch?

I can't tell him that. So I just go, "I just *know* they did it, okay?"

But he's looking at me in that way adults always do when they want you to think they have an open mind, when really they're just sitting in judgment.

"So did you do it?" he asks, drumming his fingers on a pile of papers.

"No!" they say in perfect unison.

"We would never do that," Kristi adds. "And I'm really sorry to hear that Rio thinks we did." She gives me a disappointed look and continues, "Besides, I think you know me well enough to know that I would *never* willingly touch a piece of doggy excrement."

I swear that's what she called it.

And then she adds in a quiet little voice, "I feel bad suggesting it, but maybe Rio did it. I mean, she's probably feeling sad because her ex-boyfriend asked me to the Moondance, so now she's, like, you know, desperate for attention."

"That's ridiculous!" I say, looking at Principal Chaney, but he just leans back and adjusts his striped tie, like he's actually considering *that*.

Then he looks at me and says, "Rio. It seems you've had some trouble adjusting to our curriculum."

"What?" I ask incredulously.

"If you remember correctly, you were in this office on your very first day of school, and you received a week's detention. I was hoping that would enable you to see the kind of commitment we require, but sadly I can see that it hasn't."

"What's that supposed to mean?"

"I think you need to take some time to reflect on the kind of conduct we expect here at Sea Crest High." He retrieves a golf ball from his top drawer and rolls it between his thumb and forefinger.

And I just sit there in that crappy chair, staring at the floor, because I can't believe this is really happening to me.

"Mr. Chaney, can we please be excused, so we can get back to class?" Kristi asks.

He nods, and I watch Kristi, Kayla, and Jen Jen smile at him and glare at me as they walk out the door.

"Are you going to call my mom?" I ask, getting up to leave.

"Should I?" He gives me a stern look.

"I'd really rather you didn't." I look down at the ground.

"I won't call her this time, because I'm going to give you the opportunity to handle this on your own. But if you wind up in here again, I'm afraid the consequences will be quite serious."

I'm almost out of there when he goes, "Oh, and Rio,"

I stop.

"You can drop by the custodian's office for the supplies you'll need to clean up your mess."

My mess?

But I don't say anything, I just walk out the door and head for the janitor.

Thirty-eight

I didn't go to English, because it took me that whole time just to clear out the dog shit and disinfect my locker. And even though the janitor felt sorry for me and offered to help, I wouldn't let him. I figured he had enough on his hands just having to clean up after us on a normal day.

But before I started with the heavy-duty scouring, I searched my tote bag for my camera so I could take pictures of this mess, just in case I needed the evidence for later. But I couldn't find it. And after dumping out the contents of my purse, backpack, tote bag, and locker, it was still nowhere to be found, and I was pretty sure Kristi stole it as part of her prank. But with no way to prove that, and no one to believe me, I pulled on some rubber gloves and started scrubbing.

When I get to Art, I go straight into the darkroom so I can be alone. I stand near the door, allowing my eyes to adjust to the dimness, then I walk over to the corner where I locate the folder of prints I was working on for my project.

It's filled with like a hundred pictures of my stupid, vain, horn dog ex-boyfriend in various lame poses. God, I can't believe how cool I thought he was. Not to mention how cool I thought I was for being with him.

I flip through the stack of useless prints and somewhere in the middle I come across one of Kristi. She's standing by her customized car, talking on her pink rhinestone cell phone, while smiling and waving at the camera. I stand there looking at it for the longest time, wondering how I could have been so stupid to trust someone so awful.

I *know* she defaced my locker and lifted my camera. I also know that she's really not too delicate to handle "doggy excrement." But apparently I'm the only one who knows all that.

I grab a black Sharpie pen from my bag, and draw big pointy devil horns, a spiky goatee, and a long sharp tail on her. Then I add a big pitchfork with the Louis Vuitton logo all over it. I hold it up and admire it, wondering if I should submit it to the Santa Ana exhibit. They can rename it *One Hundred* and One *Artists See the Devil.*

Except that I'm not really an artist.

I'm not really sure who I am anymore.

I hear someone come in, so I quickly shove the picture in my folder, and start acting all busy.

"Oh, hey," he says, coming over to stand next to me.

"Hey, Jas."

"How are you?" He leans against the table and looks at me. And even though it's dim, believe me, we can still see each other.

"Good," I say, still faking busy.

"Are you sure?"

"Yeah, why?"

"I've been kind of worried about you. You know with everything that's going on . . ." he trails off.

"Well that's very nice, but don't waste your time. I'm totally fine." I pick up my folder of useless photos, and prepare to bolt. Because while it's nice that he cares, the truth is I can't stand knowing that he pities me.

"Listen, if you ever want to just hang out and talk."

"Okay," I say. "See you around."

And right when I'm about to exit he goes, "Oh, I almost forgot, here."

He has my camera!

"Where'd you get that?" I ask, totally confused. I mean, how did he get my camera if Kristi stole it?

"You left it in here last Friday, and I didn't want anyone to lift it, so I took it home."

I look at him for a moment, trying to determine if he's telling the truth, but his eyes remain neutral. And when he hands it to me my fingers accidentally brush against his. So I quickly pull away, open the door, and hurry back to my table where I spend the rest of class ripping up pictures of Tyler.

Thirty-nine

This is a typical day in my life now:

1. Wake up full of dread, but earlier than usual.
2. Get dressed in something cool enough to fool my mom, but not so cool that people will think that I think I'm cool.
3. Drink coffee and make small talk with my mom about the stupid Moondance that I'm no longer going to, while desperately wishing I could find a way to tell her the truth.
4. Pretend I'm meeting Tyler outside the gate for a ride to school. Then actually walk outside the gate and all the way to school. (See number 1 about waking up early.)
5. Walk through the quad while people "accidentally" bump into me, "accidentally" trip me, "accidentally" throw stuff at me, and "accidentally" knock the books out of my arms.
6. Listen to groups of girls calling me "Stuck-up bitch" when I walk by.
7. Go to class and get bombarded with flying objects every time the teacher leaves the room.
8. Go to Art and spend long periods of time in the darkroom, accomplishing nothing, while successfully avoiding Jas and Mason.

9. Eat lunch in the library, alone. Since even the library geeks won't talk to me.
10. Listen to everyone hurl insults from their cars as I walk home.
11. Go up to my room and log onto my computer only to be deluged with nasty e-mails and instant messages.

But today was different. Because today, during break, I had to go to the bathroom. Usually I try to avoid going anywhere near there during that time since that's when everyone else is in there, but I just couldn't hold it any longer.

I'm just getting ready to exit the stall when I hear some girls walk in, and one of them goes, "Oh, my god, you guys, remember how Rio was always bragging about her mom being this big-time supermodel?"

What??? I freeze, dreading what I'll hear next.

"Well, Amber was over at Caitlyn's, and Parker and Hunter were there and they were fooling around on the Internet, and they totally saw pictures of her mom on this porno site!"

"No way!" they squeal.

"Way. They said, it looked *just like her!* It was totally *her!*"

"Like mother like daughter," one of them says.

"What a loser!"

"Fucking skanky whore!"

Listening to that makes me feel totally sick to my stomach. But hiding from it makes me feel worse. I throw the door open so it bangs loudly against the side and when they see that it's me, they exchange these phony, horrified looks.

I head straight for the sink they're standing next to, and begin filling my palms with pink grainy soap from the dispenser, watching them through the mirror as they rifle through their purses, and elbow each other.

I rinse my hands until the water runs clean, then I grab a paper towel and dry off. And the second I leave, I hear them burst out laughing.

ℱorty

Friday when I got home from school, the living room had changed—again. This time there was no Tuscan Villa, French Country, Moroccan Royalty, or even Indian Palace, because this time it was completely empty.

"Where's the living room?" I ask, dropping my bag on the floor and staring at the open space.

"I couldn't live with it," my mom says, coming over and handing me a glass of iced tea. "Katrina says she read an article in *Interiors* about minimalism being the next big thing."

"So you're leaving it empty?"

"*No.* I'm just going to find a new decorator with more pared-down tastes."

"I thought you said Michael was a genius?"

"I did. But Katrina says—"

"Oh, I'm sorry, I didn't realize Katrina lived here," I interrupt.

"What's that supposed to mean?" She frowns at me.

"Well, it's *our* house, but it seems like you're decorating it for everyone but us. I mean, why is Katrina's opinion more important than your own?"

"It's not that simple, Rio." She shakes her head. "People judge you on your home, so making a good impression is imperative."

"Oh, I think I might know a thing or two about being judged," I say, reaching for my bag, and heading up the stairs.

"So how was practice?" she asks, following closely behind.

"Okay." *God, I never should have lied about getting to school early and staying late for cheerleading tryouts. But how else was I supposed to explain my new schedule?*

"Why don't you show me," she says, coming into my room.

"Show you what?"

"Your cheer."

"Not, now," I say, lying on my bed, and closing my eyes.

"Why not?"

"Because I'm tired." *God, I wish she'd just leave me alone.*

"Well, I still think you should have let me hire a coach. You've never been a cheerleader, and Katrina says that's how everyone makes it on the squad."

"Oh, well." I shrug, eyes still closed.

"Also, you have to decide on your dress for the dance. It's tomorrow night! You can't keep putting it off."

"Okay," I mumble.

"Oh, and one more thing."

"What?" I ask, opening one eye to peer at her.

"Mario called and he wants *you* in the Gap ad!"

"Why me?"

"Well, it seems all of us models have children now, so they decided to do some family shots. And you *cannot* say no! This is a perfect opportunity for you—you'll get great exposure! Just think, a national Gap ad on your very first shoot! I had to do a year of catalog work before I got something like that. What do you think?" she asks excitedly.

"Whatever," I say. But I say it just to placate her because there's no way I'm doing it. I've had about all the "exposure" I can handle thank you.

"Great. I can't wait to tell Mario! Oh, and we'll just be having salad tonight, since we need to slim down for the shoot. And you might try to join me for yogalates, you know, just to tighten up a little beforehand."

"Whatever."

"Great! I'll call you when it's ready," she singsongs.

And the second she's gone, and my door is closed, I grab some scissors.

Then I go into my bathroom, and cut off all my hair.

Well, most of it. I mean, I'm not *bald* or anything.

And it's not like it was easy since it was all the way down to my waist. But now it's up to my ears. And there's a big heap of honey-blond on the floor, and on the counter, and even in the sink. So I scoop it all up and throw it in the trash. Then I look at myself in the mirror and trim up the front and sides.

And when I'm finished, I smile at my reflection.

Because I really do feel better.

That hair was becoming a burden.

~~F~~orty-one

When my mom calls me for dinner I put on some lip gloss, run my fingers through my two-inch strands, and go down the stairs, two at a time.

I grab my usual seat, and when she walks in carrying the big wood salad bowl she looks at me and screams.

And I mean *screams*. Like a scary movie scream.

"What. Did. You. Do. To. Your. Hair?" she asks, standing there all stiff, with her mouth wide-open.

"I cut it," I say, suddenly feeling a little self-conscious.

"*Why?* I don't understand! *Why* would you do this to yourself?" she asks, carefully setting the bowl on the table, while maintaining a safe distance from the newly shorn crazy person.

"I wanted a change." I reach for the salad tongs, wishing she would just sit down and stop gaping at me. I mean, it's *rude*.

"*Now?*" she asks, while her right hand searches in vain for her nonexistent hip, eventually settling for the back of her chair. "*Now*, you want a change? Oh, I don't suppose this has anything to do with *the Gap ad* then does it?"

She's glaring at me, but what she doesn't understand is that I'm used to being glared at and it just washes right over me. So I reach for the olive oil, extra-virgin (like me!), and drizzle it over my greens.

"Answer me!" she says, barely controlling her rage.

But I don't answer her. "Please just sit down," I say.

"Not until you tell me what's going on!"

"You really want to know?" I look right at her.

"Yes."

But I can hear the hesitation in her voice, like maybe part of her really doesn't want to know. Well, that's just too bad, because now I'm finally ready to talk. "If you'll sit down and stop yelling, I'll tell you."

She slips slowly onto the seat across from me and takes a sip of her chardonnay, and I play with the salad tongs, wondering where I should start. Finally, I take a deep breath and say, "I just wish you would stop putting so much pressure on me."

"I don't know what you mean." She sounds really defensive.

"You're always interfering with what I wear, what I eat, who I hang with. It's like nothing I do is ever good enough. I can never live up to your expectations," I tell her.

"That's not true! You always look beautiful, and you know how wonderful I think your friends are."

"But that's just it. They're *not* wonderful. And they're *not* my friends, not anymore. They all hate me." I look down at my salad, determined not to cry. "I haven't told you what's going on, because I didn't want you to know. But I'm tired of lying all the time just to keep you happy."

"Rio, what's going on?" she asks, and she almost looks scared when she says it.

"Okay." I force myself to face her. "The truth is I'm *not* trying out for cheerleader, and I'm *not* going to the dance this weekend. Tyler and I broke up, and he's going with Kristi, so it's fine if you want to return all the dresses. Also, no one will drive me to school anymore, so I walk."

"You. Walk. To. School?" She looks even more shocked and horrified than when she first saw my hair.

"It's not that bad." I shrug.

"Rio, how did this happen? Why haven't you said anything?"

"Because I didn't want you to know what a total loser I am. And I didn't want you to judge me."

"Going through a rough patch does not make you a loser," she says. "I'm sure whatever happened between you and your friends will work itself out, and everyone will get back together." She's actually smiling now.

"It's not a rough patch! You can't sugarcoat it like that! And I don't want to get back together! And I don't want to be a cheerleader! And I don't want to be a model! I just want to be *me,* whoever that is, and I want it to be good enough for *you!*"

"But you *are* good enough."

"Then why are you always trying to make me into someone I'm not? Why can't you just let me be a big geek who likes photography? What's so wrong with that?"

"But you can be so much more! You have so much potential," she says.

"Those are *your* dreams, *not mine*."

"Well, you should have just said something, you didn't have to cut off all your hair!" She shakes her head.

"I *have* told you, like a million times, but you refuse to listen. You just go on and on about my friends, and boyfriends, and school, and how it's all so great. But you have no idea what you're talking about. You have no idea what anyone is *really like*. And I'm so tired of having to pretend that I'm happy and that my life is perfect. It's like you put the same pressures on me at home that I have at school. And being at school is a total nightmare."

"Why is school a nightmare? Rio, what's going on?"

"I told you, everyone hates me."

"But why?"

And then I tell her everything. About the party, about the drugs, about the hooking up, about the dog shit, about the principal's office, about all the girls calling me a stuck-up bitch. I leave nothing out.

And by the time I'm done she's sitting next to me, and she's hugging me, and she's crying, too. And it feels so good to finally tell the truth again.

After a while she goes, "I know I've told you all about growing up poor. But I never told you about all the teasing I suffered because of it. How all the kids made fun of my secondhand clothes, and the way I looked in them all gangly and skinny. Skinny Bones Jones they called me." She stops and looks at me. "And much worse. Well, when I was going off to model in Paris, nobody believed me. People said I was pregnant and going to a home for unwed mothers. And when I returned a year later, I couldn't wait to show everybody what I had become. I thought wearing designer clothes and having my face in magazines would make them sorry for treating me so badly. Well, it didn't. And believe me the rumors just got nastier. Then my career took off, I moved to New York, and I never looked back. But I never forgot what that felt like." She looks at me and runs her thumb lightly across my cheek. "All I ever wanted was for you to be happy. And I honestly thought if you got in with the popular crowd you would be safe from that kind of bullying." She shakes her head and sighs. "Rio, I think you're so beautiful, and talented, and smart, that it kills me to think I made you feel otherwise."

I wipe my nose on my sleeve, but it's worse than I thought. So I reach for my napkin and blow.

"But what's happening to you at school is unacceptable and I won't allow it. I think we should call your father and file a lawsuit against them for failing to provide a safe environment."

"Mom, no! Please don't do that," I beg. "You'll only make it worse!"

"I won't stand for this! That principal has no right treating you like that!"

"I know. You're right. But Mom, please. Just give me a chance to work it out by myself."

"How are you going to do that?"

"I have an idea. And if it fails, then you can step in, okay?"

"Promise?" she says.

"Promise."

"And one more thing."

"What?"

"Let's see if we can get you into my hairdresser's tomorrow. I think if we even it out, and lighten up the tips, you'll have a very chic pixie cut." She smiles.

"Deal."

Forty-two

Monday morning when my mom drops me off at school she gives me one last chance to chicken out.

"Are you *sure* you don't want me to march into the principal's office and strangle him?" she asks, mostly joking, but partly serious.

I shake my head. "Thanks for the offer, but no. I can handle this." Then I grab my backpack and close the door between us.

And right when I turn to leave she says, "Rio, I'm proud of you."

So I smile and wave good-bye and as I head toward the quad I think about how lucky I am to have her as my mom. Okay, I know, a week ago I would have never said that, but it's different now. I mean, before when she was acting like my "friend" it was no different than hanging out with Kristi, because it was all based on a lot of stuff I don't really care about, but pretended I did. But now I finally feel like it's okay to just be myself, and that I actually have her approval. Maybe it's not always gonna be so great because the truth is she's *still* a former almost-supermodel, and that's bound to get on my nerves, but that doesn't mean I can't enjoy this moment of truce.

As I walk across the quad I'm totally scanning for Kristi, Kayla, and Jen Jen, but I don't see them anywhere so I head for my locker. And as I pass this group of girls one of them looks at me and goes, "Oh, my god, did you see her *hair*?"

Oh, I totally forgot about my hair.

I lift my hand and pat my head, running my fingers through the short, spiky strands, and it feels kind of weird since I've had long hair my whole entire life (except for maybe when I was born, and then a year or two following that), so it's like every time I look in the mirror I'm still shocked.

On Saturday when my mom took me to her hip L.A. salon I was feeling pretty nervous and totally dreading the nasty lecture I was sure I would get about the perils of the self-inflicted haircut.

But instead Laurence (pronounced like he's French, even though he's from the Valley), just stood behind me, lifted a few pieces and said, "This is fabulous, but we're going to make it even better. We're going to make it magnificent!"

So after two and a half hours that involved:

1. Two shampoos
2. One protective conditioner
3. A paintbrush dipped in bleach
4. A pair of scissors
5. A razor (kind of a scary moment for me)
6. A blow-dryer
7. A straight iron
8. Molding wax
9. A complimentary makeup application

My hair was shorter, spikier, platinum blond, and totally cool and edgy-looking. And as I was staring in the mirror I was starting to feel really excited about it, like maybe cutting it all off wasn't such a bad idea after all.

Then Laurence totally wrecked it by saying, "You know, you look just like your mother. Are you a model, too?"

My mom was right beside me and she must have seen my expression, because she quickly said, "No, she likes to be on the other side of the camera. She's a very talented photographer."

Kristi wasn't in English, and I didn't see her at her locker, so I guess my big moment will have to wait until lunch. And I'm feeling kind of anxious as I head for my art class since I was hoping the whole confrontation would've been over by now.

I'm thinking about all this as I walk into the classroom and smack into Jas.

"Oh, I'm sorry," I say, bending down to retrieve the papers I knocked out of his hand. But when I try to hand them over, he just stands there gaping at me.

"Oh, my god, Rio. Your hair," he says.

And just like that I'm feeling all nervous and self-conscious about it. Which is like the lamest thing in the world, because if *I* like it what do I care what *he* thinks? So I thrust the papers at him and make a beeline for my desk. Then I start going through my bag like I'm looking for something, even though I'm not. But it keeps me busy until I calm down. Then I grab my camera, place it on my desk, and sit there wondering what the hell I'm gonna do for a project, since I've no idea what happened to the good photos I took all those months ago before I became popular.

I'm walking toward the darkroom, when Mason looks up from her easel and goes, "I like your hair."

"Thanks," I say.

"Who did it?"

"Me." I shrug.

"You did it?" She looks totally shocked.

"Well, I did the first cut. Then it took this guy in L.A. about two hours to fix it."

"You just, *cut it?*"

"Yeah, I was ready for a change, you know?"

"It really suits you." She smiles.

And I don't know why, but right when she says that I look over at Jas. But he's staring at me, so I look away.

I spend the rest of class in the darkroom looking through hundreds of photographs, and negatives, and proof sheets hoping to find my long-lost photos, and secretly wondering why Jas was staring at me. Is it because of my hair? Or is it something else?

Forty-three

By lunch, I'm on a mission. So I head straight for my former lunch table 'cause I know if I hesitate for even one second I'll totally lose my nerve. I walk right up to the edge and stand there. But they just sip their Diet Cokes and talk about the Moondance like I'm invisible or something.

"I *so* didn't expect to get Moon Princess," Kristi says, refusing to acknowledge me. "Just being nominated is an honor."

Is she kidding?

I clear my throat, and go, "Hey."

They all turn and look at me.

"Nice *hair*," Kristi says, and they all start laughing.

But I just continue to stand there, so she looks at me all annoyed, and goes, "Can I help you?"

"Yes, you can," I say. "I want you to leave me alone." My voice is a little shaky.

"Uh, hel-*lo*? You're the one standing at *my* table, it's not like I'm following you around." She rolls her eyes and they all start laughing again.

"Look," I say, anxious to get to the point before I lose my nerve completely. "I don't know what I did to make you guys hate me so much, but I'm asking you to stop. Stop spreading rumors, stop sending me nasty e-mails and text messages, stop throwing stuff at me, stop calling me names, and stop writing stuff on my locker and filling it with dog shit." *There I said it, now I can breathe again.*

"Excuse me, but I think we all know that you're the one dealing in dog crap."

"Why would I do that?" I set my bag on the edge of the table, and look at her.

"Because you're pathetic? Because you're attention-starved? Because you always have to be the center of everything?" She flips her long dark hair behind her shoulder, mocking me.

But I don't react. Instead, I look at Kayla and Jen Jen, just sitting there as usual, refusing to get involved. But by not saying or doing anything, they are involved, and by laughing at her mean jokes they're taking sides. And I just don't get it. I mean, I know Kristi hates me, but what did I ever do to them?

I look right at Kristi and say, "I'm not asking for us to be friends, I'm just asking you to back off, that's all."

"Well, guess what, Brazil? I don't know what the fuck you're talking about, because I'm not the one bothering you. I can't help it if the whole school thinks you're a nasty, stuck-up skank. You brought that on yourself. So why don't you just crawl back to your loser friends, and quit infecting our lunch table."

I look at Kayla and Jen Jen staring at their Diet Cokes. And it reminds me of me, and how I used to sit there doing nothing while Kristi tortured some poor, unfortunate dork. But now I have to do something to stop it. And I have nothing to lose. I mean, how much worse can it really get for me?

So I look right at Kristi and go, "I'm so sick of the way you call everyone who's not part of your little group a loser. Because if anyone's a loser it's *you!* People aren't nice to you because they like you. They're nice to you because they *fear* you. You intimidate, manipulate, and control everyone around you. But you couldn't scare Mason so you call her a lesbo. And you were totally into Jas, but he didn't like you back so you have your jock friends throw stuff at him."

Okay, I'm going out on a limb here because I have no evidence to back up that Jas part. It's just an idea that came to me recently, but I know I hit it when Kayla looks at me and goes, "Who told you?"

And Kristi looks at her and yells, "Shut up, Kayla!"

I stand at the edge of the table smiling.

Then Kristi narrows her eyes and goes, "Oh, and you should talk. Like you never say anything bad about anyone. Remember how you said Kayla and Jen are stupid, limited, and stuck on themselves?"

I continue to stand there, but I'm no longer smiling. Because she's right, I did say something kinda like that.

"And for your information," she continues. "I was listening the other day when you called Jen, I heard everything!"

Jen Jen looks at her and yells, "Shut up, Kristi!" Then she looks quickly at me and shakes her head, like it's not true.

But Kristi sees it and jumps up from the table, screaming, "What do you care if she knows? Like what's Brazil gonna do about it? She's a total loser!"

People are starting to gather, probably hoping to see a good girl fight. But while I'm not about to fight her, I'm not quite done yet, either, so I say (in kind of a loud voice so everyone can hear), "Your days are numbered, Kristi, because pretty soon people are gonna realize they don't have to put up with your crap. And without your little helpers, you're nothing."

Then I look at Kayla and Jen Jen and go, "Don't you guys get tired of her stupid rules? Don't you want to try new things with different people? Don't you realize that if you walked away *right now* she'd be sitting here *alone*? I mean, why are you trying so hard to please someone who's mean and nasty and boring and unoriginal?"

When I'm finished I just stand there, and even though I'm feeling kind of shaky, I also feel pretty damn good.

Then Kristi gives me her famous death stare and goes, "Fuck you, freak." Then she throws her Diet Coke at me.

But it misses, so I just shrug.

And as I start to walk away she's still screaming at me.

But Kayla and Jen Jen are looking at each other.

Forty-four

I'd be lying if I said that didn't make me feel powerful, revolutionary, and kind of like a goddess. So imagine my disappointment when I was walking through campus between fifth and sixth period and like ten different kids said something rude about my hair.

When my mom picked me up after school she looked all worried when she asked, "So how'd it go?"

"Good," I said, getting into the Range Rover and fastening my seat belt as she pulls out of the parking lot. "Nothing changed, but it went okay."

"Do you need me to step in?"

"No, they haven't changed, but I have, and that's all that really matters."

Instead of going home we drive straight to the airport since my dad is getting back in town. And I'm feeling kind of nervous to see him, since he's always made this big deal about my "long, golden mane" (his words, not mine).

We get there kind of early so instead of driving around and around in circles, my mom parks the car and we wait in the baggage claim area. I'm standing off to the side, just hanging with "The Duke," when

I see my dad coming down the escalator. He grabs his luggage off the carousel, gives my mom a big hug, and walks right past me.

So I go, "Dad? Hel-*lo*?"

And he turns and squints and goes, "Rio?" Like it was truly a question. I'm not kidding.

So I go, *"Yeah?"*

And he just stands there and blinks. Well at least he didn't do the big-screen scream like my mom. Then he says, "What happened to all of your hair?"

My mom gives me a nervous look since we didn't exactly go over our story. But I just say, "I wanted to try something new."

"I took her to Laurence," she pipes in. "Isn't it chic?"

I guess she doesn't want him knowing that the first cut was on me, since that can be a sign of insanity.

"You look so grown-up," he says.

Ohmygod, is my dad getting misty-eyed?

"Don't worry," I say, going over to hug him. "I'm still me."

We went to Morton's for dinner and it was really nice being with him, and my mom only annoyed me twice. Okay, maybe three times, but I totally refrained from rolling my eyes.

And that's when I told her that I decided to go to New York and be in the Gap ad with her.

"You don't have to," she said.

"I know I don't *have* to. Maybe that's why I want to. I mean, all the other models' kids are going right?"

She nods.

"Well, then how bad would it look if I didn't show?"

And my dad goes, "We're going to have two models in the family?"

"No, just one," I told him. "I'm hoping I can talk to Mario about interning this summer."

When we get home Kayla and Jen Jen are sitting in Kayla's black convertible Bug right outside our gate.

And when my dad asks, "Do you know those girls?" I say, "Yeah, they used to be my friends."

He presses the remote to open the gate, and I motion for them to follow. And when he pulls into the garage I say, "I'll be in later." Then I walk over to the black Bug just as Jen Jen and Kayla are getting out.

"Hey," I say.

"How are you?" Kayla asks.

"Okay." I try not to fidget so they won't think I'm nervous, even though I am.

"Um, okay, here's the thing," Kayla starts.

But then Jen Jen interrupts her and says, "We want to apologize. We're really sorry for everything that happened."

"Except for the locker," Kayla says.

"Yeah. I mean, we're *sorry* about the locker, but I swear we didn't do it. And I promise we don't know who did. It was probably Kristi, but it's not like we saw her."

I nod, but I don't say anything.

"We said some really bad things about you, and we're really sorry. It's like, today at lunch, when you were going off on us, it made us stop and think," Kayla says.

"You were so right," says Jen Jen. "She's like such a bitch and we're so afraid to go against her. She's mean to everyone and we feel bad, but we just stand there and let it happen."

"Or even worse, we join in," Kayla says. "Anyway it was really brave of you to do that and I'm glad you did. Because I am tired of it, and Jen is, too."

I look at Jen Jen. She nods.

"Well, I said some bad stuff about you, too, but I only did it so Kristi would like me—which I know is a pretty lame excuse. I really am sorry," I tell them.

"Let's just try to forget all that and move on," Kayla says.

"So what are you guys gonna do?" I ask.

"Well, we're not putting up with her crap anymore. And if she doesn't like it then she doesn't have to hang with *us*." Kayla smiles.

"So do you need a ride to school tomorrow?" Jen Jen asks.

I look at both of them and while I appreciate the offer, I go, "My dad's taking me tomorrow, but maybe the next day."

The next morning when I go downstairs for breakfast my dad looks up from the paper and goes, "I haven't seen that in a long time."

And when my mom looks at me I can see the disapproval in her eyes, but to her credit, she refrains from saying anything.

When I get to my locker Kristi breezes right past me and goes, "*Nice shirt,* Brazil. Back where you started, huh loser?"

Well, I'd rather be part of an " ape   Crew" than her crew. I'm just glad I didn't throw it away like she suggested. But since I already had it out with her yesterday, I just turn back to my locker. I mean, maybe I can't change her, but I can change my response to her.

But then the weirdest thing happens. Some girl I don't even know walks right up to her and goes, "Why don't you just leave her alone?"

Kristi turns, and in total disbelief says, "Excuse me? Did you just speak to me?"

The girl looks all red and nervous, but she stands her ground and says, "You heard me."

I stand next to my locker, watching them face off in front of a crowd of people. (Nothing like the promise of bloodshed to bring people together.) And while I think it's really nice of this girl to put herself on the line like that, I really don't want her to become a social suicide on my behalf. I'm just about to step in when I see Jen Jen and Kayla walk up.

"Back off, Kristi," they say.

Kristi glares at them. "This is none of your business," she says.

"The shitty way you treat people is everyone's business," Jen Jen says.

Kristi just stands there trying to appear calm, but if you look closely, you can see her hands shaking. "You're so gonna regret this," she says. "You're gonna be so fucking sorry!"

But they just shrug.

Then Kristi looks at everyone gathered around and goes, "Well, you're not making me late to class." Then she takes off toward English in a big hurry, even though the bell hasn't rung yet.

I slam my locker shut, and that girl walks up to me and says, "You know, I've spent the last three years trying to avoid her, because she's always so mean to me. But yesterday, when I saw you stand up to her like that, I decided it was time I did the same. Thanks for giving me the courage to face her."

We smile at each other, and then the bell rings, and we all go to class.

But by the time I get to Art I'm feeling like a loser again, because everyone's so excited about the show, and I'm no longer part of it. And as I head toward the darkroom I'm hoping I can come up with something at least halfway decent for my project. I mean, how humiliating would it be to flunk high-school art when I want to be an artist?

As I walk by Jas, he looks right at me, but he doesn't even smile or nod. His behavior toward me is really making me wonder.

So after agitating the tank, and fixing the image, I'm so anxious to see the negatives I carefully pull out a tiny bit of film to inspect it. But it's totally depressing because the first three are just more stupid pictures of Tyler. So I pour some clearing agent and agitate again, then I perform my final wash. And while I'm hanging the film to dry I check out the rest of the roll. More shots of Tyler, followed by a series of leaves blowing in the wind that make me question my ability, if not my sanity. God, it's like nothing is as good as those lost photos. But then maybe I just think that because I no longer have them. Because you know how you *always* want what you don't have.

I'm almost at the end of the roll when I get to this picture I don't remember taking. And I'm leaning in really close and squinting at it, because this may sound crazy, but it looks like the back of Kristi's head. But that's because it *is* the back of her head.

She's standing in front of my locker, writing something. And I can just make out the words "Stuck-up B—"

There are four more in the sequence, including one with her handling "doggy excrement."

I told you she wasn't so delicate.

But who took these pictures?

Ohmygod, it was Jas! He had my camera, so it must have been him!

I grab my stuff and run out of the darkroom. When I get to Mason's easel I go, "Do you know where Jas went?"

"He left," she says, setting down her paintbrush and looking at me.

"Oh." I just stand there, trying to mask my disappointment. Then I get an idea. "What are you doing after school?" I ask.

She gives me a really strange look (which makes me feel bad, but I guess I deserve it), then she shrugs and goes, "Nothing, why?"

"Do you think you could help me with a little project?"

After Kinko's, Mason drops me off at my house. "You really gotta get your license," she says.

"I know, I know. Hey, you wanna come in?"

She shakes her head and looks kind of uncomfortable. "That's okay. Jas told me your mom doesn't want you hanging with us."

I open her car door and step onto my driveway. Then I look at her and go, "That was true then, but not anymore. Come on."

When we go inside, you're not gonna believe this but I have a living room—and it's beautiful. And it's not an Epcot living room, either. I just stand there taking it all in, and then my mom walks up and goes, "What do you think?"

"It's awesome. But it's not exactly minimalism, is it?" I say, noticing all the lamps, and cushions, and framed photographs.

"I decided to tune out everyone's opinion and just do what I wanted for a change. I figured if you could do it, then I could, too." She smiles and looks at Mason, and I realize they've never actually met so I introduce them. "Is that a Norma Kamali?" my mom asks, looking at her dress.

"Circa nineteen eighty-three. I got it at this great vintage place in L.A.," Mason says.

It's like love at first sight. Before you know it my mom's dragging her upstairs to look at the time warp side of her closet, otherwise known as "the shrine that's dedicated to all things seventies and eighties." She's showing Mason all this designer stuff she snagged from photo shoots: Stephen Sprouse graffiti blouses, original Jordache jeans, she even lets Mason touch her Ramones T-shirt that Joey Ramone spit on or pissed on or threw up on or something. And watching them together makes me feel totally relieved, because the truth is I was a little worried about bringing her over.

By the time Mason leaves she's clutching a Duran Duran T-shirt (my mom has six more), and I'm walking her to her car when she goes, "Are you sure you want to do this?"

And I go, "Why? Do you think I shouldn't?"

"No, I think it's good. I just want you to be sure that's all."

I watch her get in her car, and when she starts the engine, I say, "Hey, Mason."

She turns to look at me.

"Thanks for helping me, I really appreciate it. And I'm sorry about all the bad stuff before."

"I know. I'll see you tomorrow," she says.

And I watch her drive through the open gate and down the road.

Forty-five

The next day when I come downstairs carrying the big cardboard box, my dad looks at me and asks, "What's that?"

"School project," I say, then I look at my mom nervously, but she just smiles and winks. I set it on the counter and down a quick cup of coffee. And when I hear Jen Jen's horn I grab the box and my backpack and head out the door.

I push the passenger seat forward and place the box carefully in the back. Then I lift the lid and say, "Check it out."

"I knew it!" she says, shaking her head.

By the time the first period bell rings the whole school knows. Because I took the box, placed it in the middle of the quad, removed the lid, then stood on the sidelines so I could watch.

And believe it or not, Tyler and Kristi were the first to investigate. He leaned down and picked up the first flyer I had stacked in the box. But unfortunately for Kristi it was the picture of her holding the piece of dog shit.

I mean, she was wearing rubber gloves, *but still.*

"Fuckin' sick!" he yells, looking from the flyer to her.

And before she can stop it, everyone has a copy.

When I get to English, Kristi's standing near the door, waiting for me. And for the first time ever, I can honestly say she doesn't look so perfect.

"So," she says, eyes smudged with mascara, bare lips pressed into a tight, thin line. "You must be feeling pretty proud of yourself." She crosses her arms against her chest.

But I just stand there and shrug.

"You've managed to steal everyone away from me; Kayla, Jen Jen, who knows, maybe even Tyler will take you back."

I shake my head. "That's the difference between us, I don't want to *own* anyone. And believe me, I'm not interested in Tyler. Especially now that he's been with you."

Her eyes narrow into thin, angry slits. "You think you're so important now, but it won't last. You're nothing but a cheap, pathetic, knockoff version of *me*. You'll fall apart in a week." She smirks.

"I used to want to be like you, but not anymore," I say, turning to leave.

About ten minutes into English Kristi is summoned to Principal Chaney's office. And by the end of first period, two uniformed cops are going through her locker.

On my way to Art I'm all excited to see Jas and Mason, but they're not there. And when I ask Ms. Tate about it, she says they're taking the day off so they can help with the exhibit.

"I hope we'll see you there," she says.

But I just go, "Oh, well, maybe."

Then I go back to my table and try to pick the three best prints for my Beauty project, even though I'm not exactly thrilled with any of them.

By lunch, word's out that Kristi's been expelled from school and charged with vandalizing school property, as well as possession of an illegal substance, which I assume is the coke she had hidden in her locker. Guess her dirty little secret is out.

Then right in the middle of my sixth-period chemistry class I get summoned to Principal Chaney's office, and I'm kind of nervous about why he wants to see me. I mean, I'm actually wondering if he's gonna try to bust me for littering or something, since those copies are pretty much strewn all over campus.

When I walk inside, he motions for me to sit on the couch, and even though I realize that's like some kind of big promotion compared to the chair, I just stand at the edge of his desk.

He brushes his hand through his thick, dark hair (that may or may not be a toupee), and explains how the situation has been properly dealt with, and how we should all just try to move past it, and get on with a successful school year.

I just stand there, wondering if I'll hear an apology.

"And I'm very sorry that the veil of suspicion fell on you," he says.

Pretty lame I know, but consider the source. I just nod and then I reach into my backpack and retrieve the zine Mason gave me in the library that day. "There's an article on page two that you might want to read," I tell him.

Then I walk out of his office and head back to class.

When I get home from school I'm pretty shocked to find that my mom is already clued in. Apparently Katrina Wood was called out of her yogalates session to go to the school and deal with her daughter. Then I guess the Ladies of Newport Beach Gossip Network took it from there.

My mom tells me she made our flight reservations for New York and that I'm probably going to miss a day or two of school.

"Let's make it two, I don't think they'll complain. Plus there's someone I want to visit," I say.

Then I go upstairs to my room, dial the number I still remember by heart, and ask for Paige.

Forty-six

Paige was way nicer to me than I deserved and without going into too much detail I explained that I took a little detour, but basically I was back. So we made plans to meet after the Gap shoot at this restaurant in Manhattan called Serendipity, for huge hot-fudge sundaes. I mean, I figure I'm probably really gonna need one after a day spent with former almost-supermodels who only eat lettuce.

"Do you mind if I bring Hud? Or would you rather it be just us?" she asks.

"Bring him," I say. "You know, I really am happy for you. It must be so great to have a boyfriend who's also your best friend."

"Yeah, it's pretty great," she says.

After dinner, I'm sitting in my room reading *The Grapes of Wrath,* and trying to not think about the art exhibit when Kayla calls.

"Jen and I are going to the exhibit, do you wanna come?" she asks.

"What? I thought you guys weren't into art."

"Yeah well, we're thinking we should expand our horizons."

"I don't know," I say. "I feel kind of weird about going. I mean, I was supposed to help organize it, but then I kind of dropped out."

"Don't be ridiculous. You're going, and we're picking you up in fifteen."

The minute I hang up I race to my closet and throw on some olive-green cargo pants, a white tank top, dangly earrings, some beaded flat shoes, and my little denim jacket in case it gets cold. And it's not until I'm in the car that I realize I'm wearing the exact same outfit I wore on that dreadful "date" with Jas.

We talk and joke the whole way there, but we don't talk about Kristi since we're pretty much trying to not gossip, and just move past all that. And I'm having fun and feeling pretty good for the first time in days. But when we enter the exhibit I start to feel kind of mad at myself. I mean, there are all these sculptures, and paintings, and photographs from all these different schools, and I should have something displayed here too.

Jen and Kayla go scoping for hotties, so I'm just wandering around on my own, looking at all the different perceptions of values like Truth, Justice, Faith—

And Beauty?

Hanging on the wall, in a simple black frame, is one of my lost photos. It's a close-up of a hermit crab in a tide pool, with his shiny black eyes looking huge and inquisitive, while his splayed legs and claws with their vibrant, symmetrical red, orange, and white stripes fill the background with color. I just stand there staring at it in complete disbelief. And as I reach out to touch it, someone behind me goes, "It is beautiful, isn't it?"

"Did you do this?" I turn and face him.

Jas nods.

"But where did you find it? I've been looking all over for it."

"I found your prints, sort of abandoned in the darkroom. So I saved them, in case you came back."

"In case I came back?"

"I mean, in case you ever wanted them again," he says, looking slightly embarrassed.

He's looking right at me and it makes me feel dizzy, but dizzy in a good way—if there is such a thing. "You took the other pictures, too, didn't you? And you left the film in my camera so I would find it."

"How'd that work out?" he asks.

"You must be the only one in Newport that doesn't know."

"I was in here all day." He shrugs.

"Well, I've been acquitted, and I have you to thank." I smile. "So how did you get those pictures?"

"Well, I was kind of worried about you 'cause of everything that was going on, but you didn't seem like you wanted to talk. And since I had your camera, I decided to take a picture of something funny, something that might make you laugh when you were developing it. But when I saw Kristi, I decided to help you instead. I didn't mention it since I knew you'd find it eventually and decide what to do."

He looks at me and smiles and I just can't help myself. "Oh, Jas,"

I take a step toward him, just as this really pretty girl walks up, puts her arm around him, and goes, "So which one's yours, Jasper?"

And he goes, "My sculpture's over there, and my painting's on that wall."

"Show me," she says.

Then he looks at me. "Don't move," he says. "I'll be right back."

So I stand there and watch them walk away. And then I leave. Because I've seen about all the beauty I can take.

Forty-seven

I only get as far as the bench outside, since the second I'm out the door I remember I don't have a driver's license, a car, or any idea where my friends are.

So I kick off my shoes and I'm sitting with my knees drawn up against my chest and my forehead pressed into my knees, and I'm feeling soft, vulnerable, and completely exposed, like a hermit crab without a shell.

And I remember learning about hermit crabs in ninth-grade biology, how when they outgrow their home, they go searching for a new one. But just because they're always moving into bigger digs, doesn't mean they forget where they came from, oftentimes bringing along their old friends, the sponges and sea anemones that lived on the old shell, and transplanting them right onto the new one.

I guess I'm searching for my own new shell. But this time I promise, I won't forget who I am, and there'll be room for everyone.

"What are you doing?"

I look up and see Kayla standing in front of me. "Oh, just getting some air. Do you guys wanna bail soon?" I ask.

"Are you crazy? Do you have any idea how many cute guys are in there?"

"No. I only saw one."

"Well there's tons! You've seriously got to come back in and check it out! And there's this group of freshman girls that cut their hair really short and bleached it blond to look like yours. You've gotta see it!"

"In a minute," I say, closing my eyes and pressing my face back against my knees.

But as she's walking inside I hear her go, "Oh, hey Jas. Rio? She's right over there."

I sit up straight, and run my hands through my hair, even though it doesn't really get messed up anymore. Then I smile as he sits next to me like everything's totally normal.

"I was looking all over for you," he says.

"Oh, I just wanted to get some air." I look down at my toes, so I won't have to look at him.

We sit there like that for a while and he says something about it being a nice night, but mostly it's quiet and I just can't take it anymore. So I turn to him and go, "So, where's your girlfriend?"

And he goes, "What? You mean Monique? We split a couple months ago."

Then he looks at me, and even though that's great news, I was referring to the girlfriend *from five minutes ago!* So I go, "No, I mean your date."

"I came here alone," he says.

So like a complete and total retard *who just can't let it go,* I say, "I'm talking about the girl inside, the one who calls you Jasper? Is she the same girl who was in your car that night?"

"What night?" he asks, and to his credit he really does look confused.

"The night—"

You saw me crying and hurling on the street?

"Never mind." I shake my head and draw my knees in tighter.

"Rio, look at me," he says.

But no way am I doing that.

"Okay, fine. Then listen. The girl who calls me Jasper is September, and she's my dad's girlfriend's daughter. She's a sophomore at Newport Harbor High, and she's *not* my date. She already has a boyfriend. But even if she didn't, I wouldn't be interested."

Because he's in love with the girl in the car.

"And the girl in the car is not only forty-two years old," he says, moving closer, trying to make me look at him. "But she also has a boyfriend. She's September's mother and she's been dating my dad for the past few months. But if you must know, there is someone I'm extremely interested in, but she won't even glance my way."

What kind of idiot wouldn't look at Jas?

We sit there for a while, not saying anything, but I can feel him staring at me.

And then it hits me: *Ohmygod! The idiot is me!*

I turn and look right into his topaz eyes.

"Finally," he says.

And when he kisses me it's even better than when I dreamed it.